EMBROILED
THE DRAGON CAPTURED
BOOK III

BRIDGET E BAKER

❀ Created with Vellum

WHAT IT'S ABOUT

Every blessing comes with a curse of its own...

In pursuit of the *heart* the dragons need to survive, Elizabeth has to make some difficult decisions. At least her dragon prince is there by her side through it all, ready to attack any foes that threaten.

Until the day he isn't.

When the world you knew is gone, when monsters become allies, and heroes make villainous choices, what's a warrior to do? Liz wrestles with demons, literal and figurative, trying to find a path through the darkness for her family, but it's not a simple task.

She's about to face the hardest decisions of her life as the dragons descend in force, prepared to take what they need at all costs. Will Liz be able to sort friends from foes in time to save the earth from the demons below and the dragons above? And what will she lose in the process?

PROLOGUE: LIZ

I was ten years old when the best ice cream shop *ever...* closed.

My parents first discovered Chinatown thanks to my mom's obsession with K-dramas. They found a place that sold Korean food, and right next door was a shop called Snowy Dessert Bar.

Had we gone that day with just my mom, we'd never have tried it. They didn't have many vegan options, though the tiger-milk tea was made with oat milk at least. Since my dad was with us, we got our first taste of bingsu.

It was *heavenly*.

I became *obsessed*.

My parents liked it too, so we went at least once a week for almost two years. It helped my mom survive her pregnancy with Coral, and even little Jade liked sucking down tiny bites of the cold, sweet, shaved milk, especially when she was teething.

Until, without notice, one day Snowy closed.

It broke my heart—my parents' too, but especially mine.

I refused to eat ice cream, any ice cream, for years. My parents tried to win me over with a place called Nu Cafe, which had Taiwanese shaved milk. Then they found a place called Sol Bingsu, which also had fun corndogs. They were both *fine*, probably, but after being forced to eat a single bite, I ate no more.

Because nothing could replace Snowy.

I literally mourned it.

When the topic of ice cream came up, I always felt sad. When my parents talked about getting noodles in Chinatown, I sometimes snuck off to cry. Snowy Dessert Bar had just been *so* good that everything else was a big, fat disappointment.

I knew it then.

I know it now.

No other ice cream will ever compare.

By the time I turned sixteen, my mom was *over* my attitude. "I grabbed some ice cream for your cake."

"Don't bother," I said. "I don't want it."

"Well." She slammed the Ben and Jerry's non-dairy Phish Food carton, which had probably cost her twenty bucks, on the table and huffed. "It may be your birthday, but that doesn't give you the right to be a brat."

Her tone made little Sammy cry, and then I felt pretty guilty.

"I'm sorry," I say. "Everyone else will probably love it." Or maybe not. No matter how hard they try, the vegan ice cream's never quite as good as the real thing.

"Sit." Mom arched one eyebrow, and she pointed at a chair. "It's time for you to get a little history lesson."

"Mom!" I was a pretty good kid, but I was also sixteen. "Seriously?"

"Tis better to have loved and lost than never to have loved at all." She dropped one hand on her hip. "If you can tell me who said that, you can storm out and blast music in your room."

I jutted out my lip. "Shakespeare."

"Nice try." She pointed at the chair again.

I dropped into it with a beleaguered sigh. "Fine. Just tell me whatever it is, and then I'll be sure to pretend I like the ice cream."

Mom was a pacifist, but I swear, I tried her patience. "Alfred Lord Tennyson."

"His middle name is Lord? His parents really hated him." I couldn't help my snicker.

"No, his name was Alfred, and his title was Lord Tennyson."

"So some rich guy says it's better to have something and lose it. Lesson learned." I stood up.

Mom's lips pursed.

I sat back down. "Just spit out the rest, then."

"Lord Tennyson had a best friend," she says. "His name was Arthur Hallum, and he died when he was still quite young. Tennyson wrote this for him—one of the most epic lines of poetry ever written."

"You're quoting gay poetry to me so I'll eat ice cream?" I wasn't impressed. "I'm upset about *bingsu*, Mom. It's very inclusive of you, though."

Mom's hands clenched into fists. "Elizabeth Chadwick." She breathed in through her nose, and out through her mouth. "Alfred's friend was engaged to his sister. The poet himself, Lord Tennyson, was married for forty-two years and had two children."

"He could totally still be gay," I said.

"Stop teenagering all over the place and listen." Mom sat across from me. "It's better to love and lose than never to love at all." She tilted her head. "You had the best ice cream in the world." Her half-smile was kind. "I know how much you loved it, but don't let losing it break you forever. You knew perfection, but you can still appreciate stuff that's pretty good."

"Mom."

"And you *should* appreciate that you found it, but you should also move on and love again," Mom said. "Even imperfectly. Because the alternative's giving up —and that's the same as never loving at all."

I wasn't at all convinced that was Tennyson's point.

I did think about that quote sometimes, usually whenever someone tried to make me eat ice cream. I didn't eat any that day, and I didn't eat any for several more years. I still don't love it.

I knew perfection.

Everything else tasted like disappointment.

But I was never quite sure Mom's interpretation was right. I always sort of thought Tennyson was saying that he would rather have loved, even knowing it would be short-lived. I thought he must have lived on the memory of that love. I don't think he ever tried to *replace* it with something less.

Maybe that's why he married a woman. Who knows?

Or maybe he just never found another friend quite as amazing as that Arthur guy. But when I fly out of the lava, and Axel looks at me with blank, impassive eyes?

It's pain like I've never felt before.

I decide then and there that Alfred, Lord Tennyson, is a complete and utter moron.

❧ 1 ❧

LIZ

If I had to fight my way out of a hostage situation, I could.

Probably.

I mean, I might lose an eye or something, but I bet I'd survive.

But if I was being held and tortured for information? I'm pretty sure I'd crack. I like to talk—always have.

So when Azar snatches me out of the air—still straight up can't believe I can fly—and shows me just how much better he can fly than me, I want to just tell him everything that just happened in the volcano.

One thing keeps me from doing it.

When he first bonded me, what feels like aeons ago, I had almost no leverage at all. He was a *dragon*, and I was a puny human digging through the trash for a broken umbrella to use as a weapon. I've gotten stronger, but so has he.

Now he's a nearly-invincible dragon who can take

not one, but *two* terrifying forms. He can breathe fire, and he can transform the very earth around us. A few weeks ago, that wouldn't have worried me in the slightest, because I knew he would never hurt me.

But now?

He's forgotten me entirely.

And we're no longer bonded.

He could squash me like a bug and never regret it. And what's worse, he could do the same thing to my siblings. The secrets hiding in my head are probably the only leverage I have.

I'm not sure why I could enter the volcano and talk to Freya, and I'm definitely not sure why she made *me* decide the fate of the earth dragons, but she did. I chose to make them much more powerful, but now they'll join the other dragons in being unable to lay eggs. Right now, all the earth dragons are figuring out that they've been upgraded, but no one knows it's my fault. Or, I really hope they don't.

Because the massive red dragon holding me like a squeaky toy looks angry enough to incinerate me if he had the slightest provocation.

Who are you, Liz?

Who am I?

How does he expect me to answer that question? My full name and address? My occupation? What my hopes and dreams are? That I think I'm in love with him, or I was, back when he could turn into the hottest man I'd ever seen who also made me laugh?

None of that feels. . .appropriate.

Although, what would feel right to me in this circumstance?

I'm currently dangling in mid-air, his mighty, scarlet claws clamped around my midsection. He's thankfully giving my wings space, but he's also smashing my right boob. It's not comfortable, and we're flying low enough that the ground's racing past at a nauseating speed. I'm a little worried I might puke.

He must be getting impatient, because his claws are tightening. I decide to answer his question with a question of my own. "Do you remember me at all?" I hate how much I'm hoping he'll recall something—anything at all.

Perhaps, like me, he has no idea what to say. We just keep gliding along, and my stomach is liking it all less and less by the second. I close my eyes tightly, hoping he'll either land or let me go.

I remember you shooting out from the lava while horned creatures chanted Gullveig. Nothing before that.

"You were with me in the lava—in the same place," I say. "Though you exited a little before me, apparently."

Along with Gordon and Rufus.

"I'm so glad they're alright." I shift a little, trying to find a more comfortable spot to be pinned inside his massive claws.

Are you in pain?

It doesn't sound like he really cares, so I just grunt.

He shakes me. How wonderful. *Answer my questions, winged human.*

"The name is Liz, you stupid red bully, which you know, because you said that earlier."

Bully?

"And I'm not in pain," I lie. Because there's no way I'm about to tell him how much it hurts that he's *right here,* after all that we've been through, and that he has no idea who I am. Instead of crying, I lean in to the fury flooding my body. "How am I supposed to answer questions like 'who are you?'" I twist around so that I can at least see his massive head where it's looming above me, clouds whipping past. I ignore how painfully cold the air around us is.

You didn't answer.

"Because apparently, along with your memory, you lost every scrap of intelligence. I'm clearly a human female, and I used to be bonded to you, and I just shot out of lava with a new set of wings I never had before, and now you're toting me around like I'm your enemy or my life is some kind of game to you."

I realize that I still have one of my swords—it's in some kind of leather thong that's helpfully running through the space between my two wings on my back. I reach back and yank it free, waving it back and forth with numb fingers. "Now release me before I'm forced to cut your toe off."

I expect him to squeeze me tighter, hiss, or roar in my face.

It wouldn't have shocked me if he flew me straight up toward the sun until I couldn't breathe.

I did *not* expect him to simply drop me.

I probably should have been better prepared.

The sword very nearly slips from my fingers when my wings begin pumping furiously. Even flapping fast, I can't seem to get the angles right, and I'm plummeting so fast that I'm about to collide with the snow-covered earth.

Where I'll crumple into a pile of Liz goo.

That's a twist I didn't see coming. So much for leverage.

I close my eyes, but a split second before I hit, the same unyielding red claws clamp my torso and bank to the right and upward. Azar slams into the side of a building in the process, shearing off chunks of the roof as we shoot back upward.

You're the worst flier I've ever seen.

Seeing as I've been doing it for eleven seconds. I can't seem to breathe, so answering him telepathically is my only option.

You weren't oriented the right direction. Your wings were pushing you down.

I finally draw in a breath, and then I cough until I can make some kind of sound. "I wonder how much your first flight sucked, you stupid red bully." My sword's still dangling from my hand, my fingers clenched so tightly around the hilt that I'm losing circulation in the hand. "I need to resheathe my sword."

The one you were going to use to cut off my foot?

"Not your foot—just a toe. You'd barely have noticed."

The massive, toxic red dragon who seems to hate me starts to laugh. I can tell, because he's shaking and heat's puffing around us both as he snorts.

I shiver hard when the cold air rushes back.

Are you cold?

"Is there snow on the ground, big red bully?"

Are you implying that was a stupid question for me to ask? I know only what I've researched about humans, and you're the first winged one I've ever seen.

"Me too," I say. "I'm also the first winged one I've ever seen."

Azar blows a column of fire straight out into the air ahead of us. *This entire place is quite cold.*

"Totally agree," I say. "It's almost offensive how cold it is."

He veers hard to the right until we reach the ocean, and then he follows the line of the water until mountains spring up to the left. He makes a hard turn, and lands on the top of the closest mountain, dropping me from a few feet.

I drop my sword, roll twice, wrenching my shoulder on a very hard rock, and finally stop without breaking anything. I think. If I'm limping a bit when I walk back toward my sword, well, anyone else would too.

You're fragile. You should have used your wings to balance when you landed.

"I've had wings for less than half an hour," I say. "When you saw me fly to Selfoss, that was my first-ever flight."

Selfoss. His beautiful scarlet head tilts, smoke streaming from his nostrils. *Iceland?*

I can't help my smile. He may be a bully, but he's my gorgeous, brilliant bully who studied up on Earth before coming. Before I swiss-cheesed his memory, he was doing pretty well with human stuff. "Yes, we're in Iceland. That's why it's so cold."

Why are we in Iceland? We were going to Houston.

I sigh. "You know, you could get this information from people you actually know and trust if you just head back to the volcano." I frown. "Don't you think that would be a better use of both our time? I doubt you'll believe anything I tell you anyway."

We were bonded.

I nod.

Why?

"Are you even going to believe me?" I pick up my sword and clean it on my weird white tunic. "And for the record, you never told me why you bonded me in the first place. You did it without any explanation—but I think it was a mistake. You didn't know *how* to bond a human, and you didn't know you *could* in your earth-dragon form."

Dragon? His frown hurts my heart. I remember the first time I ever saw it—it's just the same now, but it's also totally different. Because it's *not* the first time for me. *We are not dragons. We're the blessed.*

"And to us humans, you're dragons." I carefully flip the sword up and over my shoulders, sliding it into the nifty sheath Freya must have magicked thoughtfully for me before flinging me back out into the world I just jacked up.

Hey, that's my sword.

"Correction. It *was* your sword. Its partner was stuck in Hyperion the last time I saw it, but you gave them to me before you decided to forget everything, and you can't have them back."

Since I have no recollection of giving them to you, I won't be taking them back.

"Thank goodness for that."

I can't take back what was never yours. You may either return my stolen property, or I'll forcibly take it.

I'm going to ignore that until he actually tries. I glance around at the sun and decide that if I head down the way we came up and follow the line of the beach, I should be able to reach Selfoss in, say, an hour of hard flying with my new wings. I jog and then leap off a ridge, my wings pumping hard, and this time, they're turned the right way.

That's probably why it actually works.

Sure, I'm slow compared to Azar's coasting speed, but I'm just learning. I'm proud of myself. I won't get stranded on the tops of mountains, on the tops of skyscrapers, or in cells with high windows—not anymore. I've become more capable of defending myself in a world with changing rules.

I mean, I didn't really earn it, *per se*, but I think just surviving in the world I was chucked into should earn me some accolades. Azar doesn't flip out, or shriek, or blow a column of fire to incinerate me. He simply drops off the same ledge and glides along beside me.

Did we do this often?

"Fly?" I ask. "Yes."

Really? Because you're miserably slow. I hate this.

"Well, speaking of things that are hard, you didn't used to be this rude." I scowl. "But we went faster before. You carried me. Just got wings, remember? You're giving me a good reason to get faster, just to get away from you."

I could melt you and be done with all this.

"I could stab you." I refuse to look at him. It hurts too much. "You won't, though, because you want to know what happened in that volcano and why the earth blessed are so much stronger."

One massive beat of his wings and he soars out ahead of me and circles around, snapping his wings and flattening out in front of me. I can't correct as fast as he can, so I slam right into his enormous scaled chest and nearly plummet—again—toward the ground below.

His stupid claw snags me *again*, and I'm losing my patience with it.

He is too, it seems. *You will tell me* now. *How did the earth blessed grow stronger?*

I wiggle until he releases me, and then I back away slowly. "I *won't* tell you now."

He inhales sharply, and I realize he's about to melt something.

"Melting the side of the mountain won't change my mind," I say. "Because I can't tell you—I don't *remember* what happened. Unlike you, I remember everything else, so I think it's just a matter of time before it comes back to me."

Time? He's still scowling, but he's gone from bloodbath to beatdown.

"Human bodies aren't like your dragon ones. We have a whole bunch of systems that run things. The circulatory system pumps blood through so we can get oxygen and other things to where they need to go. The digestive tract helps food work its way down and sorts it into waste and energy reserves. The lymphatic system keeps us from getting sick. When we experience something traumatic, like being forcibly flung into a volcano, our body shuts down in waves to protect us."

I know—I studied the feeble human body.

"Then you probably learned about what happens when we go into shock. When your brother hurled you, me, Rufus, and Gordon into the volcano—"

Hyperion would never do that. He's defended me for centuries.

"Why ask me questions if you're convinced you already know the answers to everything?" I start to walk away.

No. You'll stay.

It's hardly an ominous threat, but I can tell from the tone of command in my head that he's losing his patience with my little rebellious act. There's a fine line between holding his attention and irritating him. I may be getting close to crossing it. I pivot on my heel, and then I trip over the ends of my new wings and fall flat on my face. This upgrade may take some getting used to. "You want to know the same things I do." I brush the ice from my white pants, my hands stinging from the cold. "Be patient for a little while, and as soon as my body relaxes and my memories return, I'll tell you what happened."

If your defective human brain can recover them.

"Exactly," I say. "But what do you have to lose?"

My sanity?

My bark of laughter actually hurts. I've missed his droll sense of humor. First he died. Then when I escaped from the human camp, I had him for mere moments before losing him again.

And now?

He's right in front of me, and he couldn't be further away.

What's wrong?

I swipe at my eyes and shake my head. "Just waiting for my brain to reboot."

Damage to your brain causes your eyes to leak? Humans really are poorly designed.

"I can't even argue with that."

Do you wish we were still bonded? His tone's light —curious.

I think about it for a moment, and I decide to tell the truth. "I do."

Why?

How much is too much? The old Azar. . .these words would have meant nothing to him. I say them as much to test him as anything else. "I loved you—the bond brought us closer. I miss that connection, just like I miss you."

But I'm right here.

"The Azar I knew is gone." As I say it, it really hits me how true it is. He's deader now than he was when they were keeping me in confinement. At least then I had hope, but now my Azar really *is* gone. Our relationships, our interactions—they're delicate. Every person we love is connected to us by an intricate web we create with our words and actions, and the trust we've built. . .once it's ripped away, who we are fundamentally changes.

I'm more powerful now. Is that what you mean?

"Sure," I say. "Yes."

His nostrils flare, and he tosses his head. *It's time to go back. Hyperion and the others will be concerned about my abrupt departure.*

He can say that again. I bet Hyperion crapped a brick—maybe a whole pile of them. "Are you offering me a ride, or are we cruising back?"

Would you accept a ride?

"I'd rather ride on your back than clutched in your claw."

I assume you did this before?

I nod slowly.

I don't like not remembering. It feels like a weakness.

And weakness wasn't allowed among the Blessed. Every person in his life would have seen it as a liability. "None of the Blessed liked me much," I say. "Not remembering me won't make you look bad. Trust me."

He's quiet as I fly up and over his shoulder and settle in on his back. The ridges are familiar, and it feels like every single thing we used to do is just one more slice on my poor heart. At this rate, I'll never heal. I may as well cut my heart out and be done with it.

Can you at least tell me why we came to Iceland?

"When you told me about the heart, I told you about something that happened to me as a child. A group of humans kidnapped me and tried to throw me into the volcano you and I just left. They kept chanting 'heart' in Icelandic."

You voluntarily shared this information? Or I compelled it from you?

"I chose to share it," I say. "I wanted to help you locate the heart and restore your people's ability to procreate."

He launches into the air then, with no notice, like he always did. I'm so much better prepared for it now that even with my unwieldy wings continually shifting and unfurling, I manage to stay on and stay crouched.

You know what I want—answers. What do you want from me?

The fact that he even has to ask. . . "The same thing I've always wanted," I say. "When you first bonded me, we made a deal. I'd be a good little ensnared human, and you'd keep my three siblings safe."

The small humans.

"And I often asked you to try to keep the human casualties as low as possible whenever dragons and humans came into conflict. That's it. Those two things are what I want."

He's quiet the rest of the way back, and I close my eyes, letting the frigid wind whipping through my hair distract me from my misery. When we reach the volcano, Hyperion's perched on the edge of the outer rim, a half dozen strike blessed gathered beside him.

"He's going to demand you throw me back in the volcano the second we land."

I'll refuse, he says.

My heart expands. He doesn't know me, but he's still the same person who bonded me to begin with. He's fair. He understands how it feels to be the little guy. He cares about people quickly. Maybe. . .maybe we'll be alright.

He lands, and then he shakes, and I slide down to the rocky ground.

"Thanks," I say. "For bringing me back. For honoring our deal."

Our deal is off, Elizabeth Chadwick, Azar says, and I can tell he's broadcasting. *We are no longer bonded, nor will we be. You will wait here until your memories return, and once we know what happened to change the earth blessed, you'll be thrown back into the volcano to continue looking for the heart.*

He snags me with one claw, plows through into the volcanic antechamber, and shoves me inside the cage bolted to the side wall that held Sammy, Coral, and Jade.

Rufus and Gordon will keep watch over them until her brain has healed.

Without so much as a backward glance, Azar flies away, Hyperion barely a second behind him. And then he's just. . .gone.

And I can finally bawl like the broken-hearted idiot I am.

I spent over a year studying humans before my father sent me here to recover the heart. I must have asked him what exactly the heart was at least a dozen times.

Each time resulted in a beating.

If I knew what it was, he said each time, *I would tell you. For a time, it was pure magic. Then it was housed in a stone of unbelievable beauty. When we left. . .* He simply trailed off, then.

The last time I asked, he closed his eyes, and I thought he was trembling with rage. . .until he spoke. *It merged with a blessed, a blessed who stayed on earth. A blessed who chose her love for the earth children over her own people.*

Then he attacked me so savagely, I thought I'd died until I woke up a few days later, barely able to move.

Euphrasia nursed me after each attack, and she answered my questions about earth as well as she could. It was never enough. Other than my father, I'm not sure any of the blessed knew quite what the heart was. Or if they did, they'd either forgotten or been frightened into silence.

I knew it would restore our people's ability to procreate. Without it, we had no future. Without it, we were doomed.

And the humans, the earth children, I was told that they would hide and protect it at any cost. Yet, this Liz says she voluntarily told me all she knew of it. What I can't reconcile is why I would trust the word of a human, any human, even one I had bonded, when it came to locating the heart.

But Hyperion insists it's true—she gave us the information that led to our trip into the volcano.

You threw me in the volcano, I ask, *because I was defending* her *and wouldn't force her in myself?*

That really makes no sense. Why would I fight with my brother? Why wouldn't I kill any and every human I met in order to find the heart? They're nothing to us. Worse than nothing, really, since by all counts, their retention of *our* heart is what has harmed us for all these centuries since our departure.

She actually killed you first, and still you begged for her life. Hyperion's expression is unbearably smug, like I'm the pitiable idiot.

It rankles because it's true. I am the idiot here. I apparently told all my people about my dual affinities, though why, I can't possibly understand. It's always been my biggest vulnerability. *Speak plainly. Tell me the things I can't remember, or I'll unleash my fury. We can see who should lead our people here in the search for the heart.*

I forgot how tiring you could be before meeting Liz. Hyperion drops to the ground, his head resting on the snow. Hissing sounds of ice melting from the heat of his body are nothing to the cloud of steam it creates. *When I arrived, you'd been here for quite some time without checking in with Father. You had already bonded the human, Liz. She was entertaining, for an earth child. She changed you in many ways. . .you were happier than I'd ever seen you. You were less. . .focused, too. Maybe that's why you protected her so fiercely.*

How? I can't help asking. *How did she ensorcel me?*

Do you not appreciate anything about her now? Hyperion lifts his head and tilts it slightly. *I find her entertaining, when she's not making me want to flame her.*

I concede she's at least. . .intriguing. *She seems remarkably unafraid around us, given the weakness of the earth children.*

Meeting her was fortuitous. Memories from her childhood helped us know where to look for the heart. You started our search in Houston, the city in which she lived. She brought us here, to the volcano where she was taken as a child. The creatures who wanted her to be sacrificed to them. . .they live in the volcano, and they appear to be demons who change into some kind of cursed form of the blessed, trapped there by magic to burn forever.

I can't help shuddering at that thought—trapped forever? I don't burn, but for creatures that do, I imagine it would also be uncomfortable.

So I met her, bonded her for unknown reasons, and then she found out that we were seeking the heart and brought us here. When and why did I tell you about my two affinities, and why did we both enter the volcano?

Hyperion stands up and begins to pace back and forth. Finally, he answers. *I threw the stupid earth blessed, the long serpentine one, and he knocked you and Liz both in.*

My talons flex. *You* threw *us in? The human was telling the truth?*

You had lost your mind. He stops pacing and his eyes flash. *You only cared about Liz. You didn't care about the heart or our people or anything else. She has a mark of a heart on her chest, and the demons were calling for her—Gullveig —chanting it over and over when they saw her.*

My own brother hurled me and my bonded human into a volcano teeming with demon-creatures, and his justification was that I was crazy. *And?*

This happened before you went into the volcano, but the humans gathered up their forces and attacked us after we traveled to Iceland, firing ice spears at you and I both. They didn't have a hope of harming us. . .until Liz made you weak. They harmed her, and that weakened you. He's scowling mightily. *Then they killed Azar.*

But I'm fine. I don't understand.

I didn't know about Axel—that he was also you. I thought you'd just died. There was a horrible hole in the earth and you burned and burned. . . I've never seen Hyperion upset, not like this.

But then when you checked, all that remained was Axel?

He snorts. *Not even close. You must have burrowed down in the earth—you didn't reveal your secret.*

Then, when?

The humans took Liz. We thought she was dead. She looked dead when they dragged her off. But she returned.

And she came to tell you that she was back?

Hyperion shakes his head again. *No, I found her with you—Axel. That's when you told me you were both. You begged me not to take her to the volcano, but the creatures called to her. I wanted to throw her into the volcano to recover the heart, and you adamantly refused.*

Once Azar was dead, you could do as you pleased.

Hyperion huffs, but doesn't argue.

I tried to stop you, but as Axel. . .

You told me you were Azar, but I didn't believe you, not at first. I thought you were just making up more lies to save her.

I revealed my secret to try and convince you to spare Liz. It didn't work. Hyperion obviously cared less about my wishes than our father's orders, and I can't blame him for that. Honestly, I have no idea why I would care more about protecting one human, bonded or not, than about Father's orders and the future of the blessed.

The volcano didn't kill her, clearly, but it did restore you —the Azar half was dead, and now it's alive. Liz came out changed as well.

Wings, I say.

Yes, but it's more than that. Hyperion sits again, his eye ridges bunched in confusion. *She's. . .sad. Or. . .I don't know. I'm not as familiar with humans as you, but something's wrong.*

She said she doesn't have a clear memory of what happened, so I locked her up until she recalls.

Throwing her in got the earth blessed a big upgrade and restored Azar, Hyperion says. *I think we should just throw her back in and see what happens this time.*

Or maybe we try sacrificing some of her smaller human family members. If they're related, that should motivate her to remember what happened, and we can test whether it's just her the volcano wants, or any human connected to her.

You really don't remember anything, do you? Hyperion shakes his head.

What do you mean?

Liz will hate you forever if you do that.

She fixated quite a lot on keeping them safe.

Other than you, and saving all the humans she can, it's all she cares about.

Maybe we can use that. I stand up. *If we threaten them.*

. .

Hyperion laughs and shoots up into the sky, trumpeting. I follow him, my body coming alive as we do what we were meant to do—fly. My brother swings around wide, circling the volcano we just left. I pick up my speed and pass him, dropping in to fly right in front of him.

His great wings beat frantically, and he's gaining on me when I notice something.

Why are so many blessed heading for the volcano? Eyjafjallajökull?

The one we just left? I wheel around and begin flying toward it, too. It's almost hard to approach. Strike blessed dart and dip, vying for the space to land by the entrance to the cave.

Earth blessed teem on the rocky ground, and as we near, I notice quite a few water blessed as well.

It's true, a water blessed says. *Azar's alive.*

What's going on? Hyperion asks.

The blessed around us all freeze.

As we circle, they shift and jostle and generally shove each other aside until there's room for Hyperion and me to land, at least.

My brother asked why you're here. I direct my demand to a group of earth blessed. They should, at least, answer the questions.

Is it true you're also Axel? Gaia's an earth blessed with

an interesting and unique brain. I like her. If I didn't like her, I might bite her head off.

Yes, I'm also Axel. Answer the question. Why are you all here?

The warrior human's no longer bonded, Halfdan says. He's fairly intelligent and was always quite strong for an earth blessed. He's even stronger now that he has grown forty percent larger. *I hear she got wings, too. Everyone wants to bond her.*

She knows me, Gaia says. *I carried her here—helped her escape the humans and find Axel again.* Her sideways glance at me is almost apologetic. *I think she'll pick me.*

She liked me too, a large, strong water blessed—Plumeria, I think?—says. *She said she would bond me if she were looking for a new blessed. And now?* She scowls at me, as if she's judging me. *She is.*

They're all here. . .to bond the winged human?

My winged human?

Who said that she could be bonded? Hyperion bellows. *The earth blessed can't even bond humans.*

Who knows? Halfdan says. *Maybe we can, now.*

The thought of some other blessed bonding Liz. . . It fills me with an inexplicable rage. I don't wait to talk or try to reason with anyone. I launch into the air, sailing over the heads of the gathered blessed, and I punch a hole through the part of the cave roof that blocks my entrance, raining chunks of rock down on the blessed below.

My eyes are trained on the cage in the corner—but it's empty.

The wind from my wings is battering every blessed in the room as I hover, casting around for the missing humans. Before I can ask about them, Liz flies across the room, zips through a wide spot in the bars of the cage, and dumps her siblings. They scurry to the back of the cage, leaving her at the front.

Liz stands there, acting like the cage was nothing to her.

I charge, furious.

Just before I reach her, my former-bonded grabs the iron bars and flexes, dragging them closed again right in front of my face. "So sorry, Your Majesty." She bobs her head and sinks down a few inches in a strange movement I don't understand. The expression on her face, however, I *do* understand.

She's mocking me.

When I land on the ground in front of the cage, I'm still eye level with her. I notice the blessed in front of the cage have scrambled back to clear a space, not that I care. They deserve to be smashed—rushing in here like scavengers trying to take what's mine. I spin around, and this time, it's not Hyperion bellowing. It's me.

This human's mine. Is that clear?

From the masses of blessed pressed back in the corner of the cave, a silver dragon emerges, her regal head held high. It's Asteria, again. I'm surprised she's even here. When we left, her parents were adamant that only one of their precious daughters could come.

But you aren't bonded, not anymore, so she most certainly isn't *yours.* Asteria never argued with me. Not once. *In fact, Liz and I talked about me bonding her long ago, when you still held her bond.*

Between Asteria and Plumeria, did my former bonded talk to every blessed she met about bonding them? *She doesn't want to bond any of you,* I practically roar. Heat's rising inside of me, and it's only a matter of time before it explodes. In this contained space, with the lava popping and bubbling and those creatures chanting incessantly, I'm not sure what would happen.

"Actually, I was just talking to the blessed who came," Liz says. "I'm not your human anymore, and I think being bonded again might help me succeed in finding the heart."

I forbid it, I snap.

"Yeah," a small voice says from the cage. "Liz isn't bonded to Azar right now, but she will be again soon."

I turn around, leaning closer to the cage. *Who's speaking?*

The tiny human smiles. "My name's Sammy. I'm Gordon's best friend."

You aren't scared of me?

His teensy head's barely two feet away, but he doesn't look frightened at all. In fact, he laughs. "You'd never hurt me."

No? When I snort, smoke billows out. *Why not?*

"You like me best of all, other than Liz."

I do? I shake my head. *I don't like you—I don't even know you.*

"I'm Sammy." He tilts his head. "You'll remember me soon, but even if you don't." He shrugs. "You'll remember Liz for sure."

Why? He's either delusional or very stupid.

"You love her," Sammy says.

Liz claps a hand over his mouth and drags him backward. "Alright, that's more than enough of that."

Love? When I glance around the room, almost all the blessed have evacuated. I don't blame them. Only

Asteria's still waiting, her expression utterly unreadable. *What?* I snap.

You really don't remember her at all.

I don't, I say. *I wish people would stop acting surprised by that.*

Why haven't you killed her, then? Asteria steps closer. *She causes all kinds of problems. She argues with everyone, she breaks out of her cage, and—*

That's why every other blessed wants to bond her? I ask.

Maybe they do, Asteria says. *But even more of them would be relieved if she was just gone, including your brother.*

She's right, Hyperion says. *I spend most of my time either hating her, or wishing I'd bonded her myself. I can't seem to make up my mind which would be better. My life would be easier, though, if she were simply gone.*

If anyone else talks about killing or taking *my* human, I really will have to destroy something. *I'm not re-bonding her, and no one else is either. The reason she's alive, the reason she's here in this cave, is that something happened in that lava, and she's going to tell us what. She's still our best connection to the heart, so she's not dying either.*

Hyperion walks closer. *I heard she was out of the cage.*

I forgot to ask about that. *How did you bend the bars?*

Liz juts out her bottom jaw. "Why do you care?"

"She's stronger," the small human with not-short, not-long hair says. "She has wings, *and* she's stronger. The world just isn't fair."

Asteria laughs. *It certainly isn't.*

Even so, she will stay in that cage until she recovers her memory. I glare.

No, Gordon says. *It's too cold for them here. They can't rest, they can't eat, and it's not healthy.* He glances at the lava. *Not to mention, this whole place is creepy.*

I agree, Rufus says. *They should come back with us to the hotel.*

I dig deep and project a red bubble around the cage. *There. That'll keep them inside, and it'll keep the blessed out. It'll also keep them warmer.*

You're making a mistake, Gordon says.

In all the years I've known him, he's never said anything like that to me. Not ever. When I turn slowly toward him, my fury must show on my face.

I'm doing this for you. Gordon lifts his much larger head, his eyes flashing.

So am I, Rufus says. *If you remembered anything at all, you'd want us to defend her.*

I'm heartily sick of everyone acting like I'm damaged, or worse, like I had gone insane. *Have you all forgotten our goal? We need the heart, and the person most likely to get it for us is right here.*

Asteria's the last blessed in the cavern, other than Hyperion, Gordon, and Rufus. But even she's walking out, at least, until she freezes. *The flame.*

"What?" Liz is pressed against the edge of the cage, her hands tightly wrapped around the bars. "What about the flame?"

What flame? I ask.

There's a flame carved on the entrance to this lava pit, Asteria says. *There are skulls underneath it.* She turns back slowly, but she's not talking to me. She's looking right at Liz. *There were three, weren't there?*

Liz nods.

There are two now.

Hyperion nearly runs me over to look at it himself. He uses a very human word to express his displeasure, and I may not remember much, but for some reason I still recognize the meaning.

What do we think that signifies? Gordon asks.

Well, Liz may have gotten wings, Hyperion says, turning. *But I think she lost one of her three lives.*

We're running out of time, Asteria says.

Speaking of running out of time, Hyperion says. *I told you I went to see Father. I told him you'd died, and he ordered me to mate with Asteria in your place to see whether proximity to the heart has allowed us to finally procreate.*

Okay. I'd always been promised to her, but I find that I don't mind at all. *Go ahead.*

Hyperion frowns. *But now you're here. You can do it. Won't he be surprised when we tell him you* could *do it after all?*

I doubt Asteria will want a two-affinity freak like me. *She doesn't have to,* I say. *She didn't know that I was Azar and Axel.* I can't help thinking about her surprise earlier, when she called me—as Axel—an idiot. *Hyperion's a better choice.*

Not for me, Asteria says. *I'm happy to fulfill your father's wishes.*

❈ 3 ❈

AXEL

As I prepare for my wedding, I can't help thinking how strange my life has become. The last thing I remember, I was leaving for Earth, tasked by my father to finally fulfill the prophecy that's been hanging over me since my hatch.

I was going to locate the heart, wrest it away from the earth children, and return it to our people.

Everyone would rejoice.

My father would finally be proud of me. I'd have a place. I'd be what he needed—what everyone needed. Only, that's not what's happened at all. I've been on Earth for months, and I've made no progress.

No heart.

No conclusive evidence of where they've hidden it.

Earth children—humans, as they call themselves— are all trying to kill us. Earth blessed have become suddenly powerful, but my secret's also been outed.

I still can't believe that I divulged it myself, voluntarily, in an attempt to protect a *human*. A very strange human with wings. A human I both hate and. . .am fascinated with against my better judgment.

There's still nothing but a blank spot where my memories should be.

The news of my dual affinities rocketed through the ten thousand blessed here, but so far no one has done anything about it. At least, not yet. Hyperion has barely even talked about it. All of our people are gathering now, preparing to herald my wedding and mating ceremony with Asteria, the princess of the strike blessed, sent to help create the first blessed egg since we left Earth.

At least, we hope.

I've known this day was coming my entire life.

I never dreaded it.

Asteria's beautiful. She's elegant and smart, and she listens. I can't think of a single blessed I'd rather mate with—our children would be powerful and strong. They'll be fit leaders one day, when she and I can't rule any longer. It's smart. It's what my father wants. And it's what I want—mating with her, producing a successful egg—it would cement my place as my father's heir.

Still, for some reason, I keep thinking about the winged human.

I shake away the stray thoughts and focus.

I only have a handful of decisions to make. When blessed marry, there's a ceremony with a very particular set of promises, and then we dance in the sky. It's beautiful, and when powerful blessed wed, the blessed all celebrate the union along with them. The air above Iceland will soon be replete with winged blessed, trumpeting their best wishes.

The ocean below will churn with water blessed, and the earth blessed will probably celebrate more than any other. It's not every day that one of their kind mates with a strike blessed. Actually, I've never heard of such a thing. Though since I've been alive, only the earth blessed have successfully reproduced, and since they can't fly, their mating's a lot less exciting and beautiful.

But now the earth blessed do have wings.

Which means I need to decide how I'm going to marry Asteria—in which form. I'm analyzing the reasons for each when Gordon interrupts me.

Again.

You have to free them. Gordon's obsessed. He's being more obnoxious than I ever recall him being, about anything in the past few centuries.

Yes, you do. Rufus has been just as bad.

They don't even seem to be scared that I'll melt them. *You do know I'm not just Axel.* I may be in my earth blessed form now, but only because I'm debating what form to take for the ceremony. I'd like to show the others in a very real way that I'm both, and what better way to do it than as Axel?

On the other hand, Azar's a more impressive sight, and he flies faster. Not a lot faster, but enough that it's noticeable. It would be embarrassing if Asteria outflew me at our very first mating.

Should we care that you're Azar too? Gordon asks. *You cared about Liz the same in both forms. We really should have known.*

I'm losing my patience. *This has nothing to do with her—she's human.*

I disagree. Now Asteria's landed next to us. *Leaving*

her in that cage was wrong. If you really don't care about her, then for a wedding gift, give her to me.

I said I don't want anyone else bonding her. We need the information trapped in her head, so we can't allow distractions. I frown. *Why would you even want her?*

I won't bond her if that would bother you, but give her and the children to me. Taking care of them amuses me, and I can help restore her memories faster. You don't remember, but she's quite a warrior among their people.

I saw that she has the earth swords.

A gift from you. Asteria walks closer. *She and I had become quite close.* Her silvery body flows around the bend in the River Ölfusá like molten metal, sinewy and smooth. When she turns back to face me, she's smiling. *Go and get her. Bring her to me.*

Until this moment, I never wanted to melt Asteria's face off. It's insane, of course. I don't care whether my future mate wants the human—what's she to me? Gordon and Rufus seem to think she's extremely important, and the information in her head may be, but she's *just* a human.

Fine, I say. *I'll bring her if that's what you want.*

I launch into the sky as much to get away from Asteria before I do something unreasonable as anything else. When Gordon and Rufus follow, it irritates me further. Until I woke on Earth without any memory of the last few months, they'd never have followed me.

I'm happy they have wings. I'm delighted they're stronger and more powerful, too, of course, but I wish they'd leave me alone already.

The way you reacted to her request. . . Gordon's tone is

smug, which is rich given how hard he's having to work just to keep up with me.

What?

Rufus finally catches up, and he's trying even harder to fly at this slow speed. *That's why we want you to free her. The way you reacted when the other blessed wanted to bond her—you may not remember her, but she's yours.*

Asteria wants her, and she can have her, I snap.

If you hand her over, you'll regret it, Gordon says.

You were supposed to mate with Asteria before too, Rufus says. *You didn't do it, and you said you never would.*

I'm heartily sick of them telling me what I want and what I said. When I finally land outside the volcano, I send the strike blessed and earth blessed I assigned to guard the cage away. On my way through the opening, I stop.

The flame emblem carved in the stone of the entrance is tiny.

The skulls below it are even smaller.

Do they really signify that Liz lost a life when she entered the volcano the last time? Can she enter again and come out unscathed a second time? Why don't I remember anything? Maybe it has to do with my Azar half dying, but then I'd expect my memory loss to extend only to that point.

"Why are you back?"

Liz is sitting on the floor of the cage, one of the tiny human's heads on her lap. The others are asleep around her, draped over her legs. As I move closer, a tiny puff of fur rises a few inches and starts making a strange sort of squeaking sound.

"Stop barking," Liz whispers. "You'll wake the babies."

The tiny fluffy thing whimpers. She pats its head with affection, and she smiles at it. Something about the interaction bothers me. I hate how many things about her I don't understand. *What is that?*

"You liked to pet her, before," she says. "It's a dog. Fluff Dog."

I can't pet things. One claw would flay her wide open.

Liz doesn't argue with me. For some reason, that feels. . .off as well.

You aren't going to insist that I did pet her as you said?

She shrugs. "Aren't you supposed to be getting married?"

Do you want to come and watch the mating?

She flinches, and that perversely makes me happy. "No, I most certainly do not." She turns her face away.

Even that small movement upsets me. I step closer, the gravel under my feet crunching. *Why not?*

Her head snaps back, her eyes bright. "Does it matter?" One eyebrow rises. "Would it make a differ-ence how I felt or what I wanted?"

I shake my head slowly.

"I thought not." She sighs. "Are the earth dragons happy that they're stronger?"

Happy?

"Are they at least relieved?" she asks. "Are you relieved to have Azar back?" She tosses her head. "Of course not. You forgot you even died." She balls up her fists and the fluffy thing squeaks. She leans down and presses her mouth to its head in a movement that makes a strange sound. "Sorry, Fluff Dog."

Do not do that.

"What?" Her eyebrows rise. "Kiss my dog?"

Kiss. Yes, don't do that.

Her lips quirk upward on one side. "You know, you're almost as scary as Axel as you are as Azar. That must be nice—no more fear."

I was never afraid.

"Liar." But then the corner of her mouth twists a lot more, and bizarrely, I know what it means. She's mocking me again.

"At least you're done with the secrets. I'm sure that's nice."

She said *you're*—the emphasis on that word—and that implies she has some kind of secret. *What are you hiding, Liz Chadwick?*

"Things you couldn't understand if you wanted to."

Try.

She sighs loudly. "A thousand tiny moments." Something glistens on her cheek, and she wipes it away. She turns away from me and inhales sharply. Then she carefully shifts the head of the child on her lap to the bottom of the cage and stands, stepping toward me.

It excites me for some reason, her moving closer. I hate the feeling.

"What secrets am I hiding?" Her laugh's bitter. "I'm not hiding them very well, clearly. You were my whole world, Axel, and you don't even remember me. Not a moment, not a glance." Her voice drops. "Not a single touch." She holds my gaze for another moment, and then she turns and walks to the back of the cage, her wings fluffing up until I can't see her at all.

I almost don't hear her, either.

"Now, go away and leave me alone. Forever, if you don't mind."

That won't work. I don't understand all her talking, all the human words and sentiments. *Asteria wants you —she asked for me to give you to her as a gift.* As I say the words, the heat of my rage rises up inside. I'm probably angry because I don't share. But now that I'm mating, I should be able to honor one small request. *You and your other small humans and the noisy fur thing will all come with me.*

"You know, there's a famous human who said it's better to love and lose something than never to love at all."

Love? What is this word, love? The small human mentioned it, too.

"That man was an idiot, but not quite as dumb as me."

What does the word mean?

"It's when you care so much about another person that you would rather be harmed than watch them struggle. You would rather *die* than watch them be hurt. You would do anything—everything—they might ever need—you would burn the world down to spare them pain."

It sounds horrible.

Her laughter sounds strange, almost like she's crying. "You're right, Axel. It is."

She says Axel, not Azar. Maybe that's because I'm in my golden form. Or maybe. . . *Did you care about Axel? Or Azar?*

"I would have been a complete and utter moron to care for either of your forms. Can you even imagine? A human being caring about the leader of the dragons who came to destroy us?"

The more time I spend with her, the more confused I become. *You didn't love me, then?*

She turns so fast that it takes me off guard. "I'm your wedding gift to Asteria now, right?"

Will you come easily?

"Why not?" Her face is blank. "You'll bring my siblings with us?"

She wanted all of you.

"Of course she did."

You don't like Asteria?

"She's much better than her sister Ocharta," Liz says. "I actually don't hate her." She mutters something else so quietly I can't make out the words, except for the word *mating*.

Are you upset I'm mating with her?

"If we were still bonded," she whispers, "you wouldn't be stupid enough to ask me that."

Which doesn't answer my question at all. Would I not ask because I'd already know? Or had we spoken about it? *Do you miss the bond?*

"I miss the Axel who bonded me." She sighs.

I am still me. You can't miss someone who's here.

"I miss you wanting me to say your name. I miss you doing nine hundred sit-ups." She sniffs and lifts her chin. "I miss you flying me places at one million miles per hour."

I can't fly that fast.

"I miss your painfully literal interpretation of everything. I miss you always being there to watch over me while I slept." The feathers of her wings tremble.

Have you remembered anything about what happened in that volcano?

"The demon creatures tried to eat us." She glances behind me.

They're there still, milling, chanting. 'Gullveig,' mostly.

"We didn't get the heart," she says. "Clearly something went wrong."

Asteria believes she can help you recover the memories.

She walks toward me, quickly. "Fine. Let's go, then." She crouches down and gently shakes the small humans who are sleeping. "Hey, guys. Rufus and Gordon are here. We're going to live with Asteria."

The small one with the shortest hair sits up. Sammy, I think. He rubs his eyes and throws his arms over his head, making a strange keening sound. "We can leave the cage?" His eyes light up. "I like Asteria."

"She's marrying Azar, right?" the one with medium length hair asks.

"This is Coral," Liz says. "Sammy's my youngest brother. Coral's the next oldest—five years older. And then barely a year older than her is Jade."

"Hi." The one with the longest hair shakes her hand at me.

"I hate the new Azar." Coral folds her arms. "He's a jerk."

"At least we get out of the cage," Sammy says. "And maybe he'll remember us soon and be nice again."

"Too late," Coral mutters.

"Stop," Liz says.

"Yeah," Jade says. "You don't get mad at something that's broken. It's not his fault."

Liz laughs.

I am not *broken.*

"Oh." Jade tilts her head and bobs it up and down. "Of course not."

Her words are respectful, but something feels wrong. I narrow my eyes.

Gordon and Rufus laugh, which confirms my suspicion. She's saying 'of course not,' but she's implying she's correct, and I just don't know.

"They're just like that," Liz says. "I apologize for their behavior and attitudes." She carefully slides her swords into some kind of strange holder that wraps around her shoulders while somehow still avoiding her wings. "Let's go." She grabs the metal bars, flexes her arms and grunts, and they slide apart easily.

We need better cages.

"Most humans would have been contained." Lix shrugs. "Bonding you and going into the volcano have changed me."

I'll carry Sammy to the celebration, Gordon says. *But Asteria can't have him.*

Or the girls. Rufus is scowling.

I turn so that Liz can climb onto my back.

"No, thanks." She launches from the edge of the cage and flies out of the cavern exit. She's only had wings for a short time, but she's already improved quite a lot.

I think she's been practicing when I'm not here.

She has, for sure, Gordon says. *There are a lot of great things about Liz, but she's not obedient at all.*

I really have no idea why I would have liked her. We catch up to her quickly, and in no time, we're landing near the River Ölfusá.

Just past the bend in the waterway bisecting Selfoss, there's a large section of open land with buildings on either side. Asteria chose this spot for the easy access to the river for the water blessed, and the wide section of land that's openly accessible.

As we draw near, I can't help notice that the earth blessed have been busy. *What is that?*

Our prince is marrying, Gordon says. *The earth blessed worked all night to make you a palace worthy of your position.*

That was a waste of resources. I doubt we'll be here for long.

It's easier than ever before to craft things, Rufus says. *And we're finding that our different strengths are even more marked now that we're stronger.*

"This is amazing." Liz lands on the rocky river bank, her face turned upward.

The earth blessed raised large amounts of stone, reshaping it into one seamless, raised dais, with the shapes of curved, sinewy blessed surging up and around the platform on all sides. Behind it, a massive palace soars—open air in parts and closed in others, but with high, soaring ceilings. Lit torches blaze on every corner so that as the small amount of sunlight for the day wanes, it'll still be easy to see.

Liz shivers next to me, and Gordon steps closer. *Do you need a warmer cloak?*

"I don't have anything that fits over my wings."

Gordon's expression falls. *I can't change shapes anymore and make you whatever you need. I'm sorry.*

She places one hand on his side. "It's alright. I understand. I'm sorry for what you've lost, too."

Losing the ability to shift into human form is no loss. I push past them all and head for the platform where

Asteria's waiting for me. The blessed are gathering around—sunset was the appointed time. It looks like everything's ready.

Earth blessed form? Asteria's words don't betray her disappointment, but I can hear it all the same.

You're disappointed.

The blessed know Azar as their Recovery Leader.

I'll shift. With one small push, I change from Axel to Azar. *Now I'm ready.*

You brought her. Asteria's eyes move past me, to Liz. *I'm surprised.*

Surprised?

And pleased. She smiles. *Very pleased that you're willing to give her to me.*

I can't keep my nostrils from flaring. I don't want to give Liz to her, but that's just part of being flame blessed. We don't share well. I'll have to practice more, now that I'll be mated.

"I'd like permission to fly into town." Liz points. "I need to look for proper coats for my new form."

"She's freezing." Coral slides down from Rufus' back. "Weak little humans like us need things like outerwear."

Liz does look a little blue, especially on her extremities. I'm not an expert, of course, but I haven't seen other humans turning that color.

After the ceremony. Asteria straightens. *Come. Watch us mate.*

I've never seen Asteria act like that—like she's enjoying the suffering of another. *Surely if she's cold. . .*

Asteria calls for the ceremony to start. *Hyperion. Now.*

Liz is shivering now, and it bothers me. A lot. I

blow heated air in her direction, unwilling to let her freeze to death while she's here. Gordon's on one side of Liz and her small humans, and Rufus has fallen in on the other. Even before that happened, all of them moved easily among the blessed for non-bonded humans.

You can't do that anymore. Asteria's gaze narrows. *She's mine. I'll take care of her. Don't worry. She won't die from being a little cold.*

Hyperion's watching us carefully, his eyes bouncing from Asteria back to me. The blessed are filling in all the open spaces quickly—wings for the earth blessed help this process happen much more quickly than it would have otherwise. The water blessed aren't pleased to have been left out of the wing upgrade, but at least they aren't openly complaining.

As all of you know, we're gathered today to celebrate the wedding and mating ceremony of Asteria Strike Blessed and Azar Flame Blessed. Hyperion's starting. *Our hope is that their union will be the first powerful blessed union that creates offspring in the millennia since we left Earth.*

And Axel Earth Blessed, Phileas, one of the stronger earth blessed warriors, says.

Hyperion's glare is ferocious, and Phileas ducks his head quickly.

He's right, I say. *I am also Axel Earth Blessed.*

The earth blessed have had offspring all this time, Phileas says, encouraged by my support. *If it works, how will we know whether he's able to create offspring because of our proximity to the alleged heart, or whether it's because he's earth blessed?*

Hyperion frowns.

I'm not earth blessed, Asteria says. *It'll still be an effective test.*

There's some grumbling, but the blessed seem to accept that.

We'll begin now, Hyperion says.

Prince Axel!

From the edge of the water, a large water blessed surges onto land, disturbing the gathered earth blessed. She's sky blue with small, delicate horns all around her face. I recognize Plumeria, and apparently, I'm not the only one.

"Plumeria?" Liz ducks underneath Gideon and disappears under a churning mass of blessed who are upset at the interruption. I start to move toward the place she just vacated when she shoots up and out, winging her way to the river's edge. She finally lands near a distressed Plumeria. "Are you alright?"

The blessed part more easily for me, and I follow Liz, pressing past the gathered celebrants until I've reached Plumeria. *What's wrong?*

It's Gaia and Gunnar, Plumeria says. *They—I think they're dying.*

Dying? I look around. *From what?*

They built almost the entire wedding pavilion, Plumeria says. *I was brought in for the fountain.* She tosses her head, and I follow her line of sight. I hadn't even noticed there was a fountain beyond the columned and raised platform I'd been standing on for the ceremony.

Where are they? As far as I can see, there's a veritable ocean of water, earth, and strike blessed. I'm not sure where she came from.

They're on the other side of the city, Plumeria says.

After they finished, they said their energy reserves were depleted. They were searching for food.

"Did they find any?" Liz asks. "Are they starving?"

Our energy needs aren't the same as a human's, I say.

"I'm aware," she says. "But when they use up energy, they need to replenish, and Gaia at least was only recently freed from human control."

And?

"She was tortured and rushed back with me," Liz says. "I doubt she's had time to eat recently, and if she helped make all of that." She points. "If they're stronger, they might not even realize how much more energy they used."

We can check on them later, Asteria says. *For now, we must continue the ceremony.*

"It's fine," Liz says. "You go on. I'll go with Plumeria to check on them."

And what exactly will you do for my people, weakling?

Liz ignores me and swings up on Plumeria's back. She does it easily, grasping the vibrant blue scales along the blessed's ridgeline, like she's done it before. "Let's go. Gaia will be happy to see me, at least."

She was asking for you. Plumeria spins around, heading for the river without even waiting for my permission.

No, I say. *I'm coming, too.*

But—

I don't wait for Asteria to complain. I'm not in a mood to hear it. If my people are dying, it could be connected to the augmentation of their power, as Liz said. *I'll return once I've determined what's wrong.* I leap into the air, hovering for the beat of a human heart before my wings pump, sending the gathered blessed careening sideways all around me.

But I'm fast enough to follow Plumeria, and that's what matters. As she said she would, she travels across Selfoss and stops on the far side, near the water. There's a pen constructed of wood containing some kind of creatures, and one of them has been killed. Its bloody entrails are spread in a grotesque line. It smells. . .good, which is hardly surprising. As an earth blessed, I've always been able to consume most anything.

Liz. Gaia calls my former bonded, not me. *You came.* Her call's weak—no wonder I couldn't hear her from across the river. *I heard the bond's gone, and he doesn't remember you.*

Liz reaches for Gaia's face and presses her hand against the great, almost-black head. "What's wrong?"

I'm so sorry—after all you've done, all that you've been through. Gaia closes her eyes, and then reopens them slowly. *If he remembered. . . he would* never. . .

"I know." Liz makes a shushing noise. "Later. We can talk about this later. Right now, we're going to help you—whatever you need."

We? When Gaia's head turns, her eyes widen. *I'm sorry you came. You're supposed to be mating. I thought Liz wouldn't want to see the ceremony, anyway.*

Why would she think that? I drag the chunk of the bloody, furry beast toward her. It's small, but it should be enough to help. *Eat.*

Gaia turns toward Plumeria. *You didn't tell him?*

Tell me what?

I've known Gaia since I was born. She's fierce and strong, albeit small, and she's brave. Her eyes, however, are sad right now. Resigned. *It's time for me to serve in a new way.*

You're not old, I say. *You have time yet. Eat.*

I tried. She shakes her head. *I can't process anything.*

You—what do you mean?

Gaia closes her eyes, so I turn toward Plumeria. *What's she saying?*

But the water blessed isn't paying any attention to me. She's crouched over Gunnar. When she turns toward me, her voice is small. *He's dead.*

Why didn't they eat? I'm practically roaring. *There's food right here.* That's when I see it.

Since we left Earth, millennia ago, only the earth blessed have been able to consume anything but the flesh of other blessed. When the others try, they ingest it alright. . .until they inevitably puke it back up.

Along with a strange, bright greenish yellow goo.

There's a pile of it next to Gaia and another near Gunnar. As Gaia dies, I begin to fear the earth dragon's upgrade might very well spell our doom. If they can't eat anything but dragon flesh either. . .we'll be stuck consuming a rapidly diminishing population, and our former meals won't be nearly as keen on sacrificing themselves now that they're not weak and won't be able to procreate.

The clock for finding the heart just sped up.

If we can't find it, the blessed are going down. Fast.

❋ 4 ❋
LIZ

I've known for a while that the strike and water dragons eat the earth dragons. It doesn't make it any easier to accept, but right now, the bigger problem is that until now, the earth dragons could at least repopulate. Thanks to my decision, my choice inside Eyjafjallajökull, there won't be any more earth dragon eggs.

I hadn't thought that through.

But that means I inadvertently did what Gideon's been praying to do since their arrival: I've doomed the dragons to die. Once they've eaten all their fallen companions, that's it. No wonder Freya was shocked by my decision. She probably didn't think anyone could be that stupid.

"No!" I wrap my arms around Gaia's great neck, shifting the black fur tufts out of the way, and I squeeze. She's such a stunning creature—like a massive black, Chinese dragon. When I get no response from squeezing, I pound on her chest. Something has to revive her.

What's she doing? Azar asks.

Plumeria clearly has no idea either.

"Her heart stopped," I explain. "If we can restart it—"

Gaia's gone, Azar says. *She'll help our people in a new way now.*

She can't. This can't be it. "No." I shake my head. "She was fine. She was strong. Surely there's something we can do." I pull both swords out of the scabbard strapped to my back, ready to threaten him into getting creative. "What else can we try?"

You can't possibly think to hurt me, Azar says.

"Why not?" I lift my chin. "You trained me to fight dragons yourself."

I don't have time for this, Azar says.

He's more right than he knows. When I think about Gaia's death and what it means for the blessed, and how it's all my fault. . .I start to cry. Again. It's so horribly embarrassing. I'm every bit as whiny and pathetic as all the humans Azar encountered before meeting me that first day. Since the moment I sprang from that cursed volcano, I've literally done every single thing that repulses him about most humans.

And I'm about to be forced to watch him mate with Asteria. I'm not really sure what exactly that entails, but it's not something *I* can do, obviously. Watching Azar marry someone else is. . .

Well, my life's become a living nightmare.

Why do her eyes leak all the time? Azar asks.

They're called tears, Plumeria says. *She was fond of Gaia and is now sad about her death. Humans leak whenever they're sad.*

"What about you?" I need to think about something else, or I'll keep leaking. If I've gotten good at anything in the past few months, it's compartmentalizing. Grief over Gaia later. Deal with pressing stuff now. My eyes scan Plumeria, who looks. . .weary to me. "Do you need to eat?"

I won't eat Gaia, Plumeria says. *We became friends.*

"What about Gunnar?" Liz's swords drop. "It's not our way—I hate it, but I don't want you to die. You did work on the fountain, and like Gaia, you were still recovering from our escape. You should eat. . .something."

Plumeria frowns, but she moves toward Gunnar.

I'm the one who told her to do it, but I still can't watch. "I'll just. . ." I wander back toward the ocean, hoping the sound of the surf will drown out the noise. While I stare out at the ocean, the wind clawing at my exposed skin and making my goosebumps return, I shiver. How did my life turn into this?

It's like every moment since the blessed came and Ocharta bonded my mom has gotten worse. The few moments of good—all of them with Axel or Azar—only make me sadder. Now I'm starting to question my basic premise from the moment I left the volcano.

Was I right to lie and say I'd lost my memory?

I'm withholding information I would normally have shared with Axel immediately, so that I have *something* with which to negotiate. But that's not something I ever did before. From the start, I was honest. I told him what I was willing to do, and I meant it. Should I just tell him what happened? Should I tell him the decision that lunatic Freya forced me to make?

What if he hates me for it?

I knew the old Azar and the old Axel. I trusted him.

I don't know anything anymore. It's like I walked out of the volcano and onto quicksand. A sound awfully close to human retching draws me back toward Plumeria. Is that how dragons sound when they eat? I *really* hope it is.

I don't want to look, but I can't help myself.

Plumeria's, unfortunately, not eating Gunnar.

She's puking him back up, along with a strange greenish goo. When she straightens, she looks at Azar, and neither of them look pleased. "What's wrong?"

Something's changed, Plumeria says. *I can't keep that down either.*

This is bad, Azar says. *Very, very bad.*

My guilt intensifies. "We need to talk," I say. "I've. . .remembered something."

Azar's head whips my way. *What?*

She means you should go somewhere with less of an audience. Plumeria's actually a delight—smarter than I realized.

"Yes," I say. "Thank you for interpreting. Maybe you should come with us." I can't help glancing around at all the other dragons who have gathered. They're all looking at the telltale neon green puke piles.

Where would you like to talk?

Before I can answer, Asteria flies overhead, circling in search of a place to land. Clearly we've been absent too long. Her royal silverness is starting to bug me. She gracefully accepted that Axel cared for me before, mostly, but now that he's forgotten me, she's a little too delighted to take advantage.

"Too late now," I mutter.

Why? Azar looks genuinely baffled.

"I need to tell you something that happened in the volcano, and I don't think you're going to like it." I try pushing my thoughts at him—just him—like I used to. I'm not sure how it'll work without the bond. It was always hard for me, but now? *Your people might be upset. I'd rather talk to you without Asteria or anyone else if possible.*

At first, Azar just stares at me.

My message must not have gone through.

But then, just as Asteria lands next to us, he snatches me with one talon again and launches into the sky, mach ten, straight at the place the sun used to be. *I'll be back later. I have to talk to the human.*

I don't consider myself to be a smug person. Usually, I try to be fair and reasonable. But watching Asteria's startled expression as we disappear is quite satisfying.

How far do I need to go?

We're high enough now that I can't breathe, and one of my swords is digging into my right wing hard enough to make me wince. "You can let me go."

He doesn't.

"I have wings, remember?"

My people are all going to die.

Apparently, we're doing this here. A million and one miles in the sky, while I'm held in his claw like a tasty squirrel. Sideways.

"I can't breathe up here." I slap his foot as hard as I can.

His head curls around, one enormous eye meeting mine. In no way does he acknowledge me or my discomfort, but he does wheel downward slowly. *Now?*

"I. . ." I swallow. I'm not sure how to start this. "I lied before," I blurt.

Clearly, I'm amazing at this sort of thing.

"I didn't trust you," I hurry to explain. "The Axel I knew was gone, and. . .I thought knowing what I knew might be the only defense I had to keep my siblings safe." My breath catches, even as we go lower. Thinking about how Hyperion threatened to chuck them into the volcano still makes me sick.

You care about them a great deal.

"I do."

You love them?

"Yes," I say without thinking. "Very, very much."

More than anything else?

I'm not sure I can answer that, not with the painful ache in my heart around Azar. "But when I was in that volcano, I met someone. Her name was Freya."

The blessed oracle?

"She was human, or at least, she looked human to me." I shrug, or at least, I try. It's hard to shrug when bands that are stronger than steel are binding your shoulder blades together and holding you at a forced sixty-degree angle. I slap his foot again. "Can we please land on the ground? This is really uncomfortable."

When he snorts, tiny flames shoot out, but he heads down in a tight spiral, and then he nosedives. I forgot how much of a punk he was before our bond strengthened and he started feeling what I felt. It almost gives me hope, recalling how much he changed, but not really. Most of our breakthroughs came when he was in human form—a form he can no longer take.

"I made a mistake."

He slams into the ground, the rocks underneath his feet compressing with a terrible groaning screech. Most of this island's just a pile of lava rock in some stage of breakdown. We've clearly found a more-rock-than-dirt area. *Explain.*

"When I slammed into the volcano, Freya appeared and fished me out to talk. Meanwhile, you, Gordon, and Rufus stayed trapped. Those creatures— the horned ones—were *eating* you."

Azar frowns.

"Can you shift to Axel?" I know it's stupid for me to ask.

You prefer him? His expression's strange. Guarded, maybe?

"It's not that I prefer him. You're the same—I do know that. I don't much care what color your scales are, but you're so *big* as Azar that I can't see your face well from down here." I can't help my half-smile. "I really miss human-sized Axel."

I was never that *small.*

"Oh, but you were," I say. "When you first came to Earth—when you bonded me, in fact, you were in human form."

He blinks.

"As an earth dragon, you could and did shift. Often."

I shifted into human form frequently? He arches one incredulous eyebrow.

"Well, maybe not *often*, but fairly often."

He stares at me for a moment, but then he shifts. He's still way, way bigger than I am, especially since his upgrade, but he's not towering over me by quite so much. As if he actually cares what I think, he drops down on the ground, his enormous head actually below mine. *Happy?*

Not even close, but I don't bother saying that. "Freya asked me to choose—three times, in fact. Each time she didn't just ask me to choose something in words. She shoved me into real scenarios, and she made me pick how to handle them. At first, I didn't even realize I was in a scene that didn't exist, but I figured it out."

He looks confused, and I can't blame him. I was confused too, and I was there. "She made me pick something pretty big at the end." I cringe. "You had died—as Azar, and then as Axel you were being destroyed." My voice cracks on *died*, and I want to curl up and hide. "And—it was my fault both times."

Hyperion said.

"Of course he told you." I kick at a rock, and it goes flying, but the wind that whips by me in that moment is terribly icy, and I curl inward.

Axel's head rises, and suddenly the air around us warms.

"You just used your flame powers in your earth form. Is that new?"

I've never tried before today.

Because he was hiding his abilities until now. That just reminds me that he also divulged his most dangerous secret to try to keep me safe, right before we were hurled into the volcano.

"The thing is, I felt really bad about all of it— trying to get you to stop hurting the humans and getting Azar killed. Having this weird connection with the volcano that got you chucked by your own brother into the lava. Both things were my fault, and if I'd been able to change them, I would have. I didn't ever mean for you to be hurt. I was trying to keep the dragons and humans from fighting, and someone I trusted. . ." I close my eyes. Thinking about Gideon still hurts. "The person I trusted the most, before I met you, betrayed me."

That's why you should never trust anyone.

"I trusted you." And Axel trusted me with his secret, but I don't say that. He'd just say it was a weak moment—a mistake. He might not even be wrong.

Trusting me was stupid, he says. *I don't even remember you.*

Not gonna lie; that one stings. Because. . . "That's my fault, too." I clench my hands. "I made a deal with Freya. She said she'd restore you—Azar would live again—and she'd strengthen the earth blessed so they'd stop being eaten. They'd be stronger, and they'd get wings."

But. . .?

"I was watching as you and Gordon and Rufus were being eaten by the horned devil things."

You made the deal for us?

"Yes, she saved the three of you by making the earth blessed like the other dragons—you can't reproduce any more, but you're stronger, more powerful, and you can fly." I wince. "She didn't mention that you wouldn't be able to eat anymore."

You traded the lives of three *of us for the future of all the blessed?*

In a large red poof, he shifts into Azar, and he *roars,* and then seconds later, fire erupts upward. As he drops his head, still spewing flame, he melts the partially broken down rock underneath us into bright red, flowing lava.

Without a second thought, I explode upward, winging my way back and away from the destruction. I knew he'd be upset, but this is excessive. He flames the earth for long enough that the lava flow reaches the ocean.

"Sure. It's probably a great time to blow all your power in one spot," I say. "Since you can't really replenish that energy by, say, eating. . ."

He spins around, eyes flashing. *You're a half-wit.*

"That might be a little harsh. Freya clearly tricked me."

Didn't you know why we came here?

He has me there. I did know why they wanted the heart—that they were hoping to restore the very thing I traded away. I should come clean about all of it while he's already this angry. I should tell him I traded his memories of me for the return of Azar, but I can't bring myself to do it. I can't tell him that I ignored his choice. I can't admit that I gave up on us, even though he won't understand or even care about it now.

It matters to me.

Which is exactly the point. It's only hurting me. I'd probably do the same thing again, as long as it contained the misery to me.

"I did know why the blessed came here," I finally admit.

And you just figured, 'Who cares?'

"I asked Freya what would happen to the other dragons, and she said it was unknown, but when she asked me to choose, to let Gordon and Rufus die, to let the earth dragons continue to be abused and eaten by the others, she simply told me they'd be stronger, they'd lose their power to shift—you never liked your human form anyway—and they'd lose the power to procreate. She never mentioned starving to death."

Why was a human making these decisions?

"I wish I knew the answer to that. I might think it's because Freya's human—she looked like one. But she also said she was Odin's wife."

Azar snorts. *A human married to my father? Ridiculous.*

"Or." I frown. "What if, like the earth blessed, like the cursed who shifted from demonic forms to dragon ones. . .what if she can shift?"

Then why can't the rest of us?

I don't have an answer for that. "I'm sorry," I say. "I really—I thought I was doing the right thing. None of the options were great. I was watching you and Rufus and Gordon being eaten and I panicked."

Hyperion threw us in?

I nod.

It's the doom the prophecy spoke of. His expression's grim. *It said he'd destroy us all.*

"But you can save your people," I say. "It said that, too." I stare at him for one moment, and then another.

Until Gordon finds us. He's wheezing when he lands, but he looks pleased. *Not everyone can't eat.*

"What?" Not everyone can't? What does that mean?

Gordon breathes a few times, inhaling deeply and exhaling slowly. He blinks. Then he finally sends another message. *The blessed that ensnared a human can eat—anything. All of them.*

How can that be? Azar looks almost angry.

We think it's tied to the earth blessed being unable to bond humans. They could eat on their own before now, but the strike and water blessed couldn't. At least, not until they ensnared humans.

"You're saying all the dragons who bonded a bright. . .they can eat?"

Gordon nods.

"For how long?"

Gordon doesn't look pleased. *It's been the case for a while, apparently. They didn't think it was relevant to share.*

My eyes widen—every dragon will want to bond a human now, and I know of three who are close. "Where's Sammy? And Coral and Jade?"

Rufus fled with them—straight to the Hotel Selfoss.

"We need to get back right away. Three tiny, unbonded brights? It's too dangerous to ever leave them alone."

Four, Gordon says. *Don't forget yourself.*

I can already imagine Hyperion's next move. He'll take a massive army of dragons and start invading human cities everywhere, just to steal brights. We're about to ensure that human-dragon relations can never, ever be repaired.

Unless I can stop it.

$\mathbf{\mathscr{H}}$ *5* $\mathbf{\mathscr{H}}$

AXEL

When I hatched, Gordon was already the second in command among the earth blessed. The prince, at the time, was the largest and meanest of the earth blessed. He did quite a few things badly, but top of the list was forcing any blessed he disliked to be offered as food to the other blessed.

It was effective—he stayed in power because his enemies died.

At least, it *was* effective until he decided the pretty golden dragon, although I was still quite young, was a threat. I'd shown a lot of promise from hatch, but as I grew, I could clearly do things that other earth blessed couldn't. Most earth blessed had something they were great at—manipulating metals, encouraging new growth in plants, tunneling, shaping stone, or using some combination of materials to defend against other attacks.

I could do it all.

As word about me grew, Uriah knew he had to take

action. The solution was simple, really. Each month, the earth blessed were expected to cull the older, the weaker, or the problematic blessed from their numbers —to feed the other blessed. Before they started voluntarily culling, the strike, water, and flame blessed would simply attack when they got hungry. It was chaotic, and there was a lot of collateral damage to all parties. By the time I was born, submitting a list of fodder to the other blessed was already established practice.

When my name showed up on the list, I wasn't even very surprised. Euphrasia was the only one I could address it with. *I'm not sure what to do,* I said. *I can't very well submit to the demand.*

No, I doubt a simple execution would be enough to kill you, even if you were inclined to allow it, Euphrasia said. *Not to mention, the prophecy says our people need you.*

But I can't disclose that, either. No one can know.

Which means it's time. Euphrasia's smile was soft. *Uriah has been a terrible leader—you shouldn't regret replacing him. You're doing a service to the others.*

A challenge for leadership requires a ratifying vote, however. One of the earth blessed would have to support me when I challenged Uriah. It was a practice that made sense. Otherwise, every blessed named on the list would challenge Uriah, and he'd be stuck fighting every single blessed who was sent off as a sacrifice.

But ratifying someone's challenge was risky.

If the person you ratified didn't win, you'd find your name on the chow list the following week.

What if no one supports me?

Euphrasia shook her head. *Then I guess your double affinities will be revealed.*

I had a very nervous heart when I challenged Uriah. On the one claw, if I challenged him as Axel and lost. . .that would be bad. The threat of dying should be enough, really. But if I challenged him and no one ratified my claim? I'd have to out myself.

That might be worse.

It was still my best chance. When all the earth blessed gathered to see that week's tribute off, I projected loudly. *Axel Earth Blessed challenges Uriah, Prince of the Earth Blessed, to a fight for leadership.*

Uriah laughed.

So did his supporters, which was basically all the earth blessed in attendance. He might have been feared rather than loved, but that was a common theme among our people. No one was beloved. It's not our way.

Will anyone ratify this upstart hatchling? Uriah looked with a scowl. Every blessed there knew that if they supported me, they might die, too.

When no one spoke up, I began to catch individual earth blessed's attention. None of them wanted to die, so they all slowly shook their heads.

Until Gordon. *I ratify Axel Earth Blessed.* He didn't stop there, though. *He should not have been named. He's neither old, nor weak. His challenge is just.*

Gordon wasn't quite as large as Uriah, but he was fast. He was also quite strong, and his strike was vicious. I'd seen Gordon kill many earth blessed in challenges, and I'd seen him kill two water blessed and a strike blessed in altercations between our people.

Even if I failed to defeat Uriah, I thought Gordon might have a chance against him.

That day, I had no idea what inspired him to speak against his ruler. Perhaps I should have known he had a good heart, but I didn't really learn that until later. On that day, I simply knew that without him, my secret would have become common knowledge. My father might have killed me the second he discovered it.

I was an abomination, but Gordon's support kept me alive, and after I defeated Uriah, ripping his head from his body, Gordon congratulated me on my success and asked to stay on as my second-in-command. He's been by my side ever since.

I trust him.

He's earned that trust by supporting me in everything for centuries. Together, we turned the earth blessed into a stable, strong group, in spite of the terrible lot we'd drawn of keeping the other blessed fed.

That's part of the reason his insubordination over this human rankles so much. *You should bond Liz to keep her safe.* If it had been *anyone else* who worried more about the well-being of my formerly-bonded human than me, I would have removed their head.

This isn't about her. It's so much bigger than a human.

"He's right," Liz says. "I'm absolutely positive that once Hyperion hears this news, he'll round up all the dragons he can and attack human settlements, forcibly bonding brights until all the blessed have a bonded human."

As he should. My irritating, winged human actually just pointed out something interesting. For the first time *ever*, we've found a way to feed all the blessed. . .without killing any others of our kind. *Maybe this isn't as terrible as I thought. We just need to round up enough humans.*

You can't just bond any human, Gordon says. *Only the bright humans can be bonded—and we're not sure whether the earth blessed can even bond humans. They couldn't before.*

"And I know you don't remember this," Liz says, "but before we left Houston, you forced the dragons to release any humans who didn't agree to the bond— you gave the humans the choice they never had."

The humans did use the ones we left behind to kill the blessed they were bonded to, Gordon says.

"Which was only possible because they shouldn't have bonded humans who didn't want to be bonded in the first place."

Ensnaring Liz must have impaired my judgment. *Leaving bonded humans behind was a major error in judgment. It left all their blessed vulnerable.*

Liz looks like she wants to argue, but she doesn't.

Let's go, I say.

"If you allow the blessed to forcibly bond my siblings, you'll regret it," Liz says.

Oh? I look her up and down. She's fierce, for a human, but so small, and so weak, I can't really credit her threat, even with my swords.

"I'll kill myself if you allow it, and then who will you chuck into the volcano to retrieve your precious heart?"

She threatened the same thing before, Gordon says.

Liz rounds on him. "Whose side are you on?"

Axel's. Gordon frowns. *Always Axel's.*

Liz huffs, like she can't believe he's saying that. "He doesn't even remember whose side he's on."

Ignoring her muttering, Gordon continues. *When you first bonded her, she threatened to kill herself, thereby weakening you when the humans attacked, unless you kept her siblings safe.*

And I agreed?

Gordon slowly nods.

That was a bad decision on my part, wasn't it? I watch Liz carefully when I say, *I think that this time, I'll do the opposite. Any blessed here can bond her siblings—it's a matter of life or death.*

Liz crouches and then launches into the air, her wings pumping. Apparently she plans to protect them against more than ten thousand blessed all by herself.

Gordon and I follow, and I can't help my curiosity. What in the name of the heart does this little person think she's going to do? She has no power, no real leverage at all. If she actually tries to kill herself, we can probably stop her, and if she succeeds, we'll find another way to reach the heart now that we know where it is.

Once Hyperion and the other blessed learn it's her fault the earth dragons can no longer reproduce, they'll be more than happy to end her short and insignificant life.

Everyone's already gathered, thanks to the planned mating, so when we arrive, Liz lands in the center of the dais, next to her siblings. She wasn't wrong in her guess. The blessed are already clamoring to bond them.

They all fall silent as Gordon and I land beside Liz. *We're still learning about everything that happened in the volcano, in our ongoing pursuit of the heart. However, it appears that earth blessed can no longer consume any sort of food—only a blessed who has ensnared a human can.*

And we have four right here, Asteria says. Four brights —you can witness how it works to ensnare one.

"That would be a mistake," Liz says. "Many of you will recall our Thanksgiving celebration. It was the first time I talked to most of you about the importance of humans having a *choice* in the bond."

That was fine when blessed didn't really need bonded humans except for our own convenience, Asteria says. But now it's a matter of life and death.

It's the same thing I said moments before, but for some reason it sounds wrong to me. For the humans, it would change their entire life.

"What's a life without choices?" Liz launches into the air again, flying around above the blessed. "Every single human you will bond will have family, friends, connections, and a job. Every single one will be forced to give all of that up for *you.* Their lives matter as much as yours—you should be asking if you want them to sacrifice all that to save you."

No one seems to appreciate her sentiment, because she's wrong.

Humans live shorter lives, and they're small and weak. From the research we did, they already shorten their own lives with unhealthy decisions, wars, and risky behavior. It would be difficult to value their lives as being on par with the blessed, who can live for centuries, are large, and are powerful.

If we weren't in such dire need, we would have the luxury of trying your way, Hyperion says. Our top priority now is confirming the earth blessed can bond humans, and that once they do, they can eat.

Liz lands, and she draws her swords. "And you mean to use my siblings to test your theory?"

We do. Hyperion looks almost amused. *The last time you attacked me, you were at least bonded to Axel. How could you possibly harm me now?*

"I doubt you want me dead," she says. "At least, not yet. That means all I have to do is keep you away from the children."

You can't use the children to test. They're too young, Gordon says. *We protect our young.*

Or we would, if we had any, Asteria says.

Sammy's climbing up on Gordon's back.

We can find other brights for the test. Brights who aren't children. Rufus has also moved, but it appears to be in order to shield the girls. *With more than ten thousand blessed, three children won't make any difference.*

We do need to see whether the earth blessed can even bond a human, I say.

"Why don't you ask the blessed who have already bonded humans what they think?" Liz tosses her head. "Ask them whether they think you should force these bonds."

That's not a bad idea, I say. *Ask the blessed who have been through this—they all forced their bonds, did they not?*

Liz sighs. "They did, but I think they wish they hadn't." Her voice drops to a whisper. "Or at least, I hope that's true."

I wish I had asked Alice. A water blessed—Jericho— has surged toward the front of the river bank. *She's smart, fierce, and our bond is valuable to me. We haven't entwined yet, but we're working toward it. I can feel the bond tightening.*

You forced it, and look, Hyperion says. *You're fine now.*

I think we'd have been better much sooner if we'd started in a better way. Jericho inclines his head and drops back into the water, and only then do I notice the small figure with blue hair on his back.

I also wish I'd asked for permission. Helvetica, a strike blessed, circles and lands, a human with silver hair on her back. *He and I are also close to entwining, I think, but we would already have done it, if we hadn't been enemies at the start. I think Liz is right. Forcibly bonding humans will be bad for us and for them. It will also enrage the rest of the humans. They've already attacked us on multiple occasions, and their weapons are improving. Their attacks may be a nuisance now, but they could grow worse.*

We must protect ourselves, Hyperion says. *If we don't all bond humans soon, we'll starve and die. There won't be any blessed for them to attack.*

"Then give me a chance to find you willing humans," Liz says. "I think I can."

Azar may not remember this, but every attempt he made to communicate with them was met with bombs, spears, and violence. Hyperion looks around. *He told me that himself —and then the humans* killed *him. We all watched as it happened—Liz caused his death herself. And her dear human friend, who lived among us, set the trap.*

"That's true," Liz says. "But you also know that Gideon betrayed me. Because he was my friend, I trusted him. That trust was misplaced. But there are humans worthy of trust, and I think I can find them."

You think you can find ten thousand trustworthy humans? I shake my head. *It's too many.*

"Give me a week," I say. "You already told me that you don't eat very often. We should have some time. And if it doesn't work, you can always attack and steal the humans you need." She cringes when she talks about stealing humans, but she holds the line.

In spite of myself, I'm impressed.

Not a week, I say. *Three days.*

"I can't find ten thousand brights in three days," she says. "It'll take more time than that."

Time we should be using to locate and retrieve the heart. Hyperion scowls. *If you don't want your siblings bonded, let's have an earth blessed bond you—it'll also be good to have a blessed with control over you who can keep you in line.*

She can have her three days, I say. *We can evaluate what progress she's made before we're weakened and unable to capture humans ourselves.*

We do need to determine whether the earth blessed can eat once they're bonded, Hyperion says. *If they can't. . .*

"I'll take an earth blessed with me," Liz says. "I need a blessed with me to identify which humans are able to be bonded, anyway. The first bright we find who's willing, we'll bond to that earth blessed—if it's possible—and have them try to eat."

I'll go with you. Phileas isn't the blessed I expect to squeeze his way through the gathering, straightening and shaking the frill that frames his reddish-brown head once he finds the space.

As will I, Agrippa says. She slides right past the gathered blessed, easily twisting through the open gaps, her bright green coils gathering next to Phileas. *I believe she will find humans who are willing, if she says she can.*

I'm especially surprised the two of them came forward, because they never get along.

I'm sure plenty of earth blessed would volunteer to go, if it makes it more likely they'll ensnare a human, Hyperion says.

As if he was giving them permission, they all start to clamor for the chance.

But she can't go without me, I say, turning toward Liz. *Unless you're traveling somewhere on this island. You need a portal.*

"You can open one and then return to gather us later," Liz says. "I would never impose on you to come." Standing on the top of the platform, entirely surrounded by the blessed, she doesn't even look frightened.

She must be.

But she doesn't look it.

She looks like a warrior. For the first time, I actually think a pitiful, tiny human looks. . .regal. Not in most ways of course, with her soft, vulnerable body, but with her hair blowing in the icy wind, and with her defiant expression, I can almost understand what I might have admired about her before.

You should bond Liz again, Agrippa says. *She might have gotten you killed, but I think she's learned, and I liked you better when you were entwined.*

Entwined? I glance at Hyperion for confirmation. No one told me we were entwined.

My brother nods, but doesn't elaborate.

We have a lot of work to do, I say, *and Liz has some kind of connection to the volcano where we believe the heart is hidden. No one will harm her, but we won't bond her either— the pain when that bond is broken would be too great.*

Although, apparently *I* was entwined with her, and I feel no pain at all. Perhaps the impact of such a thing has been exaggerated.

Where will you go to search? Hyperion asks.

Liz turns toward Gordon and Rufus. "I'd like them to take my siblings somewhere safe and keep watch over them while I'm gone."

Of course, Gordon says.

Asteria, who has kept quiet for quite a while, and whose wedding day was just destroyed, says, *I'll keep watch over them, too.*

Liz bows her head. "I would very much appreciate that. Thank you. And I'm sorry that today's celebration was interrupted."

Asteria's eyes narrow, but she doesn't say anything else.

Where are we going? I ask again.

Liz may need to sleep first, Asteria says. *Humans need time to recuperate each day—down time. They usually do this at night, when it's dark. Since it's dark here most of the time, I can't keep track of their rest cycles as easily.*

"I'm fine," Liz says. "I think we should go now—we have no time to waste."

To where?

"To a small town in Utah called Pleasant Grove." Liz smiles. "I made a friend a few years ago, and he owns a shop there. I think he'll be able to help us find people who will help."

You really think you can find humans who will be willing to have a blessed bond them? The blessed has all the power in the bond. We can force the humans to do anything we want.

"I think the deciding factor will be whether we offer them a choice." Liz appears to be serious.

You think they'll choose to allow us to bond them. . .because we're allowing them to choose? How is that different than forcing them? I ask.

She ignores my question and asks me another. "What do you need from me to find Pleasant Grove, Utah?"

It takes some time for the humans who are with the blessed to locate the things we need—images and geographical coordinates. They spend a lot of time complaining that we don't have something called *internet*. Apparently the other humans have disabled it somehow, but Iceland has some basic library resources, and we finally locate the information. Most of the strike and water blessed disperse, bored of waiting to hear our decisions.

Unfortunately, quite a few earth blessed have gathered.

Some are standing around, but many are practicing their flying skills, and it's a little distracting, being surrounded by dozens and dozens of blessed, all dipping, diving, and pivoting. Some are even racing above us.

Liz watches all of it with a strange expression, her lips compressed, but her eyes almost smiling.

When Agrippa beats Lars, she claps and cheers. "Brilliant!"

Why are you all here? I push the question to all my earth blessed.

Every single earth blessed freezes and turns until they can see me. No one answers, though.

Why haven't you dispersed like the others?

We want to come. Lars lands near Liz, and he turns to look at her. *Can we?*

Why are you asking her? I gnash my teeth. *I'm your leader, not her.*

Every single one of them duck their heads in respect, but *still*, none of them leave.

Elizabeth Chadwick wishes to find a peaceful way for us to bond humans, Agrippa says. *But we have seen her own people treat her badly.*

They tried to kill her, Phileas says. He's lying down behind Liz like some kind of pet.

And you would risk your life to save hers?

Yes, Phileas says.

She risked her life to save ours, Agrippa says. *And she has risked it to save yours as well. She liked you as Axel, and she never betrayed you to bond Azar. It was always you, either way.*

And she kept your secret, Lars says.

You may be our leader, Phileas says, *but we serve her by choice.*

Have the earth blessed always been so irritating? Now that they're strong, now that they're fierce, they're still desperate to serve? *She can't protect you. She can't even protect herself.*

That's why we want to come, Agrippa says. *She's trying to protect us even when she hasn't the strength.*

No, she's trying to keep her *people safe,* her *siblings,* I say.

And in so doing, she means to avoid further angering the many, many humans who are already trying to kill us, Phileas says. *You agreed to give her a chance. Let us help.*

Liz walks toward me. "We don't want the humans to notice when we travel to this small town, if we can avoid it." She turns toward the earth blessed. "I really appreciate all of you being willing to help."

They're watching her, listening.

"But we shouldn't take more than three or four of you—it'll keep us from being noticed. Even with the mountains, more than four would be pushing it."

But four can't keep you safe, Agrippa says.

I'm all the protection she needs. I straighten. *I'll take one earth blessed to test whether the bonding will work. Phileas.*

He has the worst personality, Agrippa says. *At least take someone who knows how to be pleasant while meeting a human.*

"Can they both come?" Liz asks. "If we land where I showed you, behind the main mountain, before the sun rises, it should be fine."

I can't help my nostril flare, but saying no would probably be unreasonable. *Fine.*

I'm a little worried that I'll have trouble opening a portal—who knows what dying and coming back might do—but it's easy. Easier than I recall it being, even. It *does* open a few feet off the ground, but all of us can fly, so it's fine. Perhaps it's easier because I made such a small one. The last one I made had to admit thousands of blessed across an immeasurable space. *Come.*

Liz peeks around the edge of the portal, her eyes widening.

Is it alright?

She inhales slowly and then exhales. "It's fine. I'm just—I really hope this works."

I should be enraged. She convinced all of us to trust her, and now she's expressing fear. My people's lives are at stake, but I can sense her honesty, too. She believes this is the best way for us and for the humans, so I can't fault her for pushing even with her doubt.

She squares her shoulders, and her wings spread out behind her. She's still a soft, strangely-shaped earth child, but she's growing on me.

Not that I'd ever admit it.

When she jogs a few steps and leaps into the air, her wings beating furiously, Agrippa also takes to the air, following her through immediately. I watched her win several races earlier, so I shouldn't be surprised she's a graceful flier, her wings light and quick. Phileas flies through right after, bobbing and lurching like he's too heavy for his own wings.

Once we've all passed, I close the portal and look around.

It's dark, and it's still chilly. The human buildings down below appear to be built more densely than they are in Selfoss, but they look more similar than I expected. *How will we locate your friend?*

Liz frowns. "Something just occurred to me—which means I'm an idiot."

What? Agrippa asks.

"I was assuming I could walk around and talk to the humans. . ." Liz shakes her head. "But I have *wings* now." She says a strange word under her breath and drops to the ground, kicking her feet out in front of her and dropping her head in her hands.

The strange thing is how her frustration makes me feel. Instead of being angry, or frustrated myself, I feel. . . Something I've never felt before. I want to *help* her.

And there's nothing I can do.

I feel helpless.

Something I don't like at all.

All I need to do is borrow a cell phone.

Once I've looked up the number for Blak-fyre Games, we'll be fine. I can have Norm come meet me anywhere, I bet.

But how am I supposed to get a phone, looking like this? I'm exhausted. I'm scared for my siblings. I'm terrified all the dragons will die, and it'll be my fault.

And I'm even more scared that I'll fail in finding humans and they'll basically attack, only it'll be all over the world, ensuring humans die by the millions and blessed too. The stakes are so high, and it feels like they have been for months, now. I want to cry.

But I also really, really don't want to cry in front of Axel. I remember him being so frustrated by the weak and whiny humans, but here I am, bawling all the time. I can't seem to help it.

I do the best thing I can think of and wrap my oversized white wings around myself like a feathered curtain and try to be as quiet as I can while I have my mental breakdown.

What do we do? Phileas asks. *Is she broken?*

They could at least ask on a private channel where I can't hear them.

I'm not sure, Agrippa says. *Maybe she's hungry.*

"I'm not hungry." I clench my jaw, wipe my tears, and force my panicked hysteria down where it belongs, deep inside my gut, motivating me. I wipe my face on my white tunic. "Freya, you idiot. If you can hear me, shame on you. What kind of woman sends another warrior out into the world in a white tunic?" Even looking down at myself, I can see that it's already covered with grime.

I must look like a homeless, junkie angel wannabe.

That's when it hits me.

Dragons have invaded Earth, so I'm sure that the general public is on slightly higher alert than they normally would be, but there have been absolutely zero reports of winged humans. There have been no Valkyries I've even *heard of* other than me. Humans out here, in *Pleasant Grove,* Utah, won't have even seen a dragon other than the ones on the television. To them, it must feel mostly surreal, even now.

I bet the preppers have hidden in their bunkers, and the rest of the world's starting to wonder whether it's all a conspiracy and the government's just making it up. That kind of skepticism is just human nature.

Which means, if they see a dingy angel wannabe out here, the most obvious assumption would be that I'm a lunatic, not that I'm connected to the dragon invasion. I've somehow crafted the heaviest, most elaborate wings

anyone has ever made for cosplay—that's all. As long as
they don't, like, see me flying or something, no one will
assume they actually work. As long as I can avoid some
kind of forced inpatient situation, I'll be fine.

I stand.

You're done leaking? Azar asks.

I sigh. "For now, anyway." It's still so embarrassing,
but I square my shoulders and start marching toward
civilization. It takes me about a quarter mile to
remember that we're literally in the middle of the
closest mountains and it would take me hours to hike
down to Pleasant Grove. Luckily, Azar has been
following me with the stealth of a woodchipper. I'm
assuming they all have.

"Hey, you can give me a ride while it's still dark," I
say, "right?"

Of course, Azar says.

I snort. "Not you. You're the size of a cruise ship.
I'm talking about Agrippa. She's more travel-sized."

I'm not letting you go wandering around by yourself.

"Are you worried I'll alert the local militia and
you'll get attacked?"

Of course not, Azar says. *We have your siblings.*

*And the last time she was with the humans, she attacked
them and freed us,* Agrippa says. *She's trying to find brights
to stave off a war. I trust her.*

She's still too important to risk, Azar says. *What if the
humans recognize you and attack you? With your fluffy wings
and tiny swords, they could kill you easily.*

"Not a single human here will be a threat," I say.
"Trust me."

I don't trust your judgment on this matter.

"It was so much easier when you could shift into a human form," I say.

I'm not concerned about making things easy for you.

I can't tell whether Azar's making a joke. It would have been a joke, before he lost his memory, but I think he's being serious. "Do you want me to have a real chance with this? Or not?"

Azar frowns.

"I won't be going that far." I point at the slight light over the other side of the mountains. "Hikers come up here around dawn, or I'd let you fly me over, but I can't risk them noticing you and calling the cavalry. You're bright red and massive, and it's hard to miss your magnificence." A little flattery never hurts, but even spreading it on thick, it takes me five more minutes to convince him to stay put.

"Could you at least switch to Axel? He's less recognizable."

He doesn't even argue that point.

I can sense him better when he's Axel, too, Agrippa says. When we finally head out, we're not even flying. Axel insists it's less visible and safer for us to slither through the mountainside.

It's kind of nice to lie on something—I won't lie.

I even close my eyes for a minute.

It's less that I'm exhausted, though I am, and more that for the first time since being locked in that hanging cage, I'm away from Axel. I couldn't have done this on her before—with her wings, she's far easier to grip. Snake-form-earth dragons are usually the hardest to ride, like Gordon, but with wings, I have a joint to hold. Her movements are smooth and fast, and we make good time.

The trip over the mountain's actually pretty nice.

It's cold, though. I'm lucky we're not buried in snow. Mount Timpanogos is as pretty as Norm always said it was, but it's colder than I imagined. I crouch as closely to Agrippa as I can. I have no idea how the dragons stay so warm, but I'm grateful for it. When we reach Grove Creek, I direct her to follow it until we reach the reservoir.

The sun's barely starting to be visible over the horizon now, and I'm forced to stifle a yawn.

You're tired. You need to sleep.

I shake my head. "No time. I have to get to my friend as early as I can. We can't waste a second."

Why do you believe your friend will help us?

It's an interesting question. Why do I?

"Norm's kind of a dork," I say. "Which means nothing to you, but the way I met him was. . .he was super into something called Live Action Roleplay Games—LARP for short."

I have no idea what that is.

"It's a game where humans dress up and pretend they live in a world that's not ours."

I'm still confused.

"So am I, believe me." I can't help my smile. "Anyway, Norm wanted to learn how to fight with a wooden sword on his quests. He tried a few places, but eventually, they referred him to the gym I was training at."

For what?

"Norm was a little. . ." How would the dragons describe it? "A little fluffy. He never felt like he fit in with the other humans in the games."

He ate too much. This, I've seen.

"It's not just that—the other guys he played these

games with thought he was kind of a joke. He wanted to be a cleric, which is like a religious priest or something, but they were supposed to be warriors too, and Norm wasn't much of a warrior. He worked all day at a job he hated—he was a plumber, and it paid well. So one day, he took the money he'd saved and took a vacation where he came out to Houston to learn to use a sword properly. He wanted to show them he wasn't someone to laugh at."

He wanted to become a warrior.

"Yes." I should have led with that. The blessed love their warriors. "Exactly."

And did you teach him to be a warrior?

"I was like twelve years old," I say.

How many years are you now?

"Almost twenty-three," I say.

You haven't seen this friend in a long time?

"He came out for a week of vacation almost every year after that," I say. "That's how I know the name of his gaming store. After he figured out how to handle those wooden swords, I guess he became kind of like the warrior-cleric of the nerds, and Pleasant Grove is chock full of dorky people like him."

I don't understand 'nerds.'

"Me either, sister."

We're at the reservoir, and I can't help looking around and taking it in as the sun rises behind us. It's serene and beautiful in a way not many things have been for me in months.

"I need to leave you here," I say. "I'll be back as soon as I can."

You want me to wait?

It pains me to say this, because it'll take me

forever to get back to her where Axel and Phileas are, but she can't wait here. As the sun comes up more fully and people start percolating, someone will spot her for sure. "You need to go back to Axel. I'll find you soon."

How?

"I'll get back to where we landed. You stay there, hidden in the curve of the mountain."

Agrippa looks at me for a moment, her eyes studying mine. *Be safe, warrior friend.*

"I'm sorry about Gaia," I say. "I can't believe she's gone. I'm really, really sad about it. I liked her a great deal."

She was a beautiful blessed.

"She was," I say. "And I mean to make sure we don't lose any more."

I believe you, she says. *Don't let us down.*

No pressure at all.

As I walk away, I can't help checking over my shoulder. The sun's rising quickly now, and Agrippa's still watching me. But when I walk another dozen or so paces and turn again, she's finally gone. I square my shoulders and continue onward, almost grateful for the miserable cold biting at my exposed skin. It's keeping me awake and alert.

Which is why, when the truck screeches to a stop on a small residential street, I'm ready to deal with the driver.

"You okay?" The man rubs his eyes. "You look. . .cold."

He doesn't even mention my wings. Off to a good start.

"Uh, I went for a hike," I say. "But I got in a fight

with my boyfriend, and I told him to go away." I shrug. "He listened, and then I realized that was stupid."

"What kind of jerk drives off and leaves a woman in the mountains in December?"

It's December already? Of course it is—we had Thanksgiving, then we made it to Iceland and searched, and then the humans attacked. I was there for a while, and then we had the whole escape and lava. "What's the date?"

"Don't tell me you're from sixteen hundred and four." He's smiling.

"No, just LARPing a little too hard and lost track of the real world. I think that's probably more than weird enough."

"If I were you, I'd probably have told my jerk boyfriend to take the wings and leave me a coat." He chuckles.

"Are you kidding me? I spent a year's savings on these wings. He can't have them."

Within another two minutes, the man has loaned me his phone, and even though it's six fourteen in the morning, Norm answers when I call. Bless him.

He sounds groggy, though. "Ello?"

"Norm," I say. "It's me."

The words he says next are shocking, really. "You're alive?"

I cough to make sure the truck-driving good-samaritan can't hear him. "I'm actually here in Pleasant Grove. My *boyfriend* ditched me after we got in a fight. I could use a ride. Any chance you could come pick me up. . ." I glance around.

"Uh, we're at Grove Creek Drive and 920 East, by a little orchard thing," the man says.

"I heard him," Norm says. "I'll be there in less than ten minutes."

"He's coming." I hang up and smile. "Thank you."

"You keep this." The man hands me an old, beat-up work coat. "Take off the wings and put this on before you freeze." He's smiling, though. "And next time you pick a boyfriend, find one at church instead of while wearing elf ears."

"Good advice," I say. "But I'm afraid I tend to fall for the bad boys."

"The pretty girls always do." He puts his car in drive. "Do you mind me asking what you paid for those wings?" He's squinting now. "Because that's the coolest costume I've ever seen. I swear, they almost look like they could be real. My daughter Maya would love them."

"More than you can even imagine," I say honestly. "They're the most expensive thing I've ever bought." They cost me the love of my life. Or maybe they were my consolation prize after I lost the love of my life. Either way.

He's shaking his head as he drives away.

The work coat does *not work* around my wings, but I drape it around my body from the front, hooking the shoulders over mine backward. It's not exactly warm, but it's much, much better than what I had before.

When Norm drives up, I'm relieved. Three more cars have passed me in the growing light, and two of them stopped and drove so slowly, I was worried they were calling the cops. Unfortunately, Norm drives a Kia, and it's very small. I almost can't cram my stupid wings into the car.

"Do I want to know?" He's got one eyebrow raised.

"I'll explain everything, but I need some clothing," I say. "And I'd really like a shower."

"It also looks like you could use a nap," he says. "No offense."

"I'd really like one," I say. "But I have very little time."

"I thought you died," he says softly. "They showed video clips, Liz. It looked. . .bad."

"I did, actually, but Gideon brought me back." Norm never trained at the same MMA gym that I went to with Gideon, but he heard about him plenty over the years.

"It almost looked like you were on the dragons' side," Norm says. "But clearly not, if you're here, dragon-free."

"About that," I say.

His eyes widen.

"I am kind of on their side, but it's not what you think. They never wanted to attack and kill us." I sigh. "They came for something they left here a thousand years and change ago, and without it, they're all dying."

It takes me the entire drive back to his place, but I explain what happened in broad strokes. By the time we reach his cute little green house, he's stunned. He's staring straight ahead, his hands still at ten and two.

"Wow," I say, just to say something. "Your house is great."

"Thanks." He parks in the tiny garage, kills the engine, and turns sideways to stare at me. "So why are you here? I honestly never thought I'd see you again."

"I've been helping them find the heart—the thing they need. In the process, I caused a bit of a mess."

"How so?"

"You've seen that dragons can ensnare humans," I say.

"Enslave us, you mean?"

"It's not like that," I say. "Well, I mean, it can be. Sometimes it is, but I really liked my dragon."

"You *liked*? You don't like him now?"

"He died," I say honestly. I don't explain more, in part because I'm too tired to go into it, but also because the humans think Azar's dead, and I'd rather not tell them he's not. I really do think Norm will help us, but. . .talking to him's still a big risk. And if he does betray us, I'd rather limit how much damage he can do.

"What do you need from me?"

"The dragons. . .have you ever seen cartoons like Tom and Jerry where they try to fix something but it only gets worse?"

He shrugs. "Sure."

"In trying to help them. . ." I cringe. "I kind of made things worse. The only dragons who can eat right now are the ones who are bonded to a human."

Norm's eyes widen. "What?"

"Basically, any of them who don't bond a human will. . ." I draw a finger across my throat.

"They'll *die*?" He swears again. "You're serious?"

"I'm really trusting you," I say. "Because if you told the military this. . ."

"You came to me because you thought I'd *help you* keep the creatures who are attacking Earth alive?"

I drop my head back against the car's head rest. "Listen, I told you it's more complicated than the media and the government—"

"Because if you're thinking I might betray my own country, my own people, just to bond a dragon. . ." He shakes his head. "I can see why you might think that, since my whole life has been about living in a fantasy world as much as I possibly can. . ."

My heart sinks. "I understand that you can't help me," I say. "But Norm, even if you can't risk helping us, I have to beg you not to tell—"

"You're misunderstanding me, Liz. Let me be clearer: *hell* yes, I'll do it," he says.

"What?"

"You were totally right, if that was what you were thinking, that I'd betray my own country and walk away from my entire life for this chance."

I'm still just staring at him. I do close my mouth.

"If there's any chance of me helping those majestic creatures the American military has been bent on destroying, even if I can't bond them, I will *absolutely* do it."

That's why I love Norm.

"And while we're on the topic of what I'm willing to do, can I just say that the wings are like, level one hundred out of ten amazing, but the rags you're wearing?" He grimaces. "We have *got* to do something about that."

"I just want a coat," I say. "Maybe we can cut a blanket so it will go over my wings or something."

He frowns and blinks at the same time. "Oh, no. Liz—I have a friend who owes me a favor, and she's a *whiz* with period clothing. You're about to get a complete makeover. An *angelic* one."

He's beaming.

His excitement might be just a little contagious.

AXEL

I don't even know Liz, not really.

So *obviously,* I don't care what happens to her.

The only reason I'm pacing a hole in the ground in the stupid wilderness in the middle of tiny-town USA is that she's connected to the heart. The blessed need her—without her, we might never find out whether the heart's buried in the volcano. We may never understand the origin of the demon-creatures swimming around in the angry, boiling hole of a mountain with the ridiculous name.

She's valuable to our search.

That's the only reason I'm worried.

Axel, it's going to take her some time. Agrippa sounds like she really isn't concerned. *She has to convince the humans to help us and then get back to where we are without causing a panic. And she has wings—that's not normal for humans.*

I whip around, my talons churning up piles of dirt and rock as I turn to face her. *This is your fault. If you'd told her no, I could have taken her and—*

A truck stopped near her. I hid and watched long enough to see a man hand her his hand-held talking device. You could not have gone without being spotted with your bright golden scales.

Phones, I say. *The handheld devices are called phones. You clearly know nothing about the humans. I should have gone. Then I could have determined whether the human in the truck was trustworthy or meant her harm.*

You don't even recall shifting into a human form, Agrippa snaps.

It's the first time one of my earth blessed has ever snapped at me, that I can remember. *Liz is a bad influence on all of you.*

She's teaching us to think for ourselves. Agrippa's eyes flash, and I realize *she's* worried about Liz.

I think she might be as nervous as I am.

Not that I'm *nervous,* but concerned about the recovery of the heart.

Elizabeth Chadwick's helping us, Phileas says. *Be patient and see what she can do.*

I hate every single second of *waiting*—doing nothing as the seconds pass and pass and pass. It feels like time has slowed down until it's barely passing, but eventually, the sun climbs to the highest point in the sky, and she's still not here.

That's when I start to make circles around the mountain. I do spot a few humans, but they're fairly easy to hide from—none of them are looking for a blessed, thankfully. By the time the sun has fallen low in the sky, I'm genuinely agitated. Her failure to appear puts our plans to recover the heart at risk in a real way. *What if the other humans recognized her and the military came to take her?* I spread my wings. *We should fly into the settlement and look for her.*

She's a warrior, Phileas says. *There would have been a big fight if the military humans came for Liz.*

We're on the opposite side of a mountain, I say. *We would neither have seen nor heard it, which is the point. Her caution leaves her entirely vulnerable to their attack.*

She's not vulnerable, Agrippa says. *She's one of the smartest, most resourceful beings I've ever known.*

That's hardly reassuring. One tiny human can't fight the spears and troops and war machines Hyperion told me they have—they used them to *kill* me. *We need to go right now.* I crouch down, preparing to leap into the sky.

If you're this worried about her, why didn't you just bond her? Agrippa asks. *Then you'd already know whether she was okay. You'd know exactly where she was.*

I couldn't risk it, I say. *The humans used her to weaken me last time. She's destined to go back into the volcano—if she died, that could weaken me yet again, right when the blessed need me to be strong.* A weak leader can't defend their people, and my entire life's purpose is to redeem ours.

Then let me bond her, Agrippa says.

My reasoning on bonding Liz being a risk is solid, but the idea of her being bonded by someone else? It makes me want to melt my two earth blessed subjects into goo and return to Iceland without them. The blessed are possessive, and Liz used to be mine. I'm sure that's why. *No one can bond her. What's true of her weakening me is true of any blessed who bonds her.*

I disagree, Agrippa says. *We can test whether earth blessed can bond humans, and I'm willing to risk being weak if she dies. I really like her.*

As do I, Phileas says. *We can ask her when she returns which of us she'd rather—*

She doesn't like you *at all,* Agrippa says. *She almost started crying when she was with me earlier, talking to me about Gaia's loss.*

You make her cry, Phileas says. *That's hardly a good thing.*

You know nothing about humans. Agrippa's practically snarling. *We became friends when Liz saved us from the humans, and I hear she's the reason the earth blessed are stronger. I owe her my life for that already.*

What did you hear about her connection to the earth blessed strength?

Agrippa turns toward me slowly, her eyes wide. *Nothing substantial, but the earth blessed are speculating.*

About what? I arch one eye ridge.

You were exposed before she went into the volcano—Azar and Axel. It was. . .quite the secret, and you shared it for her. Then when she went into the volcano, the earth blessed all became. . .more. Stronger. Agrippa shrugs. *Perhaps it's wrong, but it seemed like she did something to keep you safe. If you'd seen how distressed, how* broken *she was when she thought you were dead. . .*

I was dead, I snap.

As the sun begins to set, I'm done waiting. *I'm going to find her.*

At least wait for nightfall, Agrippa says. *Fewer people would see us. We shouldn't risk the humans discovering us without real cause. It could do the opposite of what you want and endanger her.*

They fury inside of me about Liz's absence swells with nowhere to go, and I shift into Azar, heat building, and I open my mouth to roast Agrippa.

Do you hear that? Phileas asks.

I freeze. *Hear what?*

Humans approach.

I'll check it out. Agrippa eyes my massive, bright red form and shakes her head with disgust. *You just can't help yourself.*

I wait, irritatingly hopeful, until a moment later, I hear them too. Humans, quite a few of them.

You can come, Agrippa says. *It is Liz!*

Tromping around the corner of this mountain is irritating in this form, my feet crushing rock, trees, and scree. Even so, I move as fast as I've ever moved as Azar without flying. And when I crash down a small decline, I slide to a stop by a rocky outcropping.

. .

And I finally see her.

My heart swells at the sight.

Liz is standing at the front of a large column of humans, all of whom are staring up at us with dangling mouths and wide eyes. There are at least a hundred of them, maybe a few more. There are females, males, and a few forms I can't differentiate thanks to the clothing and head coverings. Some are tall. Some are very short. A few are rounded. A few are bony. The hair colors that are not covered are as different as the blessed scale colors—some striped, some dark, and lots of light, golden.

"See?" Liz is smiling as she turns back to face them. "Majestic, right?"

"I want the red one." The rounded human beside her has bright red hair, and he's pointing at me. "I call dibs." He tugs on the bottom of his puffy blue jacket.

"You can't call dibs, Norm," Liz says.

"Oh, wait, is he still yours?" the rounded human asks. "Or, like, you said that's ended, right?"

I am not hers; she is mine.

Quite a few of the humans turn toward me when I declare Liz is mine. In general, I've heard that the incidence of brights among the human population is quite low. Maybe one in a few hundred or even a thousand humans seem to shine to us—those are the ones we can bond.

Out of the hundred humans Liz brought, we have been lucky if one or two were glowing.

Somehow, there are more than forty.

How did you find so many brights? Agrippa asks. *Is that what took so long?*

Liz beams. "Can you please identify which of them are brights?" She turns toward the humans. "As I told you, we're not totally sure what makes someone a person who can be bonded, but unless you shine for them, they can't bond you. I still ask that you not disclose what you're witnessing here today, even if you're not eligible to be bonded."

"You really don't want to harm humans?" the rounded one asks. "You just want to get this heart thing so you can have baby dragons again?"

If some of them do go to the government with information, I hope they'll pass along our good intentions. That would be nice.

We indeed only came to recover our people's heart, I say. *We're dying off without it, and now things have gotten even worse.*

"You really can't eat?" a woman with long, dark hair in braids asks.

That's true, Agrippa says. *A dear friend of Liz and*

mine, another blessed Liz saved when she fled from the humans who held us captive, recently expended too much energy and died when she couldn't replenish her reserves.

"Which of us can help?" a tiny human with a big ball of fuzzy hair around her face asks.

If you can line up, we'll point out the ones who can, Phileas says. *And if you're not opposed, Agrippa and I would like to try bonding two of you right away. Until recently, the earth blessed couldn't fly, and we couldn't bond humans, either.*

"Because you're earth dragons," the fuzzy hair woman says. "And only the water and electric ones could?"

Exactly, Agrippa says. *And if we still can't bond humans. . .*

"Then they'll all die," Liz says. "So we're hoping that when they got wings and a power upgrade, they also became able to ensnare humans."

Why would all of you come to join us? I ask. *Did Liz offer you something?*

The humans begin talking too fast for me to understand them.

"Their reasons differ," Liz says. "Some of them just want to help, and some of them have always wanted to find purpose in their lives, but for many of them, including my friend Norm, he's always felt like there was more in life than what he had. He's always longed to be a part of something like this—what we humans call fantasy."

Perhaps the strength in his heart called to him, I say. *Because he's bright.*

The smile on the rounded one's face is beautiful to see.

Then he begins to leak—cry. He falls to his knees and chants something I don't understand.

I want him, Phileas says. *I like the idea of having a human who wants to be bonded badly enough that he cries.*

The rounded human's head whips up, and he says, "My name is Norm."

I'm Phileas, earth blessed of three hundred and twelve of your annual cycles. My strength is in manipulating rock— useful in Iceland, and here too, it appears.

Norm stumbles to his feet, and squares his shoulders. "What do I have to do?"

Phileas steps closer. *Nothing.* His mouth curls back in a small smile. *Simply tell me that you're willing so Liz won't try to stab me with her small knives.*

"Swords," Liz says. "And they're not small. They weigh a ton." In that moment, I realize Liz has changed her clothing. She's wearing something quite different, a red and brown hide of some kind. It's not dragon hide, but it looks nice. It's much better than the dingy white tunic, and it looks warmer, too. She's also wearing a very nice black scabbard that wraps around her shoulders and under her wings. The swords are held much more elegantly than before, which I'm sure is a relief to her.

A scarlet cloak with ties in the front and openings for her wings swirls around her, and that makes me rest easier as well. I've worried about her health ever since my failed mating. She's looked cold ever since when I'm not close enough to warm the air around her.

Who dressed my Liz?

My Liz? Agrippa's fully smiling now. *Interesting.*

I ignore her.

"It was me." The tiny woman with the fuzzy head lifts her hand. "My name's Karen, and my job's making high end costumes. It allowed me to work from home —my mom's disabled. Or, she was." She swallows. "She died last month."

"No one makes clothing as beautiful as Karen," Norm says. "That's why she was one of the first people I called when I saw Liz in those rags."

"I'd never had to make anything to accommodate real wings," she says. "I'm sure I can come up with better options, given a little more time."

Liz is beaming at her.

Karen. I nod slowly. *You're both talented and kind. That must be a well-loved name for humans.*

For some reason, Liz snorts and Norm laughs.

I ignore them and continue on. *Your kindness in providing clothing for Liz is appreciated. Since you're also glowing, you may come back with us if you choose.*

She starts crying, too. This seems to be a real design flaw for humans. They're mostly made of water, but they all spring leaks in times of stress or excitement.

I'll take her, Agrippa says. *If she wants me.* She tilts her head and steps closer to Karen. *I'm a serpentine earth blessed, and I'm very fast, on the ground or in the air. My affinity is somewhat useless, however. I speed the growth of living things planted in the earth.*

"That sounds amazing," Karen says. "I'm terrible at keeping plants alive, but I love them. Maybe you can help."

I can bury you in flowers.

"She probably means that quite literally," Liz says. "Make sure you're clear with her about how many flowers you want—exactly. Dragons' sense of humor sucks until you've trained them."

I'm learning, Agrippa says. *Liz already started.*

"That's true." Liz is smiling again.

I like seeing her smile.

Shall we try? Phileas asks. *If you're both in agreement?*

Are you ready? Agrippa asks.

Karen and Norm step forward, nodding and then bowing their heads for some reason.

"Go ahead and try," Liz says. "Every human who came with me was willing to be bonded." She glances over her shoulder. "I know the rest of you are anxious to know whether you're bright—we'll point you all out as soon as this is done." Liz sounds anxious, and I don't blame her.

I, too, am concerned.

How's it done? Phileas asks. *No one ever spoke to us about it, since we couldn't ensnare.*

Liz frowns. "Azar, do you remember?"

Only what they told us before we came. Not many blessed who lived on Earth before we left came with us, so we're almost all new to this. At first, I found it strange that so few returned, but as I thought about it, I understood. Sending the younger blessed risked less of a loss as well. *They said the stronger humans, the brighter ones, would call out to us. If we sought for their energy, pulling it toward us, we could bring it into ourselves.*

"We're stronger than other humans?" Karen asks.

I shrugged. *That's what they told us, but I don't recall bonding Liz the first time. It's been a strange week.*

"Yeah, our trigger-happy government shot you," someone in the back with dark skin says. "Sorry about that."

It appears Liz was right. Not all the humans hate us. The ones who hate us just seem to have more firepower.

Agrippa lowers her head until it's close to Karen's. Her long, serpentine nose is almost touching the fuzzy halo around Karen's face. *I like your fuzzy brown fur. It makes you easy to spot. Don't change it.*

Karen's face turns bright red. Then her body stiffens, and her head falls backward. I'm not sure what the humans can see, but I watch as the light around her expands, like an explosion that moves outward to encompass Agrippa and then contracts back down to Karen. Her hair shivers, almost, and then it turns a mossy green, just like Agrippa's scales.

It's still just as fuzzy, though.

Oh, Agrippa says. *I like this better. Now we match.*

Karen may not be very smart—she's beaming like an idiot. Or maybe she's just profoundly happy.

Once we reach Iceland, I have a saddle I made for Liz when we escaped, back when I could shift into human form. Shifting allowed us to make clothing and saddles. After Liz left, I dumped it by some trees, but I think I can find it again. There aren't many trees in Iceland. Until then, you'll have to try very hard to hold on to my back. I'm slippery.

As I watch the two of them staring at each other, both of them looking a little different than before, I can't help wondering what color Liz's dark hair would become if I bonded her.

It was gold at first, Phileas says. *When Azar bonded her too, it turned red.*

Liz is looking at us strangely. "Why aren't you guys happier?"

Of course she's relieved. I am too, obviously. *We are.*

"Now you do it," Liz says. "Norm is my friend—the one I told you about. He's—"

The warrior, Agrippa says.

Norm doesn't look much like a warrior, in my opinion, but then neither did Liz. She's clearly stronger than I expected her to be, so maybe for humans, strength and ferocity look a little different.

"You told them I was a warrior?" Norm asks. "Really?"

"You are," Liz says. "No matter how other people made you feel, you dug deep and became what you wanted to be. And now. . ." She tosses her head. "You're fighting the US government to help the dragons. You're making the life for yourself that you always wanted."

I'm worried he's going to spring a leak again, but he doesn't. Instead, he straightens, his chin lifting. His hair's a little strange, but then I realize it's trapped underneath a strange cloth cover. A little red piece of fabric is wrapped around his head—humans call it a hat, but it's not like the others I've seen that look decorative. This one looks like it was made only for warmth.

Which is smart. Humans have no protection without fur or scales or magic of their own. They should use small swaths of fabric, or whatever they can find.

Like Agrippa before him, Phileas crouches and lowers his head, nearing Norm. He sniffs his strange hat, and then he lifts his head and bellows.

The sound's much stronger than I expected from

Phileas. He's always been quiet and reserved—cranky, yes—but not much for showmanship. Could this round human's warrior spirit change Phileas? It's an interesting possibility.

"Maybe less screaming." Liz grimaces. "We're really trying *not* to tell the humans we're here, remember?"

Sorry. Phileas drops his head again. *I have a very nice neck ridge that you can hold when you ride me.* He fluffs it out. *It looks thin, but my frill doesn't hurt if you grab it.*

"Can we find out who else is a bright now?" a very tall human with big teeth asks.

"Yes," Liz says. "Of course. I think they're about to bond. We'll do it right after."

Heedless of the interruption, Norm's staring right at Phileas, and then Phileas lowers his head and his frill snaps outward, and the light-glow-ball happens again. It's almost as beautiful the second time, and not only because it means they'll be able to eat, I hope.

It's also clear that they're happy. They have more light together than they had apart. Interestingly, the glow around Karen and Norm has shifted—darkened. Instead of a bright light with a golden tint, it's now a rich, dark amber color.

It's like the other bonded humans.

I suppose that's how we'll know a bright human's already ensnared.

With Agrippa and Phileas both smiling and clearly preoccupied, it falls to me to select the humans who are bright. Two steps takes me to the end of the line they've formed, and as I look at their faces, I realize that they're all hopeful.

Desperately hopeful.

For some reason, these humans badly want to

become ensnared. Liz's mother and many of the other humans who were taken before hated the idea. They left their bonds—but these humans *want* to be chosen.

Do you know what the bond entails? I look carefully at the dozen humans in front of me. *What did Liz tell you?*

"You need us," the tall man with big teeth says.

"We will go with you to Iceland or wherever you travel in pursuit of the heart," a short, squatty woman with a spiky grey mohawk says.

We don't know what will happen when we obtain the heart. My father may force us all back home—you'd have to leave your own country, and possibly, your own planet. Our people can't defy him. He'd kill us for trying.

None of them look shocked. Liz must have been honest, at least.

"I've never fit in here," the tall man with big teeth says. "I was picked on during school, I was mocked at work, but the one place I found friends was playing Dungeons and Dragons." He looks around. "Most of my friends are here with me."

"Take me away," the squatty woman says. "That's fine with me."

The man beside her takes her hand. "But if she's going somewhere, I hope I can come with her."

You're wed?

The woman nods.

The man frowns.

He can't hear me. Because he's not bright. *You can bond.* I turn toward the man. *But he's not bright—he can't.*

"How can that be?" the woman asks.

"We don't know what makes humans bright," Liz says.

"But could he come with us, even if he can't be bonded?" she asks.

Liz turns toward me.

Yes. The other humans can come if they promise to obey. If they'll join us, we'll protect them as best we can.

"My brother and sisters have been with us this entire time," Liz says. "They're not bonded, but Azar protected them anyway."

The woman nods and squeezes the man's hand. "I'm a bright," she says. "We can go with them." They both look pleased, which is strange to me, but I won't argue.

The man with the big teeth is also bright. Several others are not. But the seventh human is baffling. *He's. . .not* not *bright.*

"What are you saying?" Liz asks.

I lower my head, and the poor man with a weird patch of fur—a beard, I remember they call it—sprouting just on the bottom of his chin stumbles back. He has small red blotches all over his face, and he smells strange, but he has eager eyes.

The others glow or do not glow. He. . . I blink. *He glows a little bit.*

Agrippa and Phileas must have been listening, because they come closer.

It's strange, Agrippa says. *If I wasn't looking for it, I might not have noticed. What do you think it means?*

"Can I come with you and see whether a dragon can bond me?"

"Blessed," Liz says. "They prefer to be called blessed."

"You called them dragons," Norm says. "It threw us off."

Liz is not respectful. She sets a bad example for humans and blessed alike.

The man with the face blotches laughs.

"Can you hear him?" Liz asks.

He nods. "He said you set a bad example."

Liz shrugs. "That's true." She turns toward me. "I think they should be able to come. Maybe they can't be bonded, but it's worth a shot. Can you return them here, if they can't be bonded?"

"Or we could stay with you," the man says. "I live in my parents' basement, and I hate almost everything about my life. I'd rather come with you and try and help somehow than stay here and keep feeling like a loser all the time."

His light increases—just a hair, but enough that I can see it. I wonder whether the human light varies based on their choices. *He can come.*

A small cheer erupts.

As I go down the line of the one hundred and eleven humans Liz brought, inexplicably, twenty-nine of them are bright. Another twenty-six are partially bright.

But every single one of them, bright or not, wants to come with us.

"I need some of you to stay," Liz says. "Because we need more than ten thousand humans who can be bonded—fast."

She's right, Agrippa says.

"I only have three days to convince the dragons not to attack to find the brights they need by forcing the bond."

The humans are mostly frowning.

"It's life or death to them," she says. "And every

single human we contact is a risk."

"I have people I can contact," Norm says. "And there are quite a few people I reached out to who weren't close enough to come today."

"You'll probably want to say goodbyes, too," Liz says. "Why don't you all go home and call whoever you need to call. Gather personal belongings you treasure —one carry-on bag size each—and then you can return tomorrow. We'll take you all back then."

"I already have a backpack," one man says.

"Yeah, I brought a bag already," a woman with tall boots says.

We should take some with us now, I say. *We need to show Hyperion this is a viable option.*

And it would be nice to take a few of the semi-bright, Agrippa says. *We should find out whether they can actually be bonded.*

I'd like to figure out why so many of the humans you found are bright, I say. *I thought it was much rarer.*

"I have a theory," Liz says. "I think a lot of the people who are bright—who have a strong sense of justice, social and otherwise, the people who fight things, who don't accept what's wrong about the world, we don't feel like we really belong. We look for other ways to understand things, and a lot of them find it through fantasy, LARPing, D&D, and gaming."

Norm cheers.

So do most of the others.

"Whatever the reason is," Liz says. "We need way, *way* more humans. If you can all do whatever you can to locate more, that could save the dragons from causing another war by forcibly bonding people."

"But if just one of our friends decides to call the government," Norm says. "Then. . ."

"The entire plan would be put at risk," Liz says.

And you would be in danger, I say. *You should stay in Iceland from now on.*

"Absolutely not," Liz says. "They need to hear this from me—I've been bonded. I'm un-bonded now, and I'm still working to help you. They need my word to believe you."

"That's true," Karen says. "She convinced me."

"And her wings didn't hurt," big teeth man says.

"That's true," the tiny woman says. "The wings were the reason I believed her story."

You can't come without me, I say. *So I guess that means we'll both be traveling.*

"Norm got me a satellite phone," Liz says. "That way, at least we can communicate with them from Iceland to coordinate spots to rendezvous."

A small flock of large white swans fly past overhead —not far overhead—and Agrippa's head snaps up. She shoots into the sky, grabbing one and then another into her mouth.

When she lands, she's quite pleased with herself. *There's more food here than in Iceland.*

"Those are tundra swans," Karen says. "They're one of the few large birds that make Utah their warm, winter home."

They're also delicious.

Liz and Karen don't look impressed.

Was there some reason I shouldn't have eaten them? Agrippa's eyes are wide.

"Generally speaking, humans don't eat swans," Liz says.

Why not? You eat geese and ducks, right? Agrippa frowns. *Swans are bigger—and more delicious than the ducks I've eaten.*

"I thought you couldn't eat without being bonded," Karen says.

"The earth blessed ate just fine until they got their power upgrade," Liz says. "That just happened—and now they can't eat." She looks at Agrippa. "Unless. . ." She steps closer. "How do you feel?"

Agrippa straightens. *I feel great. You never answered about the swans.*

"They're pretty," Karen says.

"I think that's why," Liz says. "It's not a great reason, but I think that's why we don't eat them."

I'm as confused as Agrippa looks. How are we to know what we can and can't eat—the birds all look about the same to me.

"It's fine," Liz says. "It's not like we'll attack you because you ate a few swans."

At least if I bonded a human, they could explain some of these confusing human-things to me.

As if he can hear my thoughts, Norm asks, "Why haven't you rebonded Liz? When you died, it broke the bond, right? But you could rebond her now." He frowns. "Or can't you? Have you already tried?"

I can't admit it out loud, but I think I'm scared to bond her again. By all counts, I turned into a lunatic while I was bonded to her, and in spite of my best efforts to dislike her, I find myself listening to her strange human demands more and more with each passing day.

If you're going to be opening portals and defending Liz,

Phileas says, *you're going to have to bond some human or other, or you'll run your energy down too low.*

He doesn't say that I'll die, but he's right. If I don't want to bond Liz, I'm going to have to bond someone else soon.

As the humans prepare to either return home or come with us, I can't help watching her. For a human, Liz is graceful, fierce, and strong. If I have to bond one of them, shouldn't it be her?

But she's also the most dangerous, for precisely that reason.

I want her.

And I don't have the slightest idea *why*.

❦ 8 ❦

LIZ

Agrippa suffers no ill effects from eating two swans, so before we leave, Phileas manages to find a deer. I look away as he eats it, but it doesn't seem to bother Norm.

He's on cloud nine.

I wish he'd go back home to work more of his connections, but he insists he can still find people via phone, and he won't leave Phileas for a second.

I don't blame him for that, I guess. Being bonded by a dragon really is his dream come true, and as he already told me, he has no children. His parents even have *six* other kids they're way prouder of than him.

I can relate to that a little bit as well.

When we return that night, every single partially-bright human insists on coming with us. They all said they'd brought what they needed—they did all have backpacks or shoulder bags, at least—and they didn't have people to tell goodbye.

I think they were afraid Azar would change his mind.

Another ten bright humans insisted on coming. Three dozen non-bright humans are also tagging along, most of them family or friends of the brights and semi-brights we're taking. The others went back out into the world, pledged to find us more humans like them to collect tomorrow.

They've all sworn to use discretion, but any way I look at this, the risk of a leak is high and will just grow higher.

One disgruntled human is all it takes.

One military or former military person who feels more patriotic than fascinated. Technically, what we're asking people to do is treason.

Before I came, I was hopeful Norm would have friends he could reach out to. I figured we might find a handful of humans within a day's distance who would want to bond a dragon, but I didn't expect this kind of reaction, and I assumed very few of them would be brights. I'm so encouraged when Azar makes the return portal that I'm almost giddy.

Once it's open, Phileas and Agrippa fly though first, their newly bonded humans on their backs. If Karen's slipping and yipping a little bit, well, no one's likely to be critical.

Her halo of green fuzz looks like a mossy helmet, and I like it.

Twenty humans? Hyperion's been waiting for us, apparently, and he doesn't look impressed.

We found twenty more, Azar says, *but they're out searching for others as well. We'll go back tomorrow to see how many others they can contact.*

You do know there are ten thousand and four hundred of us, yes?

If I were blessed, I'd probably love Hyperion. As it is, I spend most of my time wishing I could clock him in the head with a two-by-four. Not that I could ever pick up one that would be long enough to leave a mark.

Many blessed are gathering, having felt the portal. It makes a kind of sucking then exploding sensation when Azar opens one. The first time I felt Hyperion's, I thought we were under attack.

We've found brights willing to be bonded, Azar says. *And two earth blessed have bonded humans—and eaten successfully. It was a successful trip all around.*

Dragons trumpet, roar, and shriek their delight.

The humans who came with us freeze in place. I imagine the idea of dragons is one thing, but being confronted with *thousands* of them all at once of various colors, shapes, and sizes is quite a different matter.

"The ones who are shades of blue, seafoam green, or lavender are usually water blessed," I say. "The shades of earthy green, brown, amber, orange, gunmetal grey, or even occasionally black are earth blessed."

"And we all know the strike blessed." Norm points at the sky where they're dipping and diving in and out of strikes of lightning.

"The strike blessed—shameless showoffs," I say.

Hyperion laughs. *Ah, Liz. You're more trouble than you're worth, but you are always entertaining.*

She's not wrong about them showing off, Azar says.

That's what makes it funny. Hyperion sighs. *He's a real drag, newly reborn baby Azar, huh?* Bonding with Hyperion about his brother's cluelessness is unexpected.

I kind of love it, but we have more important things to do.

"Some of the humans we brought back are semi-bright," I say. "We'd already found humans for Agrippa and Phileas when we realized a few weren't quite as bright as the others."

We only need brights, Hyperion says.

"But they do still shine, and they can hear the dragon-talk in their heads. We should probably test whether they can be bonded sooner rather than later, since we might encounter the same thing again tomorrow."

Oh good, Hyperion says. *You brought deficient ones. What blessed wants to risk being shackled to a human who might not allow them to eat?*

"I hadn't even considered that my semi-bright light might cause harm to one of the blessed." Andre was the first semi-bright we identified, and he's one of the nicest guys I've ever met. "I—they don't have to risk bonding me."

"Surely one of the dragons around here is brave enough to try." I leap into the air and take off, joining the throngs of dragons who are now flying in slow circles around our new group.

"Wow, that's amazing," Norm says. "I wanted to see you fly all day."

"Can we get some?" Karen asks.

"I would *love* wings," Norm says.

"We're not exactly sure why I got them," I say. "But who knows?"

I'll try bonding one of the lower-light humans, Elizabeth Chadwick. Plumeria slides out of the river bank and walks toward the humans slowly. Even her movement on land reminds me of the flow of water—shining scales and shimmying motion. She's such a bright, light blue that it lifts my heart just seeing her.

I'm not the only one who thinks so.

For centuries, the earth blessed have been the weak ones among us, Plumeria says. *They had no wings. They could take human shapes. They could consume food, and because they were weak, the rest of us ate them.*

I hadn't exactly shared all of this story.

Some of the humans look horrified, but a few look fascinated. They might be too dragon-blind to even process what she's saying.

Now the water blessed are the weak ones. We have no wings, and we have no prince of our people who also rules as the Recovery Leader. She pivots, sliding right between the twenty-something semi-brights and ten brights we brought back. *I understand how it feels to not be quite what everyone else wants. I can't fly, but if you're willing to join me, and if you like water, I'll try bonding you.*

You can always kill them if it doesn't work, Hyperion says, *and bond another human who can help you.*

I plunge toward him, furious, my hands reaching for my hilts while my wings flap rapidly.

We won't be killing any bonded, Azar says.

I wouldn't do that anyway, Plumeria says. *We're both taking a risk here—I'm willing to accept the consequences of it.*

It's probably for the best that I don't attack Hyperion. As I swing wide, I notice he's smiling. Clearly my anger really worried him.

"I wouldn't blame you if you did kill me." A curvy woman steps out of the crowd, right in front of Plumeria. "I'm here because I have dreamed every single night of my life, almost, that I'm a dragon rider. I've read every book I could find. I've watched all the movies. The only time I really felt *right* in my own skin was at Disney World when I rode the *Avatar* ride. If I ever harmed you in any way—" She shakes her head. "I'd rather die."

What's your name? Plumeria, without having witnessed the scene between Phileas or Agrippa, lowers her head, her eyes on level with the curvy woman. *And are you afraid of water?*

"I'm scuba certified," the woman says. "That means I love to spend time underwater, but I'm limited by the weight and timing of my heavy oxygen tank. And my name's Candi." She smirks. "My parents had a weird sense of humor. Apparently my mom gained a hundred pounds when she was pregnant with me—she ate candy nonstop. My grandma raised me after my parents died when I was ten. She died last year." A tear rolls down her face. "I've been eating too much candy myself, because there was nothing that brought joy to my life. Until now." She raises a hand toward Plumeria's face.

And then I watch it happen.

I can't see the light or whatever the dragons see.

But I watch Candi stiffen, and I watch her head fall backward. I watch the rapturous expression on her face as she squares her shoulders. "Thank you." Now she's crying in earnest.

The leaking of the humans is out of control, an earth blessed behind me mutters.

Human pains causes it often, Azar says. *It's a strange phenomenon.*

"Crying," I say. "You know it's called *crying*. You lot

could use a little crying yourselves. You're like walking, talking, stone-hearted monsters."

The dragons all laugh. *As if we'd ever leak.* Azar, especially, thinks it's funny.

Now she must eat, Hyperion says. *Let's see whether this not-really-bright human can still keep us safe.*

The other twenty-five semi-brights watch with rapt attention as their future's decided.

How do you feel about fish? Plumeria smiles.

"I prefer it cooked." Candi's smile is a little concerned.

I can help with that. Hyperion's getting funnier.

"I'm assuming she doesn't want to eat a pile of ash," I say. "How about I help with it? Candi can wait, though. The one who needs to eat right now is Plumeria."

Do you want to come with me? Plumeria's still just looking at Candi.

Hurry up, Hyperion bellows. *This is taking forever.*

"You're such a bully." I land beside Azar. "Haven't you ever done anything important? The beginning is the slow part—you have to line up everything else."

"I write books," the tall man with big teeth says. "My outline takes me almost as long as writing the book."

"See?" I point at him. "Listen to big teeth. The outline takes a while. Then the book just falls together."

A book? Hyperion snorts. *We're not talking about humans' boring little paper scribbles, Liz. That's your issue. You get all distracted and confused, worrying about things that aren't relevant.*

In that moment, another water blessed opens its

mouth and dumps four or five flopping fish on the riverbank beside Plumeria. *I've always wondered how they taste,* the deep, navy blue dragon says. It's a male—fewer facial horns that are larger—but he's still beautiful, even with the larger, less delicate face. He has strange sort of dangly flippers hanging off him around his face and legs, but they're shiny and interesting.

I always have so many questions and not nearly enough time to ask them all.

The water blessed don't come around me much, but maybe they will now, since I'm not bonded to the terrifying Azar anymore. I think they were scared of me before. It's nice to have a friend amongst their group.

I'm hoping *so hard* for Candi and Plumeria that I'm a nervous wreck as she approaches the flopping fish.

Should I eat them like this? Live?

"They're better roasted," Candi says. "But since you're in a rush. . .sushi's not bad."

Sushi? Plumeria blinks.

"Humans sometimes take the gross parts out of the inside of fish and slice them into pieces," I say. "Sometimes we add rice or other things, but we eat the fish raw. That's Candi's way of saying 'bottoms up.'"

Bottoms up?

Just grab it with your mouth and swallow it, Azar says.

Plumeria nods, and then she ducks down low, opens her mouth, and snaps it closed on one of the striped river fish. It takes some bobbing and shifting, but she manages to gobble the other three up as well, along with more sand than I'd personally care to eat, but I know nothing about dragon gastrointestinal systems. Hopefully that's fine.

She grimaces a little, and then she burps, loudly.

The rest of us watch her intently, waiting to see what happens.

I can't stop seeing Gaia's puddle of neon-green puke. Without meaning to, I find myself praying that she'll be okay. I pray for Candi too, that she'll be healthy right along with Plumeria. I really want them all to be happy together—and I hope that all the dorky, fantasy-nerd semi-brights can bond their dragons and live happily ever after in the fantasy world they always wanted.

Will you be sad you can't fly? Plumeria asks. *Since you've always dreamed of being a dragon rider?*

Candi's smile is sweet as she shakes her head. "I was moving quickly in those dreams, but I might not have even been flying." She bites her lip, and then she turns fully toward Plumeria. "I think I might have always been zooming through the water. I was just moving so fast, I couldn't understand where I was."

It's been a few moments—does that mean we're safe?

Before I can ask out loud, Plumeria begins writhing, her entire face contorted, her body collapsing inward, her claws spasming and digging large, long furrows in the sand. When she heaves forward, puking something back up, I struggle to suppress my tears. This isn't about me.

But the puke—as nasty as it smells and looks—isn't neon green.

It's not green at all.

In fact, she vomited up an entire fish, the biggest one, and it looks only partially chewed.

That one was nasty, Plumeria says. *But I think the others are fine.*

What's going on? Hyperion asks. *Did it not work?*

"I think that's a Greenland shark," Andre says. Thank goodness we're surrounded by nerds. They're exactly the kind of people who would know all about sharks.

"Care to elaborate?" I creep closer to the puke-fish. "Is the fact that it's a Greenland shark meaningful in some way?"

"I've read about them," he says. "When I was a kid, I was kind of obsessed with sharks."

"You're kidding." Since LARPing and playing D&D in every spare second of life is also a little obsessive, I'm thinking that makes sense.

"All I ever asked for my mom to get me for Christmas or birthdays were books about sharks, and the Greenland shark is a really weird one. It's actually the reason the first people in Iceland survived the winter."

"How?" I ask.

"The Greenland shark's basically the most toxic shark—maybe even fish—on the planet," he says. "The Icelandic people had basically thrown a lot of them away because they made them sick, but the sharks sort of fermented for a few months, so when they were about to die, they realized the fermentation had somehow sucked all the toxins out and while it tasted nasty, it was edible. They still eat it today—I think it's called hakarl or something."

"Does that mean she threw it up. . .because it's gross?" I ask.

He shrugs.

I feel fine otherwise, Plumeria says.

After consuming a second round of fish, she stays fine. No more sharks puked up, no neon-vomit at all. "I'm ready to call it," I say. "It was just the stupid poison shark. Otherwise, our semi-bright pioneer, Candi, was a success."

The water blessed start spreading the word. The lumpish, splotchy, slow-swimming fish with almost no pectoral fins are *not* good to eat. Avoid them.

"They're the dog-poop of the fish world," Andre says.

"But the semi-bright humans?" I can't help my smile. "Definitely not dog poop."

Not dog poop at all. Plumeria looks happy, her body practically curling around her newly ensnared human.

Within the next thirty minutes, all twenty-five of the remaining semi-brights, and all ten of the regular brights, are bonded.

Six strike blessed.

Nineteen earth blessed.

Ten water blessed.

It's a start, Hyperion says. *But you only have two more days, and we have thousands and thousands of blessed to save. Unless you were thinking most of us could just die.*

I don't even bother answering that.

As I wing my way back to the Hotel Selfoss where my siblings are probably getting ready for bed with Gordon, Asteria, and Rufus, I call with my satellite phone and start coordinating plans. I hope, as I get closer, that the kids aren't already asleep. It's nearly ten o'clock, but I want to see them before I collapse.

Two days without sleep is not good for Liz. Instead of becoming dull, when I'm all work and no play, I get ragey. When I reach the hotel, Sammy's asleep, but Coral and Jade are still awake. They're all fine—none of them were forcibly bonded.

Though a few blessed had stupid ideas, Asteria says. *So it's good we were here.*

"I'm very grateful," I say. "Thank you for being willing to watch them while I went to look for humans who wanted to be ensnared."

You're hard to hate, Asteria says. *I've tried—even without his memories, even without being able to take a human form, he still chooses you.*

"I'm so sorry your wedding was ruined," I lie.

The only good thing about Gaia's death, and I feel *horrible* thinking this, is that it ruined the mating plans. Standing there, pretending I was fine with it, felt like someone was carving out my heart and dicing it into little pieces to be thrown into a bowl of citric acid.

Their mating ritual was turning my heart into ceviche.

You aren't sorry. Asteria doesn't even sound angry—she sounds resigned. Sometimes I think Asteria understands humans better than any other blessed. She seems to share almost all our good and bad traits. "I wasn't sorry, but I wanted to be sorry."

Her laugh's a little bitter, but also real. *Yes, just as I wanted to be sorry when Azar returned. . .and didn't remember you. But I also was not.*

At least we understand one another.

I really do love him, Asteria says.

That's what makes it hard. She's a good—person isn't the right word—but she's got a good soul. Like me, she's fierce. Like me, she cares for him. Like me, they feel cosmically love-crossed.

His soul yearns for yours, but your bodies are wrong, she says.

"And he's perfect for you," I say. "In virtually every way."

Except that even without his memories, he's pining for you without even realizing it.

I wish that was true. He mostly just seems to despise me. "That must be why he tossed me in that cage and shot out of the volcano like a bat—"

Sometimes I wish we could cry, you know. It looks like it makes you hurt less.

Maybe it does. I'm not sure. "I try to avoid it whenever I can, but it's probably cathartic."

I'll let you spend time with the small ones, but I'll return early tomorrow so you can leave with Azar to try again. She pauses before launching from the giant hole Azar created. Back when he cared about us, he'd placed a large red bubble over it, but it's gone now, probably just another casualty of his death. *I hope you succeed, but I fear you're just wasting precious time.*

I'm afraid of the very same thing.

She's like the silver-scaled sister I love to hate.

I finally walk through the door into the next room, the frozen air gusting around me as I close it. The kids are bundled up in the same bed, extra blankets piled on top, even though the hotel generator has blessedly kept working. Having one not-very-well-insulated wall that's shared with the blasted-open area hasn't been great. I might need to move them further inside the poor hotel.

"I can't sleep," Coral says. "Can you tell us a story?"

"Yeah." Jade shivers. "Please?"

Mom used to tell them stories every night.

Stories about dragons.

Fairies.

About princesses saving poor, pathetic princes.

And about tiny princes who could slay the demons who were hunting the light. Sammy loved those best, since he's still so small. It's good to tell children that everything will be okay, especially when it might not be.

I lean over and stroke his face.

He stirs a little, then he opens his eyes. He does that a lot, when I come in to hug him after he's gone to sleep. I've never seen another kid more pleasant when you wake him up. Coral would bite my head off if I could even wake her up, and Jade would sometimes fall into an epic tantrum.

Never Sammy.

"I want a story too," he says.

He must have been half-awake before, probably from the sounds of Asteria leaving, even though it was on the other side of the wall.

"A quick story." I yawn. "I'm exhausted."

Instead of making one up, I tell them about the bonding of Plumeria, Agrippa, and Phileas. Real life's at least as strange as any of the stories we used to make up. Unlike all the humans who just joined us voluntarily, I'm not sure what I'd say if you offered me the chance to go back to a time before the dragons.

I might lunge at a trip to Disney if I could avoid all the misery.

Let someone else fight the fight.

But even as I contemplate that, a life that's so

different than mine, I can't help feeling that no matter how much I ran, the blessed would have found me. Once the kids are asleep, I change into pajamas and prepare to sleep on my stomach. Maybe one day I'll learn to sleep on my wings, but for now, they're so bulky and sensitive that I'm forced to lie facedown. As a back sleeper for almost twenty-three years, this feels horrible.

My boobs hate it, for one thing.

Eventually, though, I do fall asleep, hoping against hope that all the new brights we found are doing their best to locate others like them. I really hope there are more humans willing to try and help the blessed find what they need without destroying our little planet in the process.

❦ 9 ❦

GULLVEIG

Bedtime's the best part of every day.

Every day I plan to do less, but every day I wind up working all day—training, teaching, cooking, and brawling—so every part of me aches.

But especially my shoulders.

After scrubbing with the warm water Freya's servants brought, I finally feel clean. I'm about to sink down into my fluffy feathered bed when I hear them.

"Gullveig!" My brother's children miss him. I know they do. *I* miss him, too. Sometimes it's a sharp kind of misery, like a knife dragged across my palm. Other times, it's a quiet ache.

Being around his babies makes me feel better.

I think it might be the same for them—they need me when they're hurting more than any other time.

"Tell us a story!" Like me, they've had trouble sleeping ever since he died, especially Brunhilda, his youngest. It helps to know that Gorm's sacrifice wasn't in vain, but even that isn't enough. She's not a warrior, not even close, and it's still a scary world.

"Please, Gullveig! We've been asking and asking." Brunhilda's pleading tone tells me just how her sweet little face will look.

And I already know what story she wants. It's her favorite—always has been, even before we had hope for a better outcome. I *really* want to sleep, but I can't deny them.

"Fine." I chuck my coverlet back and try not to stomp into their adjoining room. It's not their fault I'm so tired.

Gorm's oldest child is a warrior through and through, but even Áki enjoys a good story. He sits up the second he sees me, his smile wide and open. At seventeen, his shoulders are broad, his jaw nearly bare of the baby fat that I loved so much. Whiskers have begun to sprout on his chin and lip.

He almost looks like a man.

It breaks my heart.

"I'm here," I say. "Only one story, though. No more. You know tomorrow's a big day."

"Tell us about the wedding," Brunhilda says. "Is it going to be the most beautiful thing we've ever seen?"

"It's not even a real wedding," Sif says. "They're getting married to keep the vanir from attacking. That's what Rut said."

"Rut was wrong."

Sif's pretty jaded for fourteen years, but I don't blame her. Losing her dad was hard. Really, really hard. I still have trouble getting up in the morning, and I'm an adult. I had lots of time with my beloved brother, and it still wasn't enough.

"Odin loves Freya, and she adores him, too.

They're staving off a war, but they're doing it with happy hearts, and the wedding will be beautiful."

"Tell us about how it all started, then." I'm shocked it took Brunhilda so long to ask. She's usually clamoring for this from the start. "More details this time. I still don't really understand it." Her eyes are bright, and her hands are twisted in front of her.

"Fine." I climb into the bed with them, and I lean back against the wall. Brunhilda scrambles onto my lap, and Sif leans against my side. Only Áki holds his position, but I'm not fooled. He's just as keen on the story as they are. I can tell.

"In the beginning, there were only earth children who lived under our sun. Jörð created us all to tend to the earth she loved, and she gave us this beautiful place where we could flourish because she loved us. We had trees, grasses, flowers, and grains. Animals were abundant. The earth children were happy and blessed, but we were also lonely. Other than birds, nothing filled the air overhead. Nothing swam in the great waters other than small fish and serpents."

"And then?" Brunhilda balls her hands into fists, her eyes bright.

"One night, as she was preparing to slumber, Jörð heard something new. She heard a great roaring, like the wind of a mighty storm, but stronger, and the skies overhead were clear of rain. She looked farther upward, marveling at the great expanse of the universe she'd never traveled. When she looked a little farther than ever before, she finally saw him."

"Veralden!" Sif says. "Right?"

I smile. "Veralden Radian was a god of the sky. He was powerful, and he was fierce, and he had traveled for thousands and thousands of years, and in all that time, he had never discovered anything he could not destroy. Because he had slain all his enemies, he was also lonely. He longed to find something more—he longed to find true beauty."

"And he did, that very night," Áki says.

"That's right," I say, wondering why they want to hear a story they already know word-perfect. "But when Veralden saw Jörð, he was utterly smitten. As he stared at her, the thunder struck all around, plunging deep into the earth. Wind battered the homes, trees, and vegetation, and the earth children ran and hid."

"But Jörð wasn't scared," Sif says. "She *liked* it."

I smile. "You're right that she wasn't scared. She had finally met someone—some*thing* like her. Powerful. Beautiful. Fascinating. As she moved, the earth rotated. The living things all shifted toward her. In her physical form she was small, but she drew on all the strength of her true nature, and as she moved toward Veralden Radian, he could not look away. She was everything warm and full of life that he'd never before seen."

Brunhilda claps.

"And then," I say, drawing this part out, "when they finally met, Jörð was drawn to the fierce Veralden. She couldn't turn away from him either. He was strange and marvelous and powerful, and she was in awe."

"And then?" Brunhilda shifts so she can see my face.

"Then, Veralden tried to take her with him, as he did with everything he wanted. Jörð laughed, and as she did, the world around them burst into bloom. Her joy filled the world with life and energy, and Veralden

Radian was entranced. Instead of *claiming her* like a possession, for the first time, he wanted to give something of himself instead. For the very first time, Veralden Radian didn't want to destroy. He wanted to create. He wanted to thank Jörð for the beauty she'd shared. So he leaned over slowly, and he kissed her."

Even Sif's smiling, though she's hiding it with her hand.

"Although they loved one another a great deal, a god like Veralden Radian could not stay—he was made to always move. His power was not in resting, but in conquering, in exploring, and in discovering. Jörð could not go with him—her whole being was tied to earth and home and growth and creation. She could no more follow him than a fish could fly. But when they kissed, something happened."

"It made the heartstone," Áki says.

"The most beautiful, most powerful stone in existence," I say. "It's the convergence of the power of the earth and the sky. And with its existence, for the first time, the magnificent Veralden Radian created children of his own, and he left them with his beloved Jörð. They could stay with her in a way he never could, thanks to the part of her she had infused in him that night."

"The children of the sky," Sif says. "The vanir and the æsir."

"Even so," I say. "They watched over the earth children and brought us excitement, magic, and power we had never known before."

"At first," Áki says. "But then, the vanir discovered that they could bond with the earth children. Through that bond, they could claim, and they could also destroy."

"That's a story for another night," I say. "It's time for bed now."

"Tomorrow, two sky children who want to protect Jörð's earth children will marry," Sif says. "To honor their father's will."

"And Freya brought us the heart stone," Brunhilda says. "Now that the æsir have it, we'll all be safe again."

I shift Brunhilda over, and I pat the bed where Sif needs to move. "That's all true. After tomorrow, the vanir won't be able to terrorize earth's children, not anymore. Our æsir heroes will keep us safe, just as Jörð and Veralden Radian always wanted."

"Dad died to help Freya escape," Áki says. "Without him, Odin and Freya couldn't marry."

"That's mostly correct," I say. "We'll talk about it more after the wedding, alright?" I pat Sif's head. "Your father was a hero, for sure, and we'll all be thinking of him tomorrow, even Freya herself."

"Will we see the heartstone?" Brunhilda's biting her lip.

"Yes," I say. "You'll see it tomorrow, and trust me. Once you've seen it, you'll never, ever forget it."

LIZ

When I wake up, I want to scream with frustration.

I still haven't seen the stupid heart-stone, but it *must* be what the blessed came back to retrieve. I didn't see it anywhere when I met Freya before, but she must have it.

She apparently wore it at her wedding.

And I was there.

Or at least, someone a great deal like me was there. When I was telling that story, I sure felt like the story I was telling was true, but come on. Earth met sky and. . .they kissed? It seems ridiculous. Maybe the whole thing was just. . .bizarre.

Though human met dragon, and *we* kissed. So. . .

I remember something Freya said to me inside the volcano. When I chose to spare the poor fighter whose mother was sick, she was surprised. She said she didn't expect a warrior like me to choose the strength to endure.

I had been angry. I told her she didn't know me.

And she had laughed. "You're right. And you're wrong."

Did she mean that she knew *Gullveig?* That I was the same. . .and I was different? Is she one of the sky children who wanted to help the earth children? It was probably just a dream invented by my brain to answer questions that have been rolling around in there for a long time, but it felt *so* real. I can't help wondering whether it could have been a memory, and that either telling my siblings a story or surviving the trip to the volcano shook it loose.

I'm more convinced than ever that Freya has answers, but every time I asked her a question, she was disgusted that I was asking the wrong ones. Did she expect me to remember things from my time as Gullveig? Or is she upset I hadn't learned more about the time of the dragons before looking for her?

It's not like Azar volunteered much information, but I blame his father for that. It sounds like Azar asked the right things, but Odin shut him down. I have some choice things to say to Odin when I finally meet him. I'm sure he'd incinerate me before I could say most of them. From what I hear, he's even worse than Freya at ducking answers to things.

I loved both of them when I was Gullveig, though. That makes me question my sanity, or at a base line, my judgment.

Not that I have time for much thought at all.

Azar wakens me with a bellow just after the sun rises—Sammy's sitting beside me, smiling when I wake. "Hey, buddy," I say. "Did you sleep well?'

"I'm glad you're back," he says.

With his speech delay, it sounds like 'I'm gwad yowa back.'

I pull him against my chest and squeeze as hard as I can. This is why I'm doing this. I'm trying to make a better future for these tiny people I love so much. A world they can't create—a world they're powerless right now to change.

A world they deserve.

Some humans are giddy the dragons are here. They're excited that the life they've always dreamed is now in their grasp. Others want to destroy every last dragon invader, without any exceptions. I can't help wondering how much of the positions we take has to do with the knowledge we have. Most of the humans are operating under mistaken assumptions, and that makes for bad decisions.

When Azar bellows again, I release Sammy and stand. "I'm coming, you great lummox."

When I'm finally dressed in the one outfit Karen made me, I storm through the connecting door, bracing myself against the freezing cold.

What's a lummox? Azar's already frowning.

"Hmm?"

You called me a great lummox. What does that mean?

"It's really impolite to yell and holler and make a lot of noise to get a woman to come outside." I drop one hand on my hip. "It's like a man honking his horn before a date."

Is it polite for a human to force others to wait? What about people who force others to help in a scheme that's likely doomed to fail?

I open my mouth to snap at him and realize that he's right. I wasn't being very polite either, and he's still helping me. But we hadn't agreed on a time or anything, so a little patience would have been nice. "In the future, I'll hurry, but maybe you can let me know when you'd like me to be ready. All that shouting will wake up everyone around us."

He sniffs. *Blessed don't sleep.*

"Ah, so you're not being impolite to them, just the weak little humans like my siblings." Now I am annoyed.

I'm not sure I need to learn a lot of human social rules.

"You asked what it meant," I say. "Stop asking if you don't care."

You're awfully snappy for someone with no power, a lot of demands, and so far, not much success.

"We'll find way more brights today—you'll see." I'm not anywhere near as sure as I sound. The more nerds Norm's friends can reach, the more brights we'll find, but we also might be caught, and that's when things might start to break down. I'm not actually afraid of the humans attacking us—though perhaps I should be—but I am worried about what happens if the human attacks force Hyperion into thinking going to war would be simpler.

"And I thought we were travelling as Axel," I say. "The last thing we want to do is let the humans know you didn't die."

Why not?

"Battle strategy basics," I say. "You always want to surprise your opponent, and we can't do that if they already know you didn't die."

You said the humans aren't really our enemies.

"You're tiring," I snap.

I agree—but that same sentiment about you.

He does switch to Axel, at least, even after being a snot about it. Honestly, though, it's easier for me when he's rude. The more I want to stab him, the less depressed I am. Before we leave, I confirm the location we're going via satellite phone with Barrett, Norm's oldest friend from Vegas. We Facetimed yesterday, though I didn't allow anyone to take photos, and the second he saw my wings, he threw his stuff in the car and started driving. Even so, he wasn't going to make it in time for yesterday's meet-up.

He says he's already waiting when I call, so I have Azar open a portal. This time, Hyperion insists on sending way more blessed with us, because an attack's more likely our second day. Initially, he was only sending six strike blessed, but then the water and earth blessed were upset they weren't being equally represented, and now we're stuck with six *of each kind*. Now our group feels like we're preparing for some kind of small attack instead of a covert op.

I can't fault Hyperion for being cautious—his brother *did* die not too long ago.

When we step through on the far side of Timpanogos, no one's waiting on us, but I've barely hiked a half mile when I find them. The humans are waiting like Barrett said they would be—which is good. When I told Azar I'd be heading out to rendezvous with them alone, he looked ready to fight me.

Thankfully, I reminded him how well it worked yesterday, and the importance of me properly preparing them for bonding.

There are way more humans this time too—three hundred and fifteen in total. Barrett made a roll call. It includes the nineteen brights we left, the other sixteen non-brights who are still desperate to join us, and almost three hundred new recruits. It's a similar mix to before—men, women, old people, and a few who are quite young. I told Norm they all had to be at least eighteen. Based on his rigorous paperwork, I'm assuming Barrett's checking.

Barrett's not even the only familiar face.

"Gary." I wave. "How did you find this many?"

Norm's business partner, Gary, spearheaded the outreach plans this time, with the help of his wife. Unlike Norm, Gary has always been happy, and he usually seemed like he fit in everywhere. He's just obsessed with fantasy stuff, which I don't really understand. Before dragons showed up, electrocuting people right up in my face, I had no interest in pretending I was part of a fake world.

"We were up all night." Gary smiles. "Norm—this is all he's ever wanted, and at first I thought he was making it up."

"What changed your mind?"

"I did recognize you on the television, so I knew he had a connection to the dragons. When Norm texted to say he wouldn't be coming back and had left paperwork naming me as the sole recipient of his business interests, I realized it might be legit."

"He's not dead," I say. "Why would he do that?" I can't help laughing. "He's so dramatic."

"Did he really bond a dragon?" Gary's wife asks.

"He did," I say. "But you don't look too excited."

Gary's unlike Norm in more ways than his temperament. He's also tall, muscular, and dresses well. According to Norm, he was quite the ladies' man among the fantasy nerds, at least, until he met Jean.

Like she was always meant to be the queen of the nerds, she's regal and a little haughty. I can see why—she's tall, she has flawless skin, and her eyes are a bright, cerulean blue—almost purplish. Even in Utah, I imagine that's a rare color. She even glances around the group slowly, like a queen surveying her subjects. "A lot of us are still worried this is a prank, or worse, some kind of scam."

The humans who were here last time laugh. The nineteen brights we left, and the sixteen non-brights who were going to help nonetheless begin murmuring.

"It's not a scam," I say. "If you'll come with me, I can easily prove it."

"Those wings do look real," Jean says. "How much did they cost?"

It's not dark, not anymore, but we're far enough from anyone with an ounce of sense that I feel safe flying back toward Axel.

The gasps behind me are quite satisfying.

When I circle back around, I notice that the humans from yesterday are all struggling with their bags, some of which look quite heavy.

"Wait here," I say. "I'll be back in a moment." I can't help a smug glance in Jean's direction when I pivot to wing my way toward Axel. It's satisfying to see her mouth dangling open, anyway.

When I reach the dragons, I smile. "Three hundred and change," I say. "Follow me."

That's not nearly enough, Axel says. *You have three days to prove to Hyperion we can find brights for ten thousand blessed. Your first day, we barely found fifty.*

"We found sixty-one," I say. "Norm, Karen, and twenty-nine other brights. Plus, the semi-brights are brights, too." I scowl. "And we have a plan for a second rendezvous today. I told you it would take time at first to do it properly."

Each rendezvous increases the risk. He's starting to sound like his brother.

"I'm aware," I say. "But surely it's no riskier than simply attacking. Can you focus for a moment?"

He begins walking, but I step in front of him.

"I think I should ride on you."

He freezes. *You have wings.*

"I know," I say. "But I'm the poster girl for this campaign, and for a lot of these people, their life's wish has been to ride a dragon. None of them have wings, and I can't promise that they'll ever get them, so I don't want to sell them on how cool it would be to be just like me."

He blinks.

"Fine." I turn. "I'll just ride one of the others."

A tall, thin strike blessed with a stunning head and an almost blue tinge to her silver scales ducks toward me.

No, Elizabeth Chadwick's mine. He tosses his head in the direction the humans are waiting. *Let's go. You slept so long, we're already losing the day.*

It's hardly an hour past sunrise here, since Iceland's six hours ahead of Utah, but I don't bother arguing. If I'm a little rough when I tuck my wings and drop onto his back from ten feet above, well, he deserves it. I hope he has a sore back for hours.

His head whips around, but his eyes don't look angry. They're flashing with what looks like amusement to me. I miss having the bond to confirm my suspicions—green was happy. Grey was satisfied, if not quite pleasant, and black. . .well. Not all the colors were great. He can keep his dark moods to himself and good riddance.

Even jogging to minimize the risk of running into anyone, the dragons, who are all following us, eat up the ground with their long strides. When Axel slides to a stop in front of the gathered humans, I try to look at them like he must see them.

The main thing I see, other than surprise and joy when we arrive, is the humans' hope. The women have done their hair—some with curls, and others with intricate braids. They're wearing stylized clothing, from warrior-wear that appears to be modeled after mine, to ball gowns for a few. The men are less obvious, but only by a little. They have fresh haircuts, shiny new boots, and they're carrying packed bags.

If you can hear me, raise both arms. Axel's volume is set rather rudely to blast, but I have to hand it to him. After realizing only the brights could hear him yesterday, I still didn't think of this.

I should have.

More than a hundred humans raise both hands—not as high a percentage as yesterday, but still really, really high.

I didn't prepare the humans here today as well as I did yesterday—we didn't hike up together. Before Axel can say more, I step in. "If you heard that command, please move to the far left." I force a smile. "I also want to thank everyone for coming today. Our time is short, but I want to make sure everyone understands why we're here, and what we're asking of you."

"We want to bond a dragon," one man in the back shouts.

He's not one of the ones who raised his hands. That makes me sad—almost two hundred of them are already not eligible.

"A few months ago, my entire world imploded," I say. "A dragon bonded me against my will. I was angry, and I had been trained to fight." I slide off Axel's back and walk closer to them. "I did what I knew how to do, and I fought the dragon who bonded me at every turn. I was surprised and disgusted, honestly, with every single human that had been bonded who wasn't fighting."

Some of them laugh, but a lot of them look distinctly uncomfortable.

"Our government knew what I also knew—the dragons were our enemies."

Everyone's dead silent, including most notably, Axel.

"But in spite of my irritating and often stupid attacks, my dragon, my bonded, never hurt me. He never fought back. He never made my life worse. He bore all of my temper tantrums with grace." I glance back at Axel.

He looks. . .curious.

"I didn't relent, though. And an old friend of mine joined me. I convinced my bonded dragon not to kill the rebel in our midst, and we pretended to be shifting our allegiance to the dragons." I snorted. "Secretly, I still wanted them dead or gone—both were fine as long as they never came back."

Now the humans look actively alarmed.

I launch into the sky and begin to fly in a slow path along the humans who have gathered. "But with a little more time, as my bonded dragon learned about my past, I came to see him differently. Instead of being the enemy, he protected me. He was angry at the way the humans in my past had behaved, and he told me the dragons hadn't come to conquer. They had lived on Earth before, for thousands of years. They were back to collect something they'd left, something they needed, because without it, they were unable to procreate. They had no future, and when they came, they had no idea what exactly they were even searching for. They'd been told only that they'd know it when they found it."

I land now, all their eyes still on me.

"And since their arrival, the blessed have done everything they could to recover this object they call the heart, but the humans have attacked them at every turn. Naturally, they fought back, and they're well equipped to do that."

A few people laugh.

"But I started helping them, and we've had a breakthrough of sorts. We located a volcano in Iceland that held clues to what we needed. In the process, something changed. The earth dragons, who had no wings and were at the bottom of the dragon hierarchy, got a massive upgrade. Part of that upgrade resulted in them being unable to eat. In fact, none of the dragons can eat now, not without growing violently ill. And without food, you can imagine what happens next."

"They'll die?" Jean looks vested now. "Really?"

"Every last one of them," I say, "unless they bond a human. Something about that bond allows them to metabolize our food sources here." I smile. "My little brother's favorite dragon's a green earth dragon named

Gordon. Do you know what his favorite food on earth is?"

No one answers.

"I thought all dragons would eat cows, or goats, or humans," I say. "I probably got that idea from movies, which always have them flying down herds and devouring them, but Gordon loves tunneling in the earth, and he finds grubs *delicious*." It makes me laugh.

I'm not the only one.

"Once he had one stuck on his cheek." I shiver. "When I pointed it out, he *offered it to me*." I shake my head. "I said no thanks, and he popped it in his mouth himself."

They're listening now.

"The first time the dragons bonded humans, they did it all wrong. They can force a bond—it's called being ensnared. They can fly into any human settlement, search for brights, and then bond them against their will. But they don't want to make a mistake like that again, even with their very lives on the line."

Some of them do, a water dragon I don't know says.

"That's true," I admit. "A great many of the blessed want to take action now, before they grow too weak to find enough humans and force them to bond. They want to just *take* the humans they need, but I envision something better. I want dragon-human pairs that will be strong. Humans brave enough to teach and guide the dragons who have come back to Earth—teach them about our ways and our life. I'm looking for warriors who will help us *and* them, but I know that it's complicated."

No one flinches.

"Based on our earlier test, less than half of you will

be able to bond with a dragon, but I'm asking for all of you to help us in another way. Not only do we need you to keep our secret, but I'm asking you to help us find others who will do the same. Because if I can't find enough humans in the next day and a half. . ."

My brother will take our people to war. Not everyone can hear Axel, but there are enough that it gets the message through to them.

This isn't a game. It's really freaking real.

The blessed who came with us each bond one of the brights we've found, and there are another hundred and six who are ready to go back with us. Thirty-seven are semi-bright, but it appears they do just fine as well.

It's still not nearly enough, I say. I shouldn't care—I don't care—whether this plan of hers works, but I don't like being associated with failure.

"We have two more places to go." Liz's flashing eyes and set jaw tell me she's not giving up until she has to. "If we get another hundred at each one—"

It's still not going to be close to enough.

"Why not?" She's fuming, pacing back and forth. "If we have more each day, and if we have the humans we find bond the dragons who are the weakest, the ones who are most in need of food first, then—"

We came to find the heart. We should be making progress on that, not spending all our time on this useless fix for the mess you made in that volcano last time.

As she clenches her fists, I notice something.

The human behind her is wearing an outfit that looks. . .like it was made of my skin. I peer a little closer, shifting as close as I can without crushing any of the soft humans. *Why's that woman wearing something that looks like the scales from both my forms?*

Liz follows my gaze, and then she smiles. "Uh, I had an outfit exactly like that." She turns to look up at me. "You gave it to me."

Are you implying I made you clothing out of my own skin? *I wouldn't do that.* Only, as I say it, I consider. For the humans to copy it, they must have seen it. Liz would have been a relatively well-known human, being bonded to the leader of the recovery.

"I'm not implying it," she says. "I'm telling you that you did. The reason she's wearing it is probably because she saw me wearing that when. . ." She trails off.

Finish that thought.

"I wish I could say you didn't always order me around before," she mutters, "but that would be a lie. You've always been this irritatingly overbearing."

A frantic human runs past us, bumping me.

Watch out, you big lummox, I say.

Liz laughs. "What did you just say?"

It's an insult, is it not? I narrow my eyes at her, challenging her to deny it.

The human who bumped me spins around, eyes wide. Clearly she's not a bright, and she's also not very bright. "Sorry." She bobs her head and scurries away.

"It is an insult," Jean says from a few feet past Liz. "Where did you hear the word?"

Liz seems slightly annoyed that Jean's a bright, especially as her husband Gary isn't. Either way, they're both coming with us now, and that will please Gary and Liz's friend Norm, so Liz's happy about it too. The human connections are confusing because I don't care about any of them much, and they all look extremely similar to me, but I'm trying to keep up so Liz isn't frustrated.

For some reason, when she gets upset, it upsets me.

I'm trying not to think about that very much. It's almost as concerning as the fact that I gave her clothing made of both my identities' skins.

"Lummox isn't a word you hear much," Jean says. "Did someone old say it?" She glances around. "That guy?" She points at a man with many wrinkles in his soft flesh.

No, Liz called me that this morning, and when I asked her what it meant, she changed the subject.

Jean lifts both her eyebrows and turns around.

"It's a word to describe a large and stupid person," Liz says. "Which you were being, with all your early-morning bellowing."

It was close to midday in Iceland when I woke you.

"I hadn't slept in two days," Liz says. "Besides, in Utah, it wasn't midday, so waking earlier would have been pointless."

Did you injure yourself, not sleeping enough? Why do I care? Why am I even asking? She's the one who appointed herself to take over this task, and how she does or doesn't do it, or how much she sleeps, shouldn't matter to me.

"Never mind."

Another human wearing something similar to the

faux dragon-hide outfit walks past. *How many of these people are wearing something like what you wore?*

Liz shrugs. "I noticed a few. Four? Maybe five?"

That's when I realize that she did it again. I ordered her to finish her thought about where they saw her gift of clothing, and she didn't. She changed the subject *again*. I step closer to her, lowering my head until I'm closer to her face. *When did they see you wearing the clothing I specially made for you?*

"We still have another location to visit." Liz gestures. "Actually, I just heard back from Jean's friend, so now we have two. All of those who are coming with us, gather together. You'll stay close to your bonded dragon to spare Axel any extra hassle or trouble."

If they knew anything about the blessed at all, they'd know Axel couldn't open portals. Luckily, the humans are all clueless, though I'm not quite sure what we gain by keeping it a secret that I didn't die. Still, I hardly want to point out to Liz that her 'battle strategy' is totally unnecessary for utterly unmatched opponents. The blessed don't need an edge. If we chose, we could utterly decimate the humans in every way.

I fear that facing that truth would upset her.

"My dragon says the gold one's the prince of the earth blessed," Jean says. "And that he's also somehow the flame dragon—the one we all saw die."

Liz frowns, but for the humans coming with us, they would have heard soon enough.

Jean presses forward. "Weren't you bonded?" She frowns. "Why aren't you now? Or are you? My dragon says you're not bonded now, and your hair isn't red anymore, so something must have happened, but he's not dead like we thought."

"We have less than ten minutes before we need to leave," Liz says. "I need to talk to the humans who are staying and choose someone who will reach out to me about a time and place tomorrow." She walks away.

Clearly I'm not the only one whose questions she ignores. In this case, I know why she wandered off. I suspect Liz would be agreeable to bond me again, with her weird nonsense about missing me. That's part of my reticence about it, honestly. Bonding Liz won't be simple. Things with us will grow even more complicated than before if I bond her again.

"I guess that's not a question you want to answer," Jean mutters.

I need to bond a human, I say. *But I find that I don't want to bond Liz, and yet the idea of bonding anyone else disgusts me.*

"I didn't grow up dreaming of dragons," Jean says. "Even without a preconceived notion of what you'd be like, you're not at all what I expected."

Maybe she'll tell me what Liz won't. *Why are so many human women wearing the strange outfits with both gold and red dragon scales?*

Jean grimaces, but she pulls her phone out of her pocket. "I could show you, but I'm not sure we'll have enough reception out here." She starts tapping on her phone. "When I tried to call my brother earlier, we were disconnected."

Reception?

"Actually, it's working." She holds up the tiniest little picture I've ever seen.

I crouch as low as I can, turning so that one of my

eyes can see the speck. It's—the humans are attacking us, and the ground is barren and in places, snow-covered. We must be in Iceland.

This is the attack where I die? I feel angry, sad, and curious. *How are you recreating the attack?* I peer closer.

Liz returns, her lip twisted in mirth. "You think they're recreating it?" She rolls her eyes. "Humans use technology to save images of things—we call them video or movies. I think you called them transmissions, probably because we sent them via satellite."

We thought those transmissions were human magic, so now I feel a little foolish. *I was jesting. I knew it was a recording.*

"Are you sure?" Liz tilts her head. "Because I feel like you making a joke is weirder than you not knowing about video recordings."

Now it seems like she's making a joke—at my expense. *I have an excellent manner with others.*

"Sure you do, Stalin. Everyone *loves* you." Liz's smirk bugs me, but not as much as it did at first. For some reason, it almost feels like I'm *in* on the joke.

Until Jean suppresses a laugh, and I wonder whether there's another joke being made that I don't get. Maybe something to do with the unfamiliar name, Stalin.

Before I can ask anything more, Liz raises her voice. "Does anyone have an iPad? Jean's phone is really small, and I'd like to pull up footage of the dragon attack in Iceland that Axel might be able to actually see."

It takes a bit of time, but eventually a large man with bright red cheeks and a large hat on his fuzzy head holds up a slightly larger screen. It's still minuscule, but I can at least make out the figures.

It's me.

Liz is riding on my back, just as she said, wearing my hide, just as she said. The humans are lined up in nice, easy-to-flame lines. It's almost like someone read a book on how to prepare troops for war in a way that one flame blessed could most easily destroy. Why would the humans be that dumb when they had fought us before?

Liz said her friend came to Houston and learned about us, and then he betrayed her. He was, ostensibly, advising them, and their military leaders had engaged with us before. Other than the ice spears, their attack makes no sense. Why would they think humans would do anything but die in this scenario?

Unless they wanted them to die.

Was it a lure?

Hyperion flies right down one line, torching an entire row of humans. I fly past next, but Liz is clinging to me in a strange way, and then she slaps my neck. I don't kill anyone. I simply fly past, roaring in frustration, but not unleashing any flames at all.

Hyperion loops around again, melting a second carefully prepared row of troops. The screams—the screams are loud. I'm sure Liz was distressed, watching and hearing and smelling her people being massacred.

I circle around again, and this time, just before I can attack, Liz leaps from my back and hurtles toward the ground. Even knowing she's alive today, watching her nearly splatter on the ground, right in the middle of a column of troops who have moved only enough to allow her to die without taking them out too, I feel awful.

My heart's pounding.

My breaths are coming quicker.

Just before she dies, she stops, suspended in air, and vibrating up and down.

I don't flame anyone, because I'm too busy watching Liz. They fire on me with ice arrows and spears, but they clatter off my hide like harmless rocks or sticks.

I swoop closer.

The troops, her own people, are pointing their projectile weapons at Liz and firing them. She finally drops to her feet, and then she redirects her efforts outward, creating a shield through which the bullets cannot penetrate. It's red—she's pulling that magic from me.

I'm *roaring*, clearly irate.

I can't tell whether I'm upset at her or at them until I watch as I swoop in another circle, a tight one, and I blacken the troops firing on her and resume my screaming. When I circle again, flying in a wider arc this time, a soldier's running toward Liz. At least he stops the others from firing on her.

I lean even closer, my breath clouding up the iPad screen.

"Ah," the man says, "let me clean that off." He uses the sleeve of his coat to wipe the screen clean, but when he holds it up again, I've missed something. The soldier's standing near Liz. He's gesturing for her to lower her shield. He even bangs on it.

She better not do it.

When he orders the troops to lower their weapons, she drops it.

I must have panicked even more then than I am right now, because I spear my way toward them, but I'm too slow. She yanks Gideon beside her, and then she throws my own shield back up to keep me out. Her eyes look almost sad as she stares up at me.

Instead of attacking, instead of doing anything that makes me look less pathetic for being betrayed by my own human bonded, I simply circle overhead like I'm her obedient guard.

Why didn't I force her to listen to me?

Why couldn't I manage one little human?

I shouldn't bond her again—I can't. She's too dangerous, if she figured out how to manage me like that.

Then the soldier she invited inside her shield—her friend—stabs Liz in the neck and she collapses beside him, the red shield blinking out.

I should keep watching. I should force myself to watch as the ice spears penetrate my scarlet scales and I plummet to the earth and explode. I should watch it to remind myself what comes from trusting humans— from trusting Liz.

But I can't do it.

I'm too upset by how I failed her. I flew in little circles while she died. I mean, we're both alive now. She is. I am. Everything's fine, only it's not. . .

She's not bonded to me anymore, which makes me inexplicably sad, even though I can't remember any of this. I wish I could truly erase it so it never happened. I would if given the chance.

When Liz walks toward us, she looks nervous. "Are you ready to go? I think we're done here."

I don't answer her. I walk far enough away to make a portal, careful to ensure it's on the ground for the water blessed and humans who are walking through. When she tries to catch my eyes, I look away.

In New Hampshire, the group we gather's much smaller. Sixty-four humans, twenty-one of which are bright enough to bond. The last stop of the day is better—we find another hundred and twelve brights, but all told, we have less than three hundred humans willing to save my people.

Hyperion's going to lose his mind. I doubt Liz will get her third day.

She knows it.

I can tell from the expression on her face.

"What about the Orlando Renaissance festival?" Jean asks. "I know it's riskier, but think about it. If we can't convince the other blessed to wait. . ." She shrugs.

She's right, and Liz knows it too.

"Tell me what you have in mind."

"Today's the last day, and since it's a Sunday, I bet there are lots of people. Nerdy, fantasy-loving people." Clearly Liz explained that not only do those people seem more likely to support us, but they also seem to have a higher incidence of brights.

Liz thinks that maybe brights are naturally drawn to fantasy. Norm believes it's because the type of person who is likely to be worthy of bonding a dragon is more likely to be openminded. Either way, there appears to be some sort of correlation.

"And?" Liz asks. "We go and walk around, trying to talk to people?"

"I was thinking of something a little more direct." Jean turns my way. "How would you feel about summoning anyone who can hear you?"

"He'd have to get close enough first." Liz spends almost an hour investigating the location before ruling it out. "It just won't work. It's right next to an airport, for heaven's sake."

"Maybe he can fly over, disguised as a plane," Jean says.

"Do you hear yourself?" Liz starts pacing. "It's lunacy."

"Seeing him like that," Jean says. "It would be a bigger draw than summoning the brights."

"How far away can you be and still talk to humans?" Liz is eyeing me strangely. "Let's test it."

Far, it turns out, but not far enough for me to call them from the wilderness on the east side of Orlando, and Liz throws her hands up in the air. "I just need more time."

We don't have it, I say. *I'm sorry.*

When she starts crying, for some reason it makes me want to melt something. I hate how much I hate it. *If we're going to return to Selfoss with less than three hundred brights, you know how Hyperion will react. There's no way we can find a human to voluntarily bond each blessed in a week or ten days, not at this pace.*

"I know," she explodes, her hands clenched, her eyes wild. "I'm well aware, and I can't even disagree with you. This method's just too slow."

"You have to gamble," Jean says.

I'll portal into the space beside the festival. There. I point at the map with my nose. *You'll be with me. We'll call whoever we can, and then we'll portal back out.*

"How many humans would we need to convince him?"

At least a thousand, I say.

"A thousand?" She kicks a rock. "If we could do five hundred today, and then—"

"It's only a matter of time until someone tells a government agency and they look into it," Jean says. "We should really try and frontload, or they'll ambush you."

"Fine," Liz says. "Fine. We try it. I'll go with Calista." She waves to the delicate strike-blessed. "She has a loud voice."

Absolutely not. You will go only *with me.*

"We can't risk you." She sets her feet and glares.

It's so cute that I almost miss the obvious revelation in what she just said. She's been insisting that we hide that Azar's alive as a part of our battle strategy. I thought she was simply mis-valuing the human's chances against us.

Her words—can't risk *me*—make it clear that was a lie. She wasn't worried about us losing to the humans. She's not that dumb. She worries about me, too.

It shouldn't matter.

It *doesn't* matter.

But for some reason, it makes me feel all tingly and strange. I want to smile and lie down on my back and roll around in the dirt and then race through the sky at mach speed. I want to give Liz a ride so fast that she whoops and slaps my neck.

All of that is entirely insane, so instead, I settle for

refusing her little demand. *We'll just return to Selfoss now if you won't let me accompany you.*

She stomps her foot and screams like a small human child. It makes me laugh. When I stop, all the other blessed are staring at me strangely.

"Fine." She lunges at me, and then backs off, like she's going to. . .hit me? "*FINE.*" She stomps off, flinging her hand out in front of her and pointing into the woods. I'm terribly worried that she believes she can order me to follow her.

My fear is confirmed when she turns back toward me impatiently. "We won't be gone long." She huffs. "Or maybe we'll both die and the water blessed will get wings and have to bond whales. Who knows?"

I'm laughing again, even more loudly, when I open the portal.

When we step through—a winged human and a golden dragon—in broad daylight, I brace myself for spears, bullets, and lots of shouting. I am *not* expecting to step onto a small field on which a man with a beard is shouting while holding a tiny skull. He's wearing a weird, woven hat with a large brim that comes to a point at the top.

He drops the skull and screams, but then, instead of running, he drops to his knees. "A real dragon!" He has the frenzied look on his face that I've come to recognize as the look of a blessed-lover.

Liz whacks my side. "Say it. Now!"

The blessed aren't your enemies.

"Not the blessed," she says. "Say dragons, lummox."

Lummox? I frown. *Now I know what that means. You shouldn't be insulting me.*

Liz's eyes widen, and she splutters. "Focus, dummy."

I *know* that's an insult, but she's right. There are a lot of people staring at us and a few more, screaming. I project the message as far as I possibly can. *The dragons are not your enemies. In fact, we need your help. Since coming to Earth, we need to bond humans, or we can't. .*

.

I stop, unsure we really want to broadcast that we can't *eat* without being bonded. *Is this wise?*

"For the love—" she climbs up on my back. "You're terrible at this. No wonder the humans attacked you instead of listening. Just repeat what I say." She sighs. "The government has been lying to you. We came to Earth to recover something we left here thousands of years ago."

She jabs me, and I repeat it.

"And now, we need your help. We don't want to harm anyone, but your bloodthirsty military keeps attacking us. If you've ever dreamed of life with a dragon, or of sailing through the sky with one, now you can do it."

Is she kidding? It sounds like she's advertising us as some kind of vacation or something.

"Say it," she hisses. "Now."

I hate it, but I do repeat her message, more or less.

"This is the most important part." She pats my neck. "Listen up."

Listen up, I say.

"Not that part. You weren't nearly this dumb before." She's really annoyed now.

Which means my plan's working. I really like irritating her, for some reason. And when she calls me dumb, or lummox, instead of enraging me, I find it entertaining.

Not that this is the right time for me to explore those feelings.

The people around us are creeping toward us slowly, wide-eyed, obviously surprised I haven't done anything aggressive. The man with the hat has taken it off, and he has no hair on his head underneath. It's entirely shiny. He smiles.

Finally, Liz tells me the last thing to repeat. "If you want to help us, and if you're willing to leave your boring life behind to do it, come to the open field with the large red tent on the west side of the Southport Community Park. We have to leave in ten minutes—and only humans who are pure of heart, valiant, and fearless will qualify to bond a dragon. Come and find out whether you're strong enough to help us with our quest."

Quest?

She kicks my side. "Hurry. The clock's ticking."

I roll my eyes like I've seen her do, and it feels good. I do my best to repeat her stupid lines, but I cringe a little while I do it. She's beaming, though.

This makes you happy?

No one comes.

"Maybe they're afraid of you," Liz says. "Tell them to approach the winged human instead. That's where they should check in."

If you want to help us, approach the winged human you'll see flying down in front of the golden dragon.

Liz smiles. "I'm so proud of you. You didn't even cringe when you said dragon."

I roll my eyes again. It's not something I've ever

seen the blessed do, but for some reason, I enjoy doing it.

Liz hops free of my back, winging her way in front of me a dozen paces or so. It's far enough from me that it makes me nervous, but I don't crowd her.

Until humans begin rushing at her from all sides.

The bald man with the strange hat is the first one, chucking the strange skulls he was holding on the ground as he rushes toward Liz.

Not so fast, I say. *She's* mine. *No one else can touch her.*

He stops dead in his tracks, turning toward her. "Are you Elizabeth Chadwick?" His mouth dangles from his face. "You—I—We all thought you died." He's crying.

But he can hear us, so I'm not surprised when I notice that he's glowing. Why are all the humans who want to help us so strange? I haven't spent much time around humans, not really, but I do know that carrying skulls and wearing odd hats isn't common behavior. It's as weird as running around with wooden swords and pretending to fight. Then again, warriors without a just war to fight might be forced to do strange things.

"If you heard him, you're one of the brights," Liz says. "That's what the dragons call the humans worthy of bonding them."

"You *are* her," the man says. He glares to his right and left as more humans come, but he continually looks back toward Liz with utter awe. "This is really happening."

Liz nods. "It is happening, but if you want to help the dragons, you have to be willing to come with us right now. You can't return home, or gather things you want to take. You have to walk away from your life and—"

"Done," strange hat says. "I'm in." He's beaming. "I'm *so* in."

I'm nervous the entire time we wait, but almost half an hour later—not the ten minutes she initially said—I absolutely insist that we leave.

"It's still not enough," Liz says. "Just a few more minutes."

But others are gathering. Quite a few others. They're snapping photos. They're shrieking and howling, and it's making me *very* nervous with Liz standing in front of me and periodically flying around and talking to the new people who reach the clearing.

I spin in a circle, spreading the people away from me, and I open a portal back to where the other humans are waiting. *Time to go.*

Liz sighs, but she nods. "Tell them to line up, and make sure each of them is a bright."

Once they're all through, we do a more thorough count. Somewhere along the way, we kind of lost track of screening children or people with small children. More than three dozen children are now in the mix, with accompanying parents, but we'll be returning to Hyperion with six hundred and forty-one adults, which is far more than I expected.

"You found more than three hundred at the Renaissance festival?" Jean asks. "That was a great idea." She shrugs.

She's a little annoying—clearly fishing for praise. *It was a good idea.*

"You know, I've always loved gold," she says. "It's my favorite color. I'm not sure whether a bond could be transferred, but if it can, I'd be happy to bond you instead."

Noted. I walk away, following Liz toward the front of the group, and I'm proud of myself for not melting the irritating woman. As satisfying as it would have been, and as irritating as the woman was being, it would have upset Liz. I'm almost entirely certain.

When I open the portal back to Iceland, it's hard, and it's smaller than the others have been, so it takes a while for all the humans to pass through.

But Hyperion's impressed, at least. *You will choose one to bond.*

I shrug. *Eventually.*

Now, he says. *You look haggard, brother.*

I'm fine.

He doesn't argue, but I can tell it's hard for him. *This bought her one more day,* Hyperion says. *But if she can't bring back even more tomorrow. . .*

I know. I'm not the only one growing tired and in need of energy.

Some of the strike blessed cornered a water blessed this morning and tried to eat him. Hyperion looks at the river. *The water blessed are angry. All of them are—we're in big trouble here.*

He doesn't say it, but now that even our horrific cannibalism doesn't work. . .we are doomed unless we can find enough humans to bond. Hyperion and I both follow the other blessed to the large pavilion where Liz is having the blessed gather to bond the newly located humans. She's asking the blessed to let the weakest ones bond first, but appeals to charity don't work for us. Weakness isn't pitied—it's despised. Still, I can't help noticing that Hyperion, Asteria, Gordon,

Rufus, and I aren't clamoring to bond anyone yet. I wonder whether they're waiting to be noble, or for the same reason as me.

Which makes me wonder who they *want* to bond but haven't. . .

And why.

❧ 12 ☙

LIZ

When you die and are brought back, but your siblings think you're dead, and then you're gone all day long every day. . .when they ask if they can come watch all the humans you brought back bond new dragons?

You say yes.

I don't want to, since they're brights themselves, but when I'm staring at their eager little faces. . .I can't say no.

"What are the rules?" I ask for the third time.

"We won't interfere," Sammy says.

"And we won't let any dragons bond us," Coral says. "Duh."

"And?" I look at Jade.

"You said there were only two rules." She's frowning. I wish she didn't look quite so old. It's barely been two months since the Boo Bash, but it feels like the kids have turned into tiny adults.

"She wants you to say the biggest one again." Coral crosses her arms. "You're being annoying. We could have bonded fifty dragons while you were gone."

I fire up my very best glare.

"No one can bond fifty dragons," Sammy says. "Dummy."

"Maybe two," Jade says.

"You can't bond two," I say, then I catch myself. "And *you guys* can't bond *any*."

"Oh my gosh," Coral says. "You've said that already, like ten times. Now let's go."

"I call dibs on getting a ride with Liz," Jade says.

"That's okay," Sammy says. "I'll ride with Gordon. And Coral, you can ride with Rufus."

It's so cute when he says Cowal, wide, and Wufus. Maybe I'm the only one who thinks that. And really, he's missed speech therapy since all this starts, so I hope I'm not permanently dooming his speech by keeping him here, but every time he misses an r, it makes me smile.

Some things are still normal, small issues.

It makes me. . .hopeful for some reason.

Life is weird and scary and dangerous, but it's also beautiful. Sammy's beautiful. Gordon bobs intentionally up and down a dozen times or more on the way over, and each time Sammy squeals with joy. It heals my heart.

That's what we need to somehow show the humans —the good in human-dragon relations.

When we reach the pavilion, there are far more than six hundred blessed present. So much for my appeal that each type of dragon should only send their two hundred weakest. I wish Azar would have supported me. They listen to him.

I'm the only one who doesn't.

And even though he and I are not what we were, I think I'm making progress. He seems to tolerate more from me now, and he even understands some of my humor, I think.

It's not enough.

Not even close.

But it's better than when I thought he was dead.

Until I think about the Axel I cared about—then my heart still aches. I'm sure that will fade in time, especially when I see him bond someone else or mate with Asteria.

Or when he sends me into the volcano himself, instead of fighting his brother to keep me safe. At least I'll go into the flames with the knowledge I did everything I could to fix the parts of his life I wrecked. Could two individuals with less in common have found one another anywhere in the universe?

Maybe Jörð and Veralden Radian, and look at the mess they made.

A tiny part of me has hoped that, somehow, Axel and I might work things out, but if my dream is true, the two who started all of this never did, and they were gods. Jörð loved Veralden, and then he just left. Her children and his have been at odds ever since.

Their love wrecked the entire world.

Which is why I can't obsess over Axel or Azar or any of it. I can't cause *more* problems because I won't let go of what's already lost. That's not what warriors do, and it's not what sisters do, and it's not what I'd do if I really cared about him. Losing him has made that clearer than it was when I was by his side—I love

Axel. I still love Azar. I feel it in every part of my body and soul.

I land with Jade in the center of the dais, and I notice that the dragons might be as excited as we are. They're milling around, and their thoughts are flying—mental conversations that are, in some ways, more confusing in large groups than audible ones. Just like our voices, some of them are louder than others, and I can hear a few of them from across the river. That's an impressive reach.

But what I'm hearing is more impressive.

-that I can find one who likes to watch fish under the water with me.

I just want one who likes to sing. Did you hear Klyde's ensnared? She sings like a bird.

—haven't had anything to eat my entire life, other than an earth blessed. I hate it. I'll put up with a lot from a human for making it possible for me to eat something else—anything else.

I want one who wants to fly. Odara has been doing tricks with hers. He leaps off her back and she spins around before catching him. She said it's great fun.

The blessed aren't the only ones who are excited—the humans are practically giddy. Most of them are watching the sky, the water, or the ground in front of us with rapt attention. That's what gives me the idea of how to get this done in an effective way with more likelihood of the teams finding a good match.

"Welcome to the blessed encampment at Selfoss, Iceland," I say. "I think I speak for all the blessed when I say how excited we are to have found humans who want to help us. As you already know, we have three types of blessed here with us who are in need of bonds with humans."

The blessed and the humans quiet down, all of them more than ready to get started.

"Tonight, I'd like to try something new. I'd like all the humans who love water, swimming, or seafood, and would be happy bonding a water blessed—along with being able to breathe underwater through their magic—to move down in front of the platform near the river bed."

Of course the chatter starts immediately.

"Can you all listen to me for just a moment before you start asking questions?"

I notice that Azar—he's changed forms again—has moved up behind me, lending me his authority. That's a relief. "Thanks," I whisper.

He inclines his head.

"If you've always had a connection with the earth, with plants or hiking, with metals or stone, or if you just like the look of the earth blessed, if you could move on the opposite side of the platform, around the back, I'll have the earth blessed start to gather there."

The blessed are reacting too, already moving to the areas I mentioned. I look back at Azar, rolling my eyes. In some ways, the blessed are more childlike than the humans.

"And finally, if you've always loved storms, lightning, or the wind in your face, and if you don't mind tempers that change as often as the weather in Texas, then if you could move to the far end of this courtyard, I'll have the darting, diving, strike blessed congregate in that area."

Not all of us are temperamental, Asteria grumbles behind me.

I laugh. "That's true, but most of you are. And with as blinged and beautiful as the strike blessed are, I thought you should come with a warning."

Azar snorts. *Then where's your warning?*

I spin around. "That's rude."

And also true. Asteria's smiling.

"What would you choose?" Coral asks. At first I think she's asking me, but then I realize she's looking at Jade.

"Strike blessed," Jade says, "if I could pick without Liz's head exploding."

"I don't want any of them." Coral looks around the gathering with a smug look.

"Excuse me?" I lift my eyebrows. "You must be kidding. I feel like you'd bond immediately if you could."

Coral scoffs. "If I can't bond a flame blessed, I don't want to bond a blessed at all."

Of course. She's a little spitfire.

Azar hasn't chosen a bonded yet, Asteria says. But she's looking at me.

I have wondered who he'll choose—I'm assuming that even with dual affinities, he'll have to bond someone. I know he won't pick me. I've been here all along, and he still hasn't said a word other than asking me if I would rebond him. I can't even push him for it, not knowing where I'm sure to be headed again. When one of those skulls disappeared after I went into the volcano. . .I'm not sure I'd ever really bond him again if he asked.

Losing your bond over and over. . . I can't think of

much that would be worse. He's suffered enough for me already.

In spite of her bold position, Coral watches eagerly as the humans chat with blessed, and then we all smile and coo as those conversations turn into bonds. Jade's just as fascinated, and each time, when a newly bonded couple leaves, it makes me smile.

Each of these bonds were chosen, and that makes all the difference.

A few moments later, the joy I'm feeling is interrupted in a big way.

"You have to," Sammy says.

I won't. Gordon straightens up, which is strange for him. His top parts rise up like a, well, like a serpent. He's so high up that Sammy can't really see him to try and stare him down anymore.

He's such a big personality for such a small person. "I'll never talk to you again if you don't."

When I step closer, I realize this isn't like their usual lighthearted banter.

I can't. Gordon's head sinks a little, and his body coils tighter. *I've tried. I even went and talked to a few humans last time, but I can't bond any of them.*

Sammy's crying now. "But if you don't, you'll die. And if you don't bond one of these humans, you might have to go to war to find one." He swipes at his face, and then he throws his arms around Gordon—they go about one thirtieth of the way around one coil. "Then you could get someone mean or someone who makes you feel sad."

When Gordon drops his head, he presses it against Sammy's side, and I realize that something strange has happened. That earth blessed loves my brother—it's not the same as the way I love Azar, but it's just as strong.

And when Gordon bonds another human—it's going to hurt, both of them. If he were my child. . .I don't know what I'd do. Gordon's Azar's strongest lieutenant. He's going to be in danger. He just is. If Sammy's bonded to him, my tiny little brother'll be thrown into danger, too.

I didn't choose to put them here, in the epicenter of the danger around the blessed, but I haven't been able to extricate them. I could now, possibly. I could have them dropped off near where I was being kept, and they might be taken to Dad. But there's also a large chance that they'll be interrogated and poked and prodded. The US military is out of control, and they might force them to weaponize what they know about the blessed to try and harm them.

That would damage Coral, Sammy, and Jade beyond words.

If I were their mother, I would know what to do. If I were their mother, I'd naturally make the right decision, but I'm not. I'm just a sister, and I've already chosen a painful path for myself. I would never allow them to follow me down this road.

Never.

I've done everything I've done to try and keep them safe. I'm starting to feel like, in this world, no one can keep anyone else safe, not ever.

"I wish Gordon could bond Sammy," I whisper. "I really do, but he's too small."

Sammy's head whips my way, and I realize that even from two dozen yards away, he somehow heard me. He beams then, and he presses his hand against

Gordon's head. I can feel it—the sucking feeling I felt when Axel bonded me, only it's not coming from Gordon.

It's coming from Sammy.

Gordon's eyes fly open and then he stiffens. That's when I realize that Sammy bonded *him*. "Liz said it's okay!" Sammy's beaming. *Beaming.* "See?" He waves at me. "I'm *not* too small."

His beautiful baby-boy blond hair shimmers and then turns dark brown, shining like fresh-turned, loamy earth. I feel sick to my stomach. My barely-seven-year-old brother just bonded a blessed. Before I can even react, I hear Jade, all the way across the platform, standing beside Asteria. "Did you see that? Liz let Sammy bond Gordon!"

You said you'd like to bond a strike blessed. Asteria arches one eye-ridge. *Did you already have one in mind?*

I open my mouth to tell Jade not to even think about it, but it's too late. My little sister, the oldest Chadwick other than me, presses her hand against Asteria's leg, and she does the same damn thing as Sammy, bonding *her.* Just like Mom's hair months ago, Jade's hair almost shivers as it becomes a bright, sparkling silver.

Beside me, Coral's eyes are wider than saucers. "Oh, shoot. That was rule one, two, *and* three, right down the drain. You're about to kill someone, aren't you?"

I wish she didn't look quite so happy about it.

Azar doesn't even understand why I'm upset. *I thought the small ones couldn't bond yet. I thought that was the reason you didn't want them bonding blessed, but look! They did, and they bonded powerful ones that we like. Right?*

"I didn't want them bonding blessed because they're too small to be at risk like that. I can't have them riding the dragons into *wars*, Azar." I shake my head and resume pacing, gripping and releasing the swords in my hands rhythmically like it might somehow ease my anger and frustration.

You're mad at Gordon? Azar still seems confused. *He tells me Sammy bonded* him.

Jade bonded me as well, Asteria says.

"I know that!" I stop pacing and flex my hands around the hilts of the swords as tightly as possible. "I just—I need to kill something right now."

For some reason, that makes Coral laugh.

I am *so* not a good motherly figure.

We're about to slaughter some animals we prepared for

the blessed who bonded tonight, Asteria says. *Maybe you could help—*

"You think I want to slaughter defenseless animals?" I scream at the top of my lungs, throwing my head back and letting all my frustration, my rage, and my helplessness out.

Azar joins me, bellowing his loudest up into the sky.

That feels nice, Azar says. *Do you feel better too?*

Every blessed and human in the entire area turns to look at us in alarm. I should probably be embarrassed, but I'm not. I can't kill someone, but it occurs to me that I *can* fly. Flying will be less distressing to the others, but maybe it'll help.

I turn toward Coral. "If you bond a dragon tonight, I will kill you." I spin around and face Rufus. "And if you bond her, I will cut your scales off, one swath at a time, until you're writhing in agony. And if you regrow them, I'll just start over."

Rufus just stares at me.

I sheathe my swords, and round on Coral again. "No. Bonding. Not any dragon, not any time, not anything at all. Got it?"

She drops her hands on her hips. "It's hardly fair since the other two both bonded one, but whatever. We *all* heard you." As I launch into the sky, I hear her mutter, "Drama queen."

That actually makes me smile, but the desire fades quickly, replaced again with a helpless rage.

It's my fault.

My siblings are now inextricably connected to this mess. Mother, if she were here, would be absolutely disgusted. Sure, Sammy and Jade did it themselves, and sure, Gordon and Asteria are the best of the blessed. But I *let* it happen. If I'd kept them at home—I know better than anyone how you can get swept up in the excitement of it. I've watched several rounds of this now—humans getting their life's dream, and dragons finding the joy of bonding with a human who *wants* to be their partner.

I should've kept them back at the hotel Selfoss. I could have just stayed there too.

Part of the reason I *didn't* is that Gordon and Rufus would have insisted on staying with them, forgoing their chance to bond a human. Now Rufus, who totally should have found someone, still hasn't, and Gordon bonded *Sammy!*

Ugh.

I'm sorry.

With the wind in my face and the sound of my wings, I wasn't even paying attention to where I was going or who might be close. Azar followed me, which he really shouldn't have done. I turn and glare over my shoulder. "You need to go back," I shout. "There weren't many humans left. If you're not careful, my little sister will be your only option."

I don't think I can handle Coral. His smirk is so familiar. *She'd flay me alive.*

"I pity the dragon who bonds her," I say. "She's a hurricane in a bottle."

Asteria's sorry too, he says.

And for some reason, that pisses me off. "Why didn't she tell me herself? Are you her messenger boy, now?" I pump my wings faster, irrationally angry. Why would stupid Freya give me wings that aren't even fast enough for me to escape from the one person I want to ditch? They're useless, like everything that I manage to get or do or be.

Are you angry? Or are you feeling sorry for yourself?

I extend my right wing, filling it with air, and pivot around to face him. "Can you hear what I'm thinking?" It feels. . .invasive and also, I find that I'm hopeful. How could he hear what I'm thinking if we're not bonded? Could some part of our bond still remain?

Of course not, he says. *But your sister Coral told me that for humans, anger is usually something called a masking emotion. It covers for something else.*

I'm going to kill her. "Sorry to disappoint. Right now, I'm just angry. I'm not covering anything else up." I spin back around, getting better at the flying thing, and start away from him again as fast as I can move, the frost-flecked wind accosting my face brutally.

I hate Iceland.

Where are you going? He sounds genuinely curious.

"Nowhere," I say. "Just. . .away."

Away from me?

"Well, it's been an utter failure if that was my plan, hasn't it?"

He laughs.

"But seriously, I have wings and swords, and all the blessed know who I am. I'm fine out here. You don't need to follow me around."

I wanted to follow you.

That hits me like an arrow to the heart, and I drop from the sky, plummeting downward. The frigid air and the tiny snow flurries pull greedily at my face and hair, and the temperatures freeze the tears escaping onto my cheeks. I hit the ground hard, snow flying in every direction. Without my wings, I'd skid and fall flat on my face, but tilting them allows me to stabilize what was an irresponsibly stupid landing.

Of course, stupid Azar follows me right down.

Have we finally arrived? Was this where you were headed? He looks around as he lands. *Because there's nothing here.*

He's right. More than anything else, Iceland's good at long, desolate stretches of nothing. I'm right in the middle of one, which is where I wanted to go.

Just not with him.

Or rather, all I've wanted since Freya spat me out was to come somewhere with him alone—but not like this. Not with him asking me stupid questions he'd know the answers to if only he'd rebonded me. Not with him following me only because he's worried his pet human has malfunctioned. I don't want him following to make sure I don't slice someone up because I'm unstable. Or to keep me alive so they can chuck me back into that volcano.

He's close to me for all the reasons I don't want.

And when he says things like, that he *wanted* to follow me, and I wish he meant it the way I wanted him to mean it, but I know he doesn't, well. I just spiral down without wanting to, feeling crazier and crazier. "I'm sorry," I whisper. "You really don't need to be here."

We need you.

I'm really sick of hearing about the stupid volcano and their precious heart. "You know what?" I spin around to face him. "I had a dream about where the heart came from."

His eyes widen.

"I—we've been so busy I didn't tell you yet." That

sounds lame, even to me. "I wasn't sure whether it was really a dream about the heart or just my own wishful thinking." Why did I bring this up? Now I sound even crazier than I felt, and he's looking at me expectantly. "In the dream, I think I was Gullveig. It was a long time ago, and I was telling the story of where the heart came from to three kids." I shake my head. "Never mind."

Azar sits like a golden retriever. I swear, it almost makes me laugh. *I want to hear the rest.*

"I—it's not much of a story." I recount how the goddess of the earth and the god of the sky met, and loved, and kissed, and how their kiss created the heartstone.

What is a kiss, exactly?

I'm reminded of him asking me before—and our practicing. My cheeks flush, and I hope he doesn't notice. "It's something people do when they love each other."

She had barely met this sky god and she already loved him?

It does feel silly. "That's just how the story went," I say.

And this made the heartstone? That's what we need? A stone?

"Apparently Freya had it," I say. "She and Odin were marrying, and I thought their union would keep humans like me and the children in the dream safe. They were part of a group called the æsir, and their enemies were the vanir." I watch his face carefully to see whether he reacts.

He doesn't.

"None of that means anything to you?" I suppose I

was hoping he'd either remember what the old woman had told us or maybe something his father had shared.

He shrugs. *Not really. We have many blessed named Freja, Freya, Frey, Frejar, and so on. You appear to believe this dream Freya is the same as the one in the volcano, and that both of them are my mother.*

"I do." I nod. "I'm surprised you don't."

It's possible, but I don't think we know enough yet. What did the heartstone look like?

I sigh. "I woke up before I saw it."

He frowns, like he's thinking about it.

"I know, it was pretty useless as dreams go. That's the other reason I didn't say anything about it right away."

If you really are dreaming as Gullveig, you could learn something important. Please tell me in the future what you dream as soon as you dream it.

"I will."

Tomorrow we have another long day, and after speaking with Hyperion, I should tell you—we would need to somehow come back with a lot of humans or. . .

"Or he'll take the other blessed to find them forcibly."

I can't blame him.

"Can you really not survive more than a week?" I ask. "Will you start dying?"

It's unclear. Three blessed died today, without any signs that they were even low energy or struggling. I think it may be more than a simple consumption of energy. I think something that changed in that volcano made my people need the bond between earth child and sky child.

"That's what they said in the dream," I say. "Humans were earth children—the blessed were sky children. Their bond made it possible for the sky children to survive on earth."

Perhaps the dream was a memory, he says. *We've always called you earth children.*

I can't help staring at him, especially when he looks preoccupied. He's so beautiful. Massive. Powerful. But somehow also delicate and perfectly crafted, in both forms.

I could stare at him all day.

Is something wrong? He peers at me. *You're staring.*

I look down at my hands.

Are you upset that I haven't bonded you?

I shake my head. I mean, I am, but that's not the real reason I'm staring. It's better for him if he doesn't comprehend all the things I'm struggling with. "I understand why you haven't," I say. "In fact, if you asked to rebond me, I'd be excited, but I'd probably say no. You should find someone to bond who isn't headed for another visit with Freya in the volcano."

He frowns. *I've been thinking about this. If you have to go back into the volcano, I'm flame blessed. I could go back inside with you. Perhaps I could even help keep you safe.*

My heart lurches a little—it's very similar to what he told me before the humans attacked. He said he'd go in with me and protect me. Not that it worked.

"The last time we went in, you writhed in agony while I spoke with Freya." I shake my head. "It has to be me, and it's not something you can protect me from, unfortunately." I pull the leather of my tunic aside and show him the heart-shaped birthmark on my chest. "You don't remember any of this, but I've apparently been marked as the proper human sacrifice since I was quite young."

He doesn't look at *all* pleased by that.

"When you had your memories, it was hard for you that I had to do this. It's probably better for you not to worry about it so much. The only reason I haven't dived back into the volcano yet is that I'm trying to help you find willing humans first. My wings seem to have become a real asset in our search."

The humans are impressed with them.

"Indeed they are," I say. "And tomorrow, we'll see if we can impress enough to stave off Hyperion a little longer."

Or we can just go to war and take what we can find. You and I were not bonded by choice, but then we entwined. His eyes look curious, but I'm not sure I can talk about that.

"We only entwined thanks to your ability to shift into a human form," I say. "We became closer that way —and it's not even possible now." Saying the words aloud hurts.

Do you miss it?

I can't talk about it, not without crying again. "I've noticed something, you know. You think attacking humans will be easy, because we're small. Physically, tigers, bears, even dogs, can all easily slay us. But from sticks to guns, we never fight fair. Forcibly taking human bonds may be more dangerous than you're anticipating."

You're worried about us?

I sigh. "I'm worried about *both* peoples. That's my problem." I laugh bitterly at myself for being so stupid. "Isn't it ridiculous? I want to keep the blessed and the humans safe, all of them."

It's brave.

"And ultimately, it's probably a futile effort that makes me hated by both sides." Neither of us talks as I fly back. When I get there, the kids are all gone. I panic, more than a little. Thankfully, with Azar's help, we discover they've all been taken back to the Hotel Selfoss, Coral riding with Rufus, and Asteria and Gordon taking their newly bonded humans.

"He ate!" Sammy's jumping up and down with joy when we arrive. "Gordon's going to be fine."

I wish I knew the same would be true for Sammy.

I'm sorry, Gordon says. *I really am.*

But there's nothing we can do about it now. "I know," I say. "I'm not angry."

"Really?" Coral slowly bobs her head. "That fast? No big deal? You're just over it?"

I point. "Do not get any ideas. This is a huge mess. Like, please tell me you're not planning on going off with your dragons and sleeping who knows where, now." I glare pointedly.

"Of course not," Sammy says. "Gordon's always slept in the room next to mine."

The open air freeze-box. Right.

"And that's close enough?"

Gordon bobs his head.

"Fine." I turn. "But what about you, Princess?"

Is that directed at me or at her? They're both the most imperious, holier-than-thou creatures I know, but at least Jade's kind. I suppose Asteria's kind enough, for a dragon.

"Asteria says she'll stay in that room as well, for now."

For now. I hate hearing that. Unlike before, I'm not in charge of keeping Jade safe anymore. I'm not the boss of where she sleeps or what she does—Asteria is.

"You're bonded to the sister of Mom's bonded." I hate that. Ocharta was the literal worst.

I'm nothing like my sister.

I can't argue that. No one could even approach her level without being at least half-devil. No matter what strange sort of rivalry Asteria and I have, I don't hate her. She seems to be mostly good. "I can't think of another dragon I'd rather see Jade bonded to," I say. "Though I'm not happy it happened. Thank you for understanding that she's very young and still needs her human family."

That night, in spite of the late hour, I take the time to tuck the kids in, hug them, and kiss them. Then I tell them a story. It's not an epic story. It's not about the love between the earth and the sky. No, that night, I tell them the story of how our mom and dad met. I talk about how they fell in love, and how, in spite of their differences, they built our family.

"But Mom kind of let you down," Coral says. "Aren't you mad at her?"

"She wasn't nice to you," Sammy says. "She didn't come see us, either, and you were bonded, but you did."

I pull them all close, Sammy against my left, Jade on his other side, Coral on the right. "Mom helped me escape when the humans were torturing those dragons. Without her, I would never have made it back." I tell them that story too, and I realize that without a bad guy, without a villain to fight, our stories don't mean a lot.

"Heroes are defined by the things they do when

life's hard, and the way they're willing to stand up and fight, even when the enemy's scary," I say. "You three are too young to become heroes or villains, yet. Do you hear me?" I press a kiss to Sammy's forehead. "No fighting or saving or anything else until you're eighteen."

"Do you think they'll wait for us to grow up?" he asks. "Or will everything awesome happen while I'm stuck in this room, growing?"

Nothing ever waits. "I hope so," I lie.

14

GULLVEIG

It feels surreal, now the moment is finally here.

I've stood here, docile and patient, silently preparing myself for what's about to happen as well as I can, but there's not much more I can do. Gorm and I were carefully chosen for our aptitude, and then we trained intensely for years—sent here for just this purpose, but now that the vanir have taken us, I can't help the trembling in my hands. My feet are grimy, the hem of my roughspun dress, ragged.

Running through the woods does that, I suppose. It was necessary, to be captured and brought here against our will. They'd never have trusted it otherwise. When we heard that Freyr and Freja had both lost their human bonded, we knew the time to be 'caught' was right.

"It's alright," my twin brother says. "We're ready."

Maybe he is.

As the black creature approaches me, its head lowered, its eyes intent, I want to huddle and cry out like a child. The vanir are so different than the æsir we love so much, so much crueler.

Then I feel it—a sensation I've felt hundreds of times, or maybe even thousands. A sensation I've been prepared to fight against almost my entire life.

The miserable moon vanir's trying to ensnare me.

I dig down deep, and I refuse.

The black scales of the moon vanir sparkle when he lifts his head and glares at me. The pressure intensifies, the soul-sucking power of his attempt to force a bond battering my internal defenses.

Not today, demon. I fling the words at him like an attack of my own.

Enraged, he sinks his massive taloned feet into the stone floor below us and he roars.

I hold on, barely. More than just my hands are trembling by the time he ceases his assault. Sweat has broken out on my brow. My entire body's shaking, but I have rebuffed every one of his efforts to ensnare me.

One glance to my side shows me that Gorm's struggling too, but he hasn't been bonded by the ice vanir who approached him either. It was painful and exhausting, but the æsir prepared us well.

We're just two earth children in a long line of the same, prepared to do our part to fight against the miserable bondage of the vanir and their ongoing mistreatment of our people. Whenever I lose my resolve, I remind myself that this war can't be won in a day, or in a month, or even in a year, and we all have to do our part, or it will *never* be won.

But we have to win.

Losing costs us far too much.

The war's about so much more than us. It's about our future. It's about all the other earth children, Gorm's children, since I'll never have any. My twin had already started his family when we were selected for this task, and he's here *because* he loves those children more than anything. We both want a better world for them. We're determined to create a world for them where the vanir aren't lurking around the corner, preparing to ensnare and enslave us, treating us as a disposable good they can use and discard on a whim.

Two more vanir attempt to bond me, one storm, and another moon. Another ice vanir comes to bond Gorm, but none of them manage it. I'm shaking now, even when no vanir are attempting to bond me.

When I finally hear the order from Bjorn, bellowed as if he's ready to explode, I know we've succeeded. *Freyr, Freja, report to the bonding grounds immediately.*

I can't help my half-smile, turning slightly toward Gorm. "Yes," I whisper. I'm not sure I could manage any other words, even if it would be safe to say them.

When we heard they'd lost their humans in the last conflict, even knowing they'd need to rebond soon, there was no guarantee it wouldn't happen before we could stumble onto vanir ground and be rounded up. We thought we could hold off the other vanir who would attempt to bond us, but we weren't sure.

There were so many holes in our plan—it was always a long shot.

But the æsir's number one targets, other than Bjorn himself who almost never enters any altercations, are his twin children, Freyr and Freja. If the æsir can destroy them, it could shift the entire tide of the war. No earth child can really make a huge difference, but our deaths at the right time will allow the æsir to attack the twins when weakened, and that just might be enough.

Bjorn sails down from their massive stone tower, his terrifyingly wide wingspan blocking the sunlight entirely as he nears. *I'm already bonded, or I'd take one of these rebellious little snakes myself.* The earth shudders when he lands. *I do so enjoy breaking the ones the æsir have built up.* He tilts his head when he looks at us, like he's examining a fascinating or frustrating puzzle.

Freyr and Freja, the two demon-cursed ice vanir twins approach from different places, but they both land mere seconds after Bjorn. *Why couldn't they be bonded?* Freja peers down at me with curiosity. *Are you sure they're really bright? Perhaps some spell made them appear—*

Bond them or the other earth children will be inspired by their miserable rebellion. Bjorn tosses his head. *Now. Do it.*

Why don't we just kill them? Freyr asks. *I've had plenty of rebellious earth children, and it's exhausting. I'd rather just get one who—*

Bjorn screams in his son's face. *Do it now.*

Freyr sighs and circles around his father, focusing in on me.

I've already picked this one, Freja says. *Take the male.*

Freyr might have complained to his father, but he doesn't seem inclined to do the same with Freja. He shifts without a single word and leans toward Gorm, clearly intent.

At the same time, Freja lowers her head near mine.

She's a real sight to behold—her scales much more impressive than the simple white of most ice vanir. They're translucent in places and they shimmer, like a rainbow has formed across them and then frozen in place. Her head's delicate, but her mouth's still wide and full of razor-sharp teeth. The scales across her head are smaller, and her eye ridges are graceful. There are no horns around her face at all. Her eyes, when she trains them on me, are the color of an iris in spring.

A bright, vibrant purple.

Alright, little one, let's not make this any harder than it needs to be.

Unlike before, I make only a token effort to block her.

Gorm's still putting up a fight—probably for show—but even he finally allows Freyr to bond him.

That was simple, Freja says. *What were the others complaining about?*

"I chose you," I whisper. "That's what made it simple."

You chose me? Freja laughs then, and it's a fine sound. *Well, that's a first, isn't it? I hope we'll get along well together, then, little one.*

Getting along with a vanir would be a first, from what I hear. The vanir and their earth children *never* get along. As the bond settles into place, I feel just what they described to me. It's like a net has been thrown over my mind, and I allow it to settle, keeping the one tidy packet of knowledge hidden in a far corner, well behind the net.

I can't help my smile, as I contemplate the next few months.

The trickiest part of our plan actually worked.

Gorm and I are here, bonded to the most powerful of the vanir, and now we just have to bide our time.

Come along, Freja says. *We have a lot to do today, so I'll just get you settled in my cavern. You can clean it while I'm gone.*

Clean it? Fabulous. At least cleaning's honest work.

She crouches down, and I'm not sure why until I realize she thinks I'm going to climb on her back. At first, I resist. The vanir don't usually allow their ensnared to ride them. They're forced to trot along below, catching up if or when they ever can. Freja has been known to take her more capable ensnared along in times of war, however. And that might make my ultimate goal much easier.

Our plan was to somehow coordinate when and how I should kill myself so that I can do it while she's at war—but if I'm with her, that's much simpler to time.

She uses the bond to push me into climbing on her back right as I decide to do it. Almost the second I've sat down, reaching my hands to gasp her shoulder joints, she leaps into the air, her wings pumping wildly. My right hand slips, and I slide down her back, almost plummeting to my death. Just before I've fallen, I manage to catch one of her back ridges, and I hold onto it with all my might.

As she banks and then drops without warning, sailing through the opening of a large cavern, I sense that she's amused. *Not bad for a newly-ensnared. You'll improve.* When she lands, I slide off her back and realize she has two dozen other earth children there already, waiting. I should've assumed. It's what the vanir do.

This is your initial team. You may be assigned others, but for now, gain control over them and set them to work. They can clean your chamber as well, which is near the end, by the entrance. It hasn't been cleaned in many days, since the death of my last bright, so it might be in bad shape.

I don't say anything in response. She doesn't appear to be looking for one.

I'm surprised when she crouches beside me. *If one of the gods offered you a gift, would you prefer the strength to endure or the power to dominate your enemies?*

"Do you jest?" I look around. "As an earth child, I'm not likely to gain the power to dominate over you, am I?"

No, I suppose not. She laughs. *You're entertaining.*

"I'd choose the strength to endure," I say. "It's the most realistic gift for me."

I suppose that's what I should expect from a slave. She eyes me for a moment, and then she turns to leave. Just before she launches from the edge, she turns back. *I've lost quite a few ensnared earth children in the past few months. I'd like to keep up with you longer. It's quite tiring, always suffering their loss and then training a new one. What do you say to receiving some education in physical combat to make you less vulnerable?*

Combat? Why would she want to train me in combat?

You couldn't use it on me, of course. She narrows her eyes, and I feel her push the command as she says the words, *You will never use a blade or any other weapon against me or harm me in any way. You will not use poison, and you will not conspire with others to poison or cut or harm me in any way.*

I bow my head.

No. She snorts. *Don't bow or scrape. I don't like it.*

I meet her eye. "I would be willing to train, if it would please you."

You know, little one, I think it would.

"Gyda," I say. "My name's Gyda."

I'll be back soon, Gyda. Be ready to learn.

❧ 15 ❧

AXEL

The moment I come for Liz this time, she's ready.

She hugs her brother Sammy, kisses her sister Jade on the cheek, and drags her sister Coral in for a hug. Coral looks irritated, but I can't figure out why.

Liz must see me watching. As she flutters down from the edge of the gaping hole in the side of the hotel, she says, "She's not bonded and her siblings are. Coral doesn't like them to have anything she doesn't."

I'm sure we can find her a blessed—

"She's insisting she'll only bond a flame blessed." Liz lifts her eyebrows. "Unless you're volunteering?"

I've learned with Liz that ignoring her is some-times the best option. *We have a lot to do today.* After I adjust my flying speed to accommodate her slow pace, I realize that it's going to take us *forever* to reach the rendezvous point for Hyperion's honor guard. I'm debating asking her to just ride me when she starts speaking.

"You said I should tell you when this happens."

What?

"Last night, I dreamed again—this time I was someone else, someone named Gyda."

And?

"Do the words vanir and æsir mean anything to you?"

The vanir are our ancient enemies. We vanquished them before we left Earth.

"I'm not sure you did," I say. "I think they may be the creatures stuck in the volcano—the vanir."

She thinks the demon creatures who can take blessed forms are the vanir? *I suppose that could be true. We should ask Euphrasia about them. She lived on Earth for a time before my people left.*

Liz's wings stop beating and she falls a dozen feet before she starts flying again. "How did I not know that already? She and I need to talk—badly."

I'll try and arrange for that today. I believe she's supposed to be in the group of water blessed allowed to bond today's brights.

"Perfect," Liz says. "Because when I was this Gyda person, guess what dragon bonded me?"

How should I know?

"Her name was Freja," Liz says. "She was a massive ice vanir, with the most gorgeous, diamond-like scales, and virtually see-through wings."

Should that mean something to me?

"Your father was married to a Freya," Liz says. "Don't you think those names are close?"

Was she the same creature you encountered in the volcano?

Liz sighs and her eyes flash. "I'm. . .not sure. I mean, the names are a little different, and the woman in the volcano was, well, she was a human *woman*. So maybe not. But it feels like it's too close *not* to be connected somehow. Freja and Freya?"

As I said, it's a common name with my people.

"But both of them were powerful and important. Both of them are somehow connected to the blessed before they left Earth. Both of them are connected to the creatures I think are the vanir. Don't you think that matters?"

Do you want to go back to the volcano now?

I never want to go back, but I can't very well tell him that. "I'm hoping I'll dream of this past world again—more than anything, I want to ask good questions when I do return. When I asked Freya questions last time, she mocked me for knowing nothing. She said what I was asking was all wrong."

What would you ask her now?

"I want to know what happened—how the vanir were trapped in that volcano. Or if they aren't the vanir, I want to know who they are."

Describe the vanir in your dream.

"They're like the blessed," Liz says. "Except instead of strike, flame, earth, and water blessed, they're moon, storm, and ice vanir."

What can they do?

Liz shakes her head. "I'm not sure. I wasn't there long. But I was there as like, a planted weapon for the æesir, like a kamikaze or something."

A what?

"In human history, the Japanese culture would sometimes send warriors in planes to attack their enemies. . . .and they'd know they were going to die.

But they would kill more of the enemy that way, and they were trained and willing to do that."

The person who you saw in your dream was sent to die?

"I was sent to bond this Freja, who was the son of the vanir's leader Bjorn, and I'm supposed to kill myself when the æsir have a chance to attack Freja. They think if they can take her down—" Liz freezes, her wings beating slowly in place. "It's actually almost the same thing Gideon did. They wanted a human who was bonded to a vanir to die in order to weaken them at the right moment—so they could defeat the vanir."

Surely you didn't think your miserable friend was terribly clever? I'm sure that's been a common theme throughout the existence of this bond. But knowing the weakness, why would this strong vanir bond anyone? Especially a human who had come from the enemy.

"I'm not sure, but Freja had lost her prior bonded, and it seemed like she had to bond another at some point, like without them. . ." Liz begins flying again, her brow furrowed. "What if they *had* to bond them for the same reason that you do?" She spins around to face me.

I nearly run into her. *In order to eat, you mean?*

"It makes sense." She's nodding. "Look, the humans are earth children, right? And the blessed or vanir or whatever, they're sky children. What if they needed that bond with the earth children, or they couldn't process sustenance from earth? What if—" She slows down even more, her hands clenching at her side.

Then your decision in the volcano didn't cause this change for us—it simply restored a situation that was already in existence before.

"The other dragons couldn't consume earth food before, right? You could just eat the earth dragons, and the reason that wouldn't work in the long run is because the earth dragons couldn't reproduce anymore. . ." She frowns. "So it is kind of still my fault, but I think we're missing something important."

Let's focus on finding humans today. At least that's something we can control.

I watch Liz carefully as we reach the top of the mountain where Hyperion had us gather before leaving. Euphrasia's here, but she looks exhausted. We need to find her a human to bond soon.

Some of you are here because you're not doing well, Hyperion says. *But most of you are here because we've now spent two days purloining humans from various places, and we expect that very soon, they'll be waiting for us to attack. You will* not hesitate *to attack, to defend, or to bond humans if that becomes necessary.* Hyperion turns to glare at me. *Liz is not your leader. She's not even* bonded *to your leader. You will not listen to her. You'll listen only to the Recovery Leader.*

"After that rousing pep talk, I'm sure you're all excited to get started," Liz says. "Thank you so much, Hyperion."

I think she enjoys making him angry.

"Now, if you'll all listen clearly, we can get those of you who are struggling a bond right away. With the bond to a human, you'll be able to process food for yourself here." She smiles. "And even though I'm not your leader, I have been coordinating the effort to find humans who are willing to work with you. If you'll listen to me today, I think you'll find this to be an enjoyable process all around." She snorts. "Don't forget, kids. Only *you* can prevent forest fires."

Hyperion looks as lost as I am, so I'm guessing it's not something I've just forgotten. *What?*

"Never mind," Liz says. "That's just a phrase from another useless pep talk they used to give us when we were kids." She waves. "Go ahead and open the portal. We'll hope for the best and expect the worst."

We travel to a place called Oregon first today, a park just outside a small town called Grants Pass. There aren't as many brights as usual, but we still manage to find fifty-four.

"Euphrasia." Now that Liz has done her presentation for the humans, ensuring they're all okay with leaving their homes and families and they're coming of their own volition, she waves down my old nanny. "Can we talk?"

Euphrasia seems to like her. She's smiling, which is rare for all the blessed, but especially for my old guardian. She wasn't friendly to most of the other blessed.

"Azar tells me you were alive before the blessed left Earth the first time."

She nods.

I can't help sliding a bit closer, hoping neither of them notice. I really want to know what Liz asks, but I also want to hear what Euphrasia says about the time before. When I asked, she clammed up every time, but Liz saying that she asked Freya bad questions has me wondering whether I might have done the same.

"I've been having some strange dreams, and I'd like to ask you some questions, but I'm hoping you can keep the things I ask to yourself."

I'm quite good with secrets.

"Yes, I know you are, which is the reason I'm comfortable asking you." Liz glances my way. "Can you make sure no one else is close enough to hear us?"

I incline my head slightly. My presence alone is usually more than sufficient, but I'm more than capable of glaring them farther away.

"Do you remember anything about the vanir and æsir?"

The vanir were our enemies. The æsir are the blessed— without the vanir to oppose, we took a new name for ourselves.

Liz blinks. "So—you really were the æsir, fighting the vanir. Why were you enemies?"

Euphrasia shrugs. *I'm not sure. It just* was, *but I know that we strongly objected to the way they treated their bonded.*

Liz freezes. "Did all the blessed have bonded humans? Before, I mean?"

We did. As children of the sky, we couldn't consume anything of earth without first forming a bond with a child of the earth. As you probably know, we draw much of our energy from other sources, but for physical nourishment, we could only tolerate it with an earth-child bond.

Everything she dreamed about appears to be true. I can't decide whether that's good or bad. Liz looks distressed, but I think it's good that we're gaining information that we didn't have.

"Why didn't you tell Azar all this already? As the return leader, don't you think he should know all of that?"

We didn't know what would be the same, or what might have changed. Many of the blessed who fled Earth were upset about our departure. That's why Odin kept most of the blessed who had lived here out of the return. He didn't want to make Prince Azar's job more difficult by bringing past biases into the search.

"I think he did the opposite. He didn't even tell Azar what the heart was."

Euphrasia tilts her head. *And do you know what it is, earth child?*

"It's a stone. He couldn't have told Azar that?"

Euphrasia's smile's sad. *It began as a stone that could not be moved, and our enemies grew in strength with its control. But that changed—it came to us for a time. In our departure, it was retaken by the vanir. That was more than a thousand years gone. We didn't know where it might have been or what form it may have taken. The heart always called to the earth and sky born alike—it was only a matter of time before the earth children found it.*

"I will never understand the blessed insistence on withholding information that might be helpful." Liz frowns. "But Euphrasia, you don't look like you feel so great. Maybe you should find one of the humans we just met. . ."

It takes her half an hour, but Liz finds good matches for Euphrasia and all the other blessed who came with us—all thirty-two of them. We gather the others into one place, and we travel to the second stop for the day. There are another forty-six brights, and at the third location, we find eighty-eight more.

"It's not enough." Liz's face is drawn, and she's clearly stressed out. "I mean, I think it's good. I'm really pleased that we've been able to find so many bondable humans who are sympathetic to the dragons, even with the government blasting that they're our enemy on every channel."

And yet, if we can't find more, my people will all die, I say. *It's not nearly enough.*

"I think we need to find another renaissance festival," Liz says. "The military will definitely be expecting that, but. . ." She groans. "I don't know what else to do. Why are they so stupid that they won't see that we're trying to do this the right way?"

Euphrasia's new human, a woman who had almost white hair before it turned silver with the bonding asks, "Have you thought about Comic-Cons?"

Liz turns slowly. "No."

Silver hair asks, "No, you don't want to try that? Or no, you haven't considered it?"

"I hadn't really considered it," Liz says.

"After the dragons came to the last one, the government canceled all renaissance festivals," the woman says. "They said they were too dangerous, but the last I heard, they weren't canceling Comic-Cons."

"In the United States. . ." Liz slaps her own forehead. "But what about other countries? What are they saying?"

"So far, you've only picked up humans in the US," the woman says. "Is there a reason for that?"

"I've mainly focused on friends of friends," Liz says. "I don't know anyone in other places."

"But the news said that you simply showed up at the renaissance festival." She shrugs. "If you wanted to try that again, maybe a Comic-Con in another country?"

Liz calls for any functioning technology and starts frantically tapping at screens. "Melbourne," she says.

"There's a Supernova Comicon and Gaming Convention." She beams at me. "This is perfect, but it'll be much larger."

Are you worried the humans will attack?

"I'm less worried about it in Australia. They won't be expecting us to show up either, I don't think."

Shall we go?

Liz laughs. "I need to do some preparing first." Her preparing involved poking around and tapping on a bunch of little screens, but eventually she calls me over. "Can you portal above a big building?" She holds up the screen to show me some images.

I can, yes.

She's showing me from another angle when a video pops up. The barely legible text says 'related to your search,' and Liz starts to click a tiny x to make it disappear—I'm learning about this internet humans love—but then she freezes. "Oh, no."

What?

She doesn't respond. She taps on the video and it expands.

"After several weeks of experiments, scientists in Iceland are finally caving to the public pressure. They'll be executing the remaining dragons who have been held in captivity on Friday, using all the newest technology they have developed for our ongoing counter-measures in the war against the invading dragons."

The screen flashes images one by one of almost a dozen blessed that are being held captive and tortured by the humans. I'm frustrated, but not surprised. We had assumed those blessed were already dead. Liz only told us about one other water blessed who was yet alive when they escaped, but it's hardly a surprise that they had another location.

Still, Liz looks shell-shocked. "We have to go back and save them," she says. "I promised Plumeria."

That sounds an awful lot like the beginning of the war you're trying so hard to prevent.

Her hands clench into fists. "But they—it's—"

The tinny voice from the small square screen starts blaring again. The video she selected ended, and it rolled right into another one. "So far, there hasn't been much consensus on what to do with the war criminal, the mother of the most famous war criminal of all, Elizabeth Chadwick."

Another voice comes on now, and I believe it corresponds with the brown man who's now talking. He's holding a microphone in his hand, which Liz told me is to amplify tiny human voices. "As you've already heard, the members of congress are split on whether Harriet Chadwick, wife to Ronald Chadwick, has committed crimes punishable by death. She doesn't even deny freeing her daughter, the former bonded to the strongest of all the invading dragons. She insists that her daughter's bonded dragon has died, but she agrees that Elizabeth Chadwick's potentially dangerous—and most of the military leadership agrees that with her departure, the humans lost their single strongest weapon against the dragons. The military recovered two swords crafted by the dragons themselves for their fiercest human warrior, Chadwick herself. Now civilians are reporting that Elizabeth Chadwick has indeed rejoined the dragons, and not only that, she's also somehow reported to have wings, along with the swords she took upon her departure."

The video cuts to a fuzzy clip of Liz flying beside me at the renaissance festival.

"While the military's doing everything in their power to regain the weapons she stole, the one thing we do have control over is the execution of her criminal mother." The man with brown skin sounds downright furious. "Elizabeth Chadwick must pay for her heavy debt to humanity, and if the only way we can punish her is by killing her mother, then so be it."

Liz is frozen in place. She looks completely shocked.

Are you alright?

She shakes her head. "I'm fine. I think we should go to Brisbane. It's nine in the morning there." She swallows and stands, handing the square screen off to one of the other humans. "It's—we have other things to worry about right now."

It's clear that she's worried about her mother, though.

Even when our trip to Brisbane is a huge success, when we manage to find almost five hundred new brights, she's still dazed. "It's not enough," she says. "We have to find another. . ." She's poking at the screen again, frustrated and shaking. "We need at least a few hundred more or Hyperion. . ." She freezes. "If they learn we hit a con, the government will shut those down next."

She stands. "We need to hit Florida Supercon today. It's *huge*."

It's too risky, then, I say. *With that many people, the military will be there.*

"Not if they're focused on renaissance festivals or tracking down people connected to the people we've taken already." She shakes her head. "If we could go back with almost two thousand brights, Hyperion would have to give us more time." She steps closer. "Come on, Axel. We can do it."

We have to drop these humans off first, I say. *I won't risk all of them, and Hyperion will insist that we take more blessed. Thirty won't be enough.*

"Fine." Liz truly looks like a warrior in that moment. She may be upset that her mother's being executed, or maybe she's angry about the blessed. Perhaps it's that her people consider her public enemy number one, in spite of her tireless efforts to save their lives. Either way, for the first time, I truly see what I might have liked before I lost my memories.

She's fierce.

She's brave.

And she's unyielding.

She's doing it, just as the humans said, to help my people, but she's also trying to help her own. Unlike most of them, she looks at the whole picture. It's a slow process, taking all the humans we've found back to Hyperion, and he's not keen on the plan. *It's too dangerous. It could lead to a war we're not ready for—the war Liz doesn't want. We might suffer heavy casualties if we go against them this way, petitioning.*

It takes a while, but Liz convinces him to allow us to go—if we take a hundred strike blessed.

They're the most capable of fighting, Hyperion says. *And I need to stay here to make sure if the humans attack while we're distracted and weak, we're protected.*

"I notice you haven't bonded a human yet," Liz says. "You need to do it immediately."

I'm waiting.

On what? I ask.

Hyperion's smile is tight. *If you don't bond Liz, I plan to do it. She's a handful, but I find that I like her more and more.*

Something inside me snaps—and fire floods my entire body. *You will not.*

Hyperion's smug smile infuriates me further. *You couldn't stop me. You're too weak.*

I lunge at him, already blasting flame and fire.

He leaps into the sky, and we both rocket upward, my wings beating faster than they have in quite a while. It feels good, releasing some of my fury. Hyperion blows his anger right back, and for the next few moments, we take turns melting the side of several different mountains.

Do you feel better now? Hyperion's smiling.

Were you picking a fight? It makes the fire rise back up inside of me. *You didn't really want to bond her?*

I do like her, Hyperion says. *I would bond her, but mostly I wanted to see whether you'd let me. I find it fascinating that you haven't bonded her yet, but you won't allow anyone else to even contemplate it.*

I hate it. And I hate that he knows it. *We'll go to Florida and find you a human now. The brightest one we see, that's your new bonded.*

Hyperion doesn't argue, but he's still smiling when we get back to Liz and the others. When I finally open the portal into Miami, I'm braced for hostilities. Instead, when we explode into the sky over Pride Park, the open area beside the convention center, there are hundreds of humans holding signs.

We ♥ Dragons!

Take me, Liz!

I'm ready to bond a dragon!

Water > electricity.

Bond me, baby, one more time!!

Liz stares at them, gape-mouthed, beside me. When they finally process that we're there, the humans begin to cheer.

Loudly.

Others *race* toward us from the edge of the convention center parking lot.

"They came!"

"They're here!"

"Take me!!"

The humans below us are frantic. Liz flies closer to them, beginning her explanation of why we're here, but she barely gets through the first twenty seconds of it when there's a loud crack.

The humans all look around frantically.

And Liz plummets toward the ground, a large hole in her right shoulder, and an even larger hole blown in her right wing. The feathers near the wound are painted scarlet.

Without even meaning to, I explode into my flame blessed form and snap my wings out to their fullest point.

Then I *scream*.

GULLVEIG

Thanks to months of training, I don't hate Freja quite as much. Unfortunately, the other vanir are just as bad as I was led to believe they were. They slaughter earth children without a single thought. They ensnare earth children who are capable of being bonded without a care for free will or anything else. We're nothing more than tools for them.

In fact, Freyr said as much.

He persists in calling Gorm 'heiðr,' because he thinks it's funny to call him 'bright.' It's how the vanir see us—earth children with more light around us. My brother doesn't deserve another name, because we are only tools.

Freja's different, though.

She's kinder. She also listens to the things I say, evaluating my words for their benefit, their truth. She's spent a significant amount of time preparing me to join her in war. The idea of going with her, of being there on the battlefield and helping her destroy my own people—it's painful.

I know that's what they need me to do, though. It's the entire reason I was trained and sent among the vanir in the first place. Gorm hasn't been training, but Freja told her twin that she was taking me to the next battle, and he said he'd do the same—our proximity will strengthen the twins. Having us far away leaves them vulnerable.

At least with Gorm going too, we'll be together when it happens.

I always imagined it that way, dying with my brother at the same time, in the same place, serving the æsir's cause to the end. It won't be a guarantee that the æsir can kill Freyr and Freja, but it's a good start. And if we can help, it's worth it. Only once the vanir are finally destroyed will the earth children finally be free to truly live.

What are you thinking when you disappear into your mind like that? Freja cocks her head sideways, her eyes narrowing. *I've never had an ensnared who did that— utterly blanked her mind.*

"It's called meditation," I say. "It helps me to focus. It clears my head of all the things that don't matter." Really, though, it's the only time I can think about what's coming, my plans. It's my one chance to prepare. Had I known she was already back, I'd have done it later. It's much harder to keep her out when she's actively trying to penetrate my thoughts.

You know, at first the brights were more plentiful. Freja circles the area where I was training with my short swords. She showed me patterns to follow—she told me it's from the vanir's study of the most successful earth children warrior patterns. *My training might keep you alive longer, but I think the vanir's careless bonding and death of so many brights has been bad for your population.*

"The brights, as you call them, are the strongest of Jörð's children, those who are still pure of heart. We used to be the guardians of the earth among her children. We're rare, and you should take a little better care of us."

Like the æsir, you mean.

I sheathe my swords in the scabbard on my back and cross my arms. "If you lose your bonded humans, you'll die here on Earth. It's not your home."

Freja laughs, as she often does with me. *It's as much my home as yours.*

"Not so," I say. "Your father was a visitor here, whereas our mother *is* the earth under our feet. You'll never be welcome in the way we are."

Do you wish you were a sky child? Freja, as always, has questions. *Do you resent us for coming here and making you feel so small by comparison?*

"I have never resented the world for the way it is. I simply make plans to change the things that are wrong in it."

Freja shakes her head. *You're the strangest earth child I've ever met. You still haven't told me how you kept the other vanir from bonding you.*

"Nor do I plan to," I say. "Some things aren't meant to be shared with one's master."

She roars then, throwing her head back. *It's almost time. I brought you something to celebrate that you're joining me tomorrow when we attack.* She drags something from the edge of her cavern where she dropped it until it's right in front of me. Then she bumps it with her nose, nudging it closer.

I lean over and reach for the long, leather-wrapped bundle. It's heavy—heavier than I expected. "What is it?"

She merely smiles.

I unwrap it carefully, which turns out to be good, because inside are two of the sharpest swords I've ever touched. "I have short swords," I say. "They're easier for me to manage than these full-length ones would be."

But these are better. She looks smug. *I spelled them. They'll slice right through æsir hide like an oar through water.*

I suppress my grimace. "How wonderful."

Many of our ensnared believe that fighting the æsir is antithetical to their entire purpose in life. After all, the æsir treat their earth children like beloved pets. But know this. She looms closer. *A pet is still a slave. At least we're honest about who you are to us.*

I think about her words all night. I knew I wouldn't be able to sleep on my last night on earth. I think about how the æsir treat us—pets, she said. But she's wrong. I watched my parents, and they loved their æsir fiercely. They did everything they were asked, and their bonded æsir cared for them, too.

They chose to bond the children of the sky.

They had families. They found many moments of joy. Small, we may always be, but we are valuable among the æsir, and until the vanir are vanquished, earth children will never really be safe.

I spend the final hour before dawn working on the forms with my heavier blades. It's slightly different, but my arms have been sufficiently strengthened thanks to my constant training.

Freja thought she was training me so I could defend myself on the battlefield. She did it because the presence of her bonded human will strengthen her. What she didn't know was that I was really training to prepare myself for taking my own life. When I sheathe my new blades, the sound of their entry into the hard leather scabbard like the whoosh of the wind past our cavern, I close my eyes and imagine how it will feel.

The blade, sliding into my body—aimed right for my heart.

It will be quick.

At least it will be quick.

Gorm's already waiting when Freja and I finally wing our way down to the gathered vanir.

As you all know, the æsir are about to begin their annual hunt for new brights. They make it into a party, pretending that they care for the earth children. Bjorn scoffs. *The idiotic earth children actually believe that ridiculous propaganda, so they'll all be gathered. We steal all the ones we can, and then we destroy as many æsir as possible.*

Freyr snatches Gorm in one claw. He's never allowed my brother to ride. That would imply a relationship between them other than master-slave. *You'll keep heiðr with your slave.* He doesn't wait for Freja to agree. He simply leaps into the air.

As usual, Bjorn isn't coming with us. He almost never leaves Vanaheim. He says he draws his strength from its walls, but I think it's something else. I think he's afraid of something else. He does open a portal for his children to lead their forces through.

The air of our home slaps me in my face.

I hate the dry, never-ending heat of Vanaheim.

The lush, gusty cold weather of Ásgarðr is like a

balm to my broken heart. If I'm going to die anyway, I'm happy it will happen here. Maybe my parents will even be able to locate my and Gorm's bodies. As soon as they see us, the æsir spring into action.

The flashes of the mighty strike blessed surge into the air on our east side. The terrifying cries of the water blessed rise up as they burst from the ocean waves, blowing ocean spray with their mighty wings as they flank us on the south.

But Odin, unlike his cousin Bjorn, doesn't hide. No, Odin and his wife Frigg take to wing as well, their brilliant crimson scales flashing in the rays of the setting sun. The sight fills me with pride and hope.

With such warriors fighting for the earth children, how could the vanir prevail? I wish we knew why the vanir always seem stronger in each fight. No one's quite sure, but we fear it may be the way they treat their ensnared humans.

The vanir don't wait for the æsir to mount a defense. The tiny moon vanir scatter, using their magic as well as they can to keep the æsir from being able to see their opponents.

You can't attack what you can't see.

And the storm vanir bring the wind to bear, buffeting the strike and water blessed to and fro, forcing their lightning and water attacks to fly wild.

But it's Freja and Freyr who face off with Odin and Frigg. Just before Odin can flame them, Freyr drops Gorm. Freja veers off and dives straight down, snatching Gorm out of the sky and arrowing toward the gathered earth children. Their goal, after all, is to steal their much-needed brights, and also to simultaneously teach the æsir a lesson: they can't protect the weaklings.

Only sky children matter.

Gorm catches my eye, and then I see a single tear fly from his cheek. *I'll always love you.* He's smiling when he drags a dagger across his own throat. I force myself to watch as he dies.

In that moment, Freja screams.

Because Odin and Frigg saw us, they know why we're here—they know what we know. This is their moment. There's never going to be a better time for the æsir to deal a terrible blow to the vanir than *right now*.

Freja realizes what Gorm's done and drops him. His eyes have only just gone dull when he falls, limp like a rag doll. His body slams into the brights below like a rock hitting a smooth pool. The earth children fall, several crushed by my brother's body.

And now it's my turn.

But before I can follow in his path, I notice what's happened.

Freyr, realizing he's been tricked, darts down from where he was flying to intercept Odin and slams instead into Frigg. Also a flame blessed, her much smaller form isn't able to withstand the force of him. As the two of them collide, claws scrabbling, tails twisting, and wings battering the other, they lurch and begin to fall.

Freyr's ice erupts from his open maw, slamming into Frigg like a massive ballista, and she turns bright blue. As they crash into the ground below, Frigg goes from blue to bright gold.

And then she explodes.

Chunks of Frigg and Freyr cover *everything*. Earth children, marauding vanir, and defending æsir alike. In that moment, something dawns on me, like the sun, cresting over the tops of the mountains, like the first frost on the blades of grass around our keep, and I realize the world is different than I knew.

No matter what I do, no matter what sacrifices we all make, no matter what plans we set in motion. . .this conflict will never end. The æsir and vanir go round and round, killing one another, slaughtering us, and they always will.

The destruction will never end.

Gorm's death, Freyr's death, Frigg's death, they all chase one another round and round. No matter who we're able to kill, everything simply starts over. Death, death, and more death.

Would I rather have the strength to endure, or the power to dominate? That's the question Freja asked on the day she forced my bond. It was the first thing that day that surprised me. The rest of the things that happened were expected, planned for, even.

I said the strength to endure, because it's what I expected she wanted, but in truth, they're both an illusion. There is no enduring. We all eventually die, even the sky children. And anyone who dominates is also sure to fall.

Someone worse, someone more powerful, *always* comes along.

The force of the explosion knocks Freja backward, and she slams into the side of a looming mountain, rolling down head over tail repeatedly until we come to a stop in front of the gathered brights she wanted to destroy.

I pull my swords and leap from her back.

I stand to face her, holding the blades that Freja gave me herself.

Instead of killing myself, perhaps I could kill her.

It would be a resounding win. Both twins gone—a terrible blow for the vanir. But then Bjorn would bide his time until his other children were old enough to attack again. None of our efforts will truly fix anything. The cycle of death will simply continue on and on and on until we change something. Until we knock ourselves free of the cycle.

But how?

The other earth children behind me are assembling—many of whom I know. They're not armed with magicked swords, but they have the things the æsir provide. Darts, poisoned daggers, slings and rocks, and arrows. They're not just walking— they're sprinting—toward us. They're eager to knock the evil vanir back. With the way Freja's reeling from her crash and her brother's death, and the other vanir they're slaughtering, they might be able to harm her, especially if I kill myself.

An entire contingent of strike blessed are taking form not far away. I should do what I came to do, and make it easier for them to destroy Freja.

But I have another idea.

A crazy, insane idea.

An idea that very well might turn my own people against me.

"I was sent to kill you." I turn to face Freja. "You probably figured that out. The reason I could block the vanir's attempts to bond me is that I trained for just that. I came to the vanir to bond *you*. My brother Gorm did the same."

Freja stares, dumbfounded.

Her head turns slightly, gazing at the site where her twin just died.

"We both lost a brother in the last few moments, and we should be trying to destroy one another."

Freja's head whips my direction. *I could end you with one breath.*

"That's true," I say. "But you won't be able to kill them all as well." As if my words summoned them, the other earth children surge over the edge of the mountain, and the strike blessed swoop closer, almost within striking distance.

The first poison dart strikes her shoulder, incapacitating her right claw.

I turn and unsheathe my swords. "I could use this gift to kill you, or to kill myself, weakening you."

You're— Her nostrils flare. *I'm a fool, for liking you.*

Her words reaffirm my decision. She *likes* me. It's more than I've ever heard any other vanir say. "Instead, I'm choosing to defend you. Now, fly home while I block these darts." I spread my arms, throwing the shield that she taught me up and outward.

A dozen darts are caught in it.

"Go!" I shout. "Now—I'm not sure how long I can block them."

Why would you help me? She glares. *You conspired to kill me.*

"I guess both of us learned something today," I say. "But for me, I just realized how senseless all of this is." I turn for one second. "Now, go, please."

Freja snatches me with her one good front claw

and throws me up into the air, flinging me over her shoulder and back onto her body. *You're coming with me, ensnared. We have much to discuss.*

She's right, I suppose. If she's willing to talk, then we do.

I hold the shield until they're too far to harm us, and just before the strike blessed lightning hits us, we dive toward the small portal Freja's capable of making. Her father will have to bring the others home, once she explains.

But when we reach Bjorn, all she tells him is that Freyr killed Frigg, but died in the process. She doesn't mention Gorm, or my plan to kill her, or my decision to help instead. Her father leaves to recover the others, whoever hasn't perished, and we're left alone.

After flying to our cavern, I send the other earth children away. Before I can say anything, before I can explain, Freya sinks to the cold stone floor, her head collapsing on the ground.

I have something important to show you, Freja says. *It's the source of all my father's power, and I think it may be the key to finally changing the world we live in, once and for all. It's the source of my magic as well.*

When she looks at me again, I see something I've never seen from her before, not once in all the time I've been here.

Hope.

Liz's body has nearly hit the ground when I reach her, my claws closing around her bleeding and broken form *just* in time. Even so, the impact of my talons on her soft human body when I wing my way upward can't be good.

The strike blessed fry several men in uniform firing guns before I rip open a portal and wing my way through. They follow me back almost immediately.

Hyperion hasn't even left the area. *What happened?*

Liz. I gently set her on the ground. *Find someone with an ensnared healer of some kind. The humans shot her.*

Hyperion flies away without a single word of argument. I crouch over her tiny body, listening for the telltale sound of her heartbeat. It's faint, but it's there. Only, it sounds erratic. Instead of the steady boom boom boom I'm accustomed to hearing, it's staccato.

Boom.

Boom boom boom.

Pause.

I use just one claw to prod her gently.

She gasps, and blood spurts from the hole in her shoulder. Her eyes fly open. "Azar."

I bring my head closer, my nostrils almost touching her.

"Throw me in the volcano. If I'm dying anyway, I may as well bargain with Freya before it happens."

No. You aren't dying.

When she laughs, blood sprays from her mouth.

What if she's right? Is she *dying?* From one little bullet?

Asteria lands beside us. *What's wrong with you, moron?*

"Yeah," Jade asks. "Why are you letting her die? Do you hate her that much?"

Hate her? No. Not at all. In fact, sitting here and looking at her, worrying she'll die feels worse than any injury I've ever endured. It feels. . .devastating. Horrible in every way I can't even explain or understand.

Bond her, stupid, Asteria says. *I don't understand why you haven't already.*

All my reasons fade—if that could help her. . . *You really think she's dying?*

Jade rushes to her side, pressing her hand against Liz's forehead. "She already looks dead, to me."

Her heart. . .is it beating? Am I already too late? I reach for her then, pulling on her soul with all my might. But there's nothing to pull *on.*

It's gone.

I'm too late.

When humans' hearts stop beating, they die.

"Shock her," Jade says, her eyes pleading with Asteria. She takes Liz's hand and squeezes. "It's the only chance we have. Please."

What?

"It's what the doctors do in movies when someone's heart stops," Jade says. "They zap them with electricity—not a lot. A little. Then a little more if that doesn't work."

You want me to. . . Asteria creeps closer, her face studying the cold, pale form of Liz. She looks worried. *I might hurt you.*

Jade releases Liz's hand. "Now."

I suppose now it's my turn to beg. *If there's even a chance it will help. . .no matter how you feel about her, please do this for me.*

I don't hate her, Asteria says. *I'm jealous. That's not the same. But winning because she died. . .* She shakes her head. *The only thing worse would be causing her death myself. You'd never forgive me for that.*

"Please." Jade's crying now, and she leans one hand against Asteria.

The strike blessed princess isn't cold, but she's hardly warm. In that moment, though, she looks at Jade with affection. *Alright. Step back.*

I watch intently as Asteria zaps Liz.

Her soft body spasms, more blood oozing out.

"That might have been too much." Jade peers at her.

Nothing happens.

"Or maybe try just a little more." Jade's eyes are wide.

Do you have any idea what you're asking her to do? I want to rend Jade into tiny pieces for not knowing.

"I don't know." Jade's crying furiously, now. "Their

bodies jolt around like that in movies, too. They shake and spasm."

The ground around Liz is now reddish brown, sticky with her blood. Her heart's not beating. She's pale—so pale—except for her mangled wing. It's scarlet in one large section, and that part's glistening brightly.

Asteria leans over her again, and she zaps her harder this time, the lightning visibly arcing from her face to Liz's chest.

This time, Liz gasps and half-sits up, gasping and then wheezing.

I don't wait for her to die again. I pull as hard as I can on her very soul, and she spins toward me, her eyes wide and terrified. The bright light that's the core of my warrior expands, burning like a supernova, and then it explodes around us.

I've never seen anything like that in my life, Asteria says. *What just happened?*

"What was weird about it?" Jade asks. "I mean, her hair turned red, but it did that before—I didn't see anything else. Is she going to be alright?"

It was too bright, Asteria says. *Like the sun.*

Liz collapses again, her body convulsing, her now-red hair strewn across the ground underneath her head like just another a pool of blood.

That wasn't the golden light of a normal bond, Asteria continues. *At least, it wasn't only that. It was brilliant gold, but also red, and then layered inside the red, a bright, vibrant green.*

"Maybe it's because she bonded Axel and Azar at once," Jade says. "It wasn't really a normal bond."

I couldn't care less how it looked. I lean closer to Liz, hoping that it worked. She looks pale—too pale. But then I remember to listen. I'm relieved to hear a heartbeat—boom, boom.

Then nothing.

Again.

No, I say. *She's—is she still dying?*

As if I prompted her, a great, pulling weight claws at my magic, and I shove the strength toward her. *Yes, take it,* I say. *Take whatever you need.*

Then, right in front of our eyes, the hole in her chest begins to close, red tissues knitting together, and then skin closing over it too. I sit back on my haunches, horribly relieved.

"Oh, good. It worked, plus, now Azar can eat," Jade says. "It's great news all around."

I'm not at all sure Liz will agree, especially since the attack kept us from recovering enough humans to satisfy my brother. Six hundred and fifty isn't likely to make Hyperion happy. I'm not happy with it either, if I'm being honest. I appreciate that Liz doesn't want to force the humans, but we can't very well let the blessed *die* in droves because she's not a fan of how we're ensnaring them. And if the blessed were to be attacked by the humans right now. . . we'll break apart like rotten fruit smashed with a hammer.

By the time Hyperion returns with Memna—a strike blessed who apparently bonded a human nurse —Liz's wing has already almost healed on its own.

The humans with guns were waiting on you? Hyperion's expression is flat.

Let's talk about this when Liz wakes up, I say.

Bonded for one moment and already letting the human dictate our actions again. He snorts. *Just as pathetic as when you remembered everything about her.*

Look at you, I say. *You're scared to bond a human at all. You're afraid of what you'll do for yours.*

Actually, I was serious. He tosses his head. *I wanted to bond that one.* He sighs. *I suppose I'll have to choose another, but now that we're going to have to fight them either way, we may as well simply go to war and ensnare all the humans we need all at once.*

"It's not that simple," Jade says. "Brights aren't easy to find."

Your sister's been finding hundreds of them a day—they've been coming to her, begging to come even when they can't be bonded, Hyperion says. *How hard can it really be?*

I heard that it's not always that easy, Asteria says. *Ocharta told me it took them days to locate the hundred or so they bonded in Houston.*

All the more reason to get started right away, Hyperion says.

"I should have known you'd be here, already yammering." Liz heaves herself up to seating, cradling her head in her hands. "Ouch. What in the world happened?" She freezes, slowly turning to look at the strand of hair in her right hand. "Why is my hair. . ." She turns toward us.

"Axel finally bonded you," Jade says.

Are you sure she didn't arrange for someone to shoot her? Asteria asks.

I know Liz's feeling better when she glares at Asteria. "Not everyone is as pathetic as you."

I expect to have to defend my newly bonded human, but Asteria laughs. *You're the worst.*

"Right back atcha, big silver."

I don't understand the relationship between them at all.

No, Liz says. *You didn't understand before, but now that you've forgotten everything I ever taught you, you're really hopeless.*

She's always been able to communicate with me this way, but she hasn't until now. She must not see a point unless she needs to tell me something privately. I can't help being pleased, even if she's not sharing anything substantial. What she said finally registers with me. *Everything you taught me? What did you teach me, exactly?*

"Don't worry," Liz says out loud this time. "I'll start over right away."

I can't tell you how pleased I am that you two are sharing private conversations again. Asteria doesn't look upset, even though her tone sounds like she is. I'm even more confused now.

Whether you bonded Liz or not, we still have to find more humans, Hyperion says. *It would probably make Azar happy to go right back to where they shot you and roast some of those soldiers.*

"There were quite a few humans willing to come with us before those military people tried to kill me," Liz says. "They had signs."

Ridiculous signs, I say. *That's what distracted me.*

"And you can't make shields anymore," Jade says. "Because you're not entwined anymore."

"I'll miss the entwined perks." Liz shrugs. "But Azar can make them for me." She nods. "And if we have to fight anyway, we may as well fight the soldiers where we know there are willing humans. Maybe some of them will still want to come with us, even after that mess."

"Plus, if any of them do come, we know they aren't scaredy cats," Jade says.

Brave humans are better than the alternative, Asteria says.

I feel Liz's pulse of pride in her sister—Jade may be small, but she's smart. I also doubt she'd run away from a fight, which probably upsets Liz. "You can't come with us, though," Liz says. "You have to stay put."

As if I'd risk Jade's life for something like this, Asteria says. *Give me a little credit. I only got a human yesterday. I wouldn't even consider flinging her into a conflict a day later.*

"Thank goodness." Liz groans as she shoves up to her feet. She shifts her shoulders forward one at a time. "I swear, the part of me that hurts the most isn't even the place I had a hole blown in a while ago." She rolls her head around on her neck. "It's the parts on my back that were lying on these cursed swords." Her eyes widen, and she bites her lip. It's terribly cute, but it's also clear she's thought of something.

What is it?

She shakes her head. "I—" She gapes at me. *I keep forgetting that we can talk this way now.*

What did you just realize?

It happened again. She sighs. *I was her—the woman named Gyda who was bonded to that Freja, the ice dragon.*

And?

She swallows. *And Freja gave me* these *swords.* She stares at me. *The ones that are on my back right now.* Your *swords, the one you said were left for the earth dragons.*

We all know you're talking privately, Hyperion says. *It's extremely rude.*

You know what's worse? I snap. *Losing all my memories, and I know how that feels, because you shoved me into a volcano.*

Now Hyperion's laughing. *Did you finally regain those memories, brother?*

I glare. *Why would you ask that?*

You're acting just like you did before—one minute. That's how long it took from when you bonded her again to when you started snapping and snarling at anyone who so much as looks her direction. It's truly amazing. Hyperion looks ticked—pacing back and forth in a place where there isn't really room for a blessed of his size to pace. He barely gets three steps in before he has to turn around to keep from falling off the edge of the mountain. *Sammy, even without a bond, had Gordon following him around like that Fluff Dog creature. Jade bonded Asteria yesterday and she's already ordering her to fly over and heal her sister. And Asteria's listening. Now you're already mimicking Liz's rudeness.*

Not to interrupt, Asteria says. *But I'm going to drop Jade off at the hotel and return. If we don't hurry, the blessed-loving humans might have already been escorted offsite.*

"She's getting smarter," Liz says. "We should hurry, and we should come from the other side."

"Shouldn't Axel eat something first?" Jade asks.

It's not a terrible idea. I toss my head toward my back so Liz will climb on.

"I can fly."

I snort. *Didn't you just say we should hurry?*

Liz scowls. "Hyperion was right. You're rude."

I can't help my smile. *Asteria, you drop off Jade, round up a few more volunteers, and once I've eaten, we're going to find any humans who want to join us. . .and let them.*

And we're going to roast some soldiers who want to kill us, Hyperion says. *Your sister Coral was telling me about the human Christmas celebration, but this sounds better than that to me.*

Before Liz has climbed all the way up my back, she freezes. "Hyperion Flame Blessed, when and why were you talking to *Coral?*"

My brother frowns. *Does it matter?*

Liz's hands tighten on my scales. "If you even so much as *look her way*, I will slice you to ribbons. Are we clear?"

My brother launches into the sky without answering.

Are your wings alright? I expected her to fly her way up to my back instead of climbing.

"They're fine," she says. "I'm just not pressing it."

I feel the bond to see whether she's telling the truth, and it feels like she is. *Good decision.*

I'm not about to admit that having her on my back feels *right* somehow, and I wish I hadn't waited so long to bond her.

Liz directs me toward the pens to the west of Selfoss where the earth blessed were keeping the animals. "Unless you prefer grubs." Her eyes are sparkling. "I hear that's Gordon's favorite, and he said that while Iceland isn't great for bug life in general, there are some really great ones hiding in the black sand areas."

I shudder. *Definitely not.*

"That's good—he wasn't really very keen to share."

Within half an hour, I've eaten—with Liz averting her eyes and plugging her ears—and we're ready to open the portal.

"Do we have a plan?" Liz asks.

Don't die, Hyperion says. *And kill any of them who so much as look sideways at Liz.*

"No, that's a bad plan," Liz says. "You only kill a solider if—"

He's right, I say. *If any of them even look at you, I will incinerate them. No fighting us about that, or we'll leave you here.*

"Not you, too." Liz kicks me, as if that might bother me. "Listen, we're going to try and find brights, remember?"

No, you're going for brights. I say. *I'm going to make them sorry they ever tried to harm you, and to make sure that none of them ever—*

Liz pulls on my energy again, which is kind of cute, and she broadcasts as far as she can. *What Azar meant to say was that we saw lots of humans there who wanted to join us. We're going to try and make sure they don't change their minds by acting unnecessarily aggressive.* She pauses her yammering long enough to scowl at me and Hyperion. *Now that Azar can shield me, you won't have to worry about me being harmed. So if you can't shield your ensnared, leave them here. We'll be back with more brights, hopefully very soon.*

She kicks me again. "Now, portal."

I'm not your dutiful horse.

That makes her smile, which isn't what I wanted exactly, but I don't hate it either.

Before I can say anything else, Hyperion opens the portal. *Let's just go already. You two are as disgusting as ever.* He flies through before anyone else, but in spite of his words, he's smiling as he does it. *Hello humans,* he shouts. *We're baaaaack.*

"Has someone been showing him old movies?" Liz asks. "Because he should *not* be watching those. I think they're warping his already strange brain."

But then we're through the portal, and the teeming chaos below demands all our attention. The soldiers are actively shoving, clubbing, and threatening to shoot the sign-holding fans of the blessed.

"If you're interested in coming back with us," Liz shouts. "We're ready to take you now. As you may have already noticed, I'm healed from the military's vicious attack, and I brought even more friends."

A soldier opens fire, aiming for Liz again, but this time, I'm ready. A bright red bubble pops into place, and Liz shakes her head.

"Not again, guys. That first shot was just beginner's luck."

Asteria swoops down low, bullets ricocheting off her belly and striking some of the humans.

"Wait," Liz says.

But Asteria has already zapped the line of soldiers, and they all shudder and fall to the ground.

"I said that we shouldn't—"

Calm down, Asteria says. *I told my strike blessed to stun, and that's what I'm doing too.*

Liz is practically beaming, but Hyperion's ticked. *This is no fun at all. Definitely not as good as Christmas.*

An hour later, we've identified six hundred and forty-three brights, incapacitated over three hundred soldiers, some of them repeatedly, and portaled the brights home. After the last portal closes, he finally stops grumbling.

It was probably faster than attacking randomly, my brother grudgingly admits. *Especially since they came with us, giddy and pleasant. That's better than drooling or kicking and screaming.*

Liz is always right. That's what I'm learning.

I can't help being a little proud of her—she is *mine,* after all. That thought makes me shiver with satisfaction. It greatly exceeds any frustration I felt about Hyperion saying I behave strangely with Liz. What does he know about strange? He's saying things that make no sense and talking about Christmas. He's changed so much himself, he wouldn't even recognize himself anymore.

After we're all back without a single injured blessed, Liz says, "Tomorrow, let's try and save my mom and the blessed they've been torturing." She yawns. "But not until after I've slept."

Save—who? Hyperion looks confused, so I fill him in. The glint in his eye is. . .predictable. *Maybe* this *will be our Christmas.*

"Your brain is so twisted," Liz says. "We're going to *save* dragons and my mother. Not to start another war —and starting a war is bad. Christmas is about love and peace and spending time with family."

That's why I said this would be our *Christmas,* he says. *Yours sounds terrible.*

"What makes killing people wonderful for you? Do you just like burning things?" Liz asks.

I can't tell who she's asking.

Yes, Hyperion and I say at the same time.

She rolls her eyes and flies away.

I nearly trip over Hyperion when I race to fly after her.

You don't have to sleep, Hyperion says. *And now that you can eat, you don't need to worry about running out of energy. We could fly somewhere. Or, if you're angry, you could attack me again.*

No thanks. I can't help my smug smile. *You need to bond a human,* I say. *Then you won't be so needy.*

Hyperion's insulting me when I fly off after Liz, but I don't care. Not much, anyway.

By the time I catch Liz, she's flying through the hole in the side of the Hotel Selfoss. *Who blasted this hole? I've been meaning to ask.*

You did, she says on a private thread.

I like that you're speaking to me this way. I can't help my smile. *You must be pleased to finally be bonded again?*

Liz points.

Gordon's coiled up in the corner, like he has been for the past few nights, but when I look closer, I notice why she's pointing. Sammy's lying on top of the pile. Gordon's not asleep. He's staring at Sammy, smiling idiotically.

Like an idiot.

Which is probably how I've looked. Ugh.

Right by the exit, Asteria's curled up, too, and right next to her, nestled in a pile of blankets, is Jade. Her chest is rising and falling, her eyes closed. Asteria's not smiling like an idiot, but she looks wistful.

I understand now, Asteria says. *It's. . .you just want to take care of them. Doing so makes you feel. . .satisfied. Complete.*

"I think it's like that because you're both happy

with the bond," Liz whispers. "It's certainly not always like that."

Shh, Asteria hisses. *Don't wake her up.*

"They're bonded now, dummy," Liz whispers. "As brights, they could always hear your telepathic hissing." *Which is why I was using the private communication with you.*

That hurts a little—I thought she was using it with me because she wanted to, not because she didn't want to wake her siblings. But why do I care? I'm shaping up to be just as bad as Gordon.

I don't hiss. I sound elegant. But Asteria lowers her tone quite a bit, I notice.

"You can go," I say. "I'll be just fine here."

I look pointedly at Asteria and Gordon, responding to her privately. *I don't want to sleep in some communal opening while you just disappear.*

Liz rolls her eyes. "Well, too bad."

We're bonded now. That means I can stay.

Yes, we all know, Asteria says. *You don't have to brag. I'm sure you'll be entwined again any moment.*

But how did we entwine? Did we do it quickly?

His missing memory annoys even me, Asteria says. *It's made him an idiot.*

She's changed—the old Asteria was never crabby. They've all changed—Hyperion, Gordon, Rufus. They're all different than they were when we came here. I might not have noticed before, since I was changing too, but the humans—Liz—has changed them all. Jade, Coral, and Sammy, they've changed us too.

Now that I'm finally catching up, I don't hate it.

I'm not leaving. I land and follow Liz. *I wish you'd stay on this side.*

She stops and turns, placing her hand on my leg. *Azar.*

When she touches me, I like it.

But when she says my name, I *really* like it.

She yanks her hand away. *Stop being so clingy.* She glares. *You only bonded me so I wouldn't die. I understand that. Believe me. And you can't follow me through that door. You're too big.*

I shift into Axel.

She rolls her eyes again. *Still too big.*

I drop to the floor, my head now on level with hers. *You almost died today.* I want to say more—I want to tell her that it scared me. I want to tell her that I can't have her walk away, not when I just got her back. I want her to touch me again and say my name. I want her to curl up next to me if she's cold, and I'll keep her warm.

I want the chance to incinerate anyone who threatens her, and I can't do that if she's not beside me.

"Apparently my near-death turned you into a golden retriever."

A golden what?

"It's a dog, Axel. A dog that won't leave its owner alone."

As if her words called it, the little dog in the other room starts barking. Liz whips the door open and crouches, and Fluff Dog leaps into her arms, licking her face.

Stupid lucky punk.

I want to lick her face.

It's a strange thought, but even as I want to discard it, I can't. I want to touch her face, and I want to touch her mouth, and I want. . .Hyperion's right. There *is* something wrong with me.

Liz starts walking through the tiny doorway with the fluffy thing.

Why does he *get to go with you?*

Liz spins then, setting Fluff Dog on the floor to yip and bounce and nip at her pants. She points. "Coral's in there all alone," she whispers. "I'm going to go and spend some time with her, alright?"

You should let her bond a blessed, too.

I expect her to argue, but she just arches one eyebrow. "I'm going to teach you something your mother should have." She looks utterly serious. "Two wrongs don't make a right."

After spouting that bizarre, unintelligible phrase, she slams the door in my face. And that's how I get stuck waiting on her while she sleeps—alone. At least the other blessed who are as pathetic as I am are all lying with or beside their bonded humans.

Almost an hour later, Rufus shows up.

He probably understands somewhat. Like me, he's all alone.

You need to bond someone tomorrow. I hold his gaze. *I mean it.*

His half-hearted nod isn't very reassuring.

Why haven't you?

He shrugs again.

Tell me.

Rufus drops his head on his front legs and sighs. *I'm happy Sammy and Gordon, and Asteria and Jade are bonded, but they're the humans who taught me what humans*

*should be. None of the other humans really feel quite right. I
guess I'm just looking for a good fit.*

And if you don't find one?

I've already lived much longer than most earth blessed.
He closes his eyes. *It's enough.*

We've all changed, alright. I'm just not sure all of
it's good. It looks like loving someone who doesn't love
you as much is just another way to experience pain.

GULLVEIG

In the aftermath of the failed attack and the loss of her brother, Freja's away a lot. I start to worry. I made progress, helping her. It meant something to her. She said she wanted to show me something, but I haven't really seen her since.

Until she flies in like she's racing, nearly knocking me over.

He's finally gone.

"What?"

My father—he's gone. He was called out to look at—doesn't matter. We have to go now.

"Go where?"

Freja tosses her head and waits.

I scramble onto her back.

She crawls to the edge of her cavern and looks around, and then she drops off the edge, only using her wings to guide the direction we're falling until we're about to slam into the ground.

I close my eyes, prepared for the worst, but instead

of a terrible impact, we bank hard right, and then dip again. When I open my eyes, we're in a cavern I didn't even know existed, and then we're dropping *again.*

"Where are we going?"

Hush.

It takes several moments of terrifying drops and spins around tight corners, weaving through dark caves before we finally stop.

"What is this place?"

Ice shimmers in all the corners, and it drips from the roof. I shiver, but not just from the bone-chilling cold. In the center of the enormous cavern, there's a pillar of what looks like *pure gold.* Streaks of gold, twisting veins and lines snake toward the column from all sides, above and below, all of them angling into the solid pillar. I slide from Freja's back and walk toward it carefully.

Ice patches covering the ground make the already rocky floor even more treacherous. Our training helped me become more sure-footed, but it's still slow as I make my way toward the pillar. Even if the strange, bluish, glowing ice didn't provide enough light, I could almost follow the gleamingly jagged lines of gold from the floor toward the column.

In the very middle of the pillar of gold pulses a strange, sparkling stone. It's large—the size of my fist—and almost circular, if it weren't angular around the edges.

I reach my hand toward it.

Don't, Freja says. *That's the heartstone.*

I blink. "That story's true?"

Jörð and Veralden Radian? Freja nods. *It's true, at least, the part where they met.*

"What does that mean?"

Freja's sigh is tired. *Your people tell a very different story than mine. Yours is a story of ill-fated love—Veralden wanted to stay with his beloved, but he couldn't. As a creature of sky, he had to move on. But after he left, he sent his children to her. It was his way of staying with her forever.*

"It's tragic, but also kind of beautiful," I say.

The vanir tell a different story.

I never heard that. "What is it?"

Veralden Radian traveled to earth, and he met Jörð, and he was entranced, just as in your tale. But Jörð was uninterested. She was wise, and she knew someone like him could not stay. She refused to have anything to do with him, but our great lord Veralden was stronger. Because he was more powerful, he did what he always did, forcing his attentions upon the weaker Jörð.

"That's awful."

Freja shrugs. *In your tale, the stone was left here out of love and desire, a gift to the children of both of them. It's a symbol of the bond between star-crossed lovers.*

"In yours, it's a. . ." I shudder. "It's what? Some kind of curse—stuck here to torture Jörð forever?"

Which one is true? I'm not sure we'll ever know. The one thing I know for sure is that the stone's very powerful. My father built Vanaheim here on purpose. He could never best your Odin—ice always yields to fire in the end. But with the heartstone underneath us, Bjorn has always been able to enforce his version of the story—the sky children take from the earth children, just as their father before them.

"The war really never will end," I say. "No matter who we kill."

I tried to remove it once, Freja says. She looks. . .tragic, as though *of course* she tried and failed to betray her own father. *I've always liked the æsir version of the story better. I've always thought the world would be better if it was true.*

"But?"

I nearly died, down here in this cave. When my father found me—he knew what I'd attempted. Rather, he thought I was attempting to steal it to best him, *not to defeat him and join the æsir, but he hasn't trusted me since. When we returned, he told me he wished I'd been the one to die, not Freyr.*

"That's horrible." Tears well in my eyes. "I'm sorry for Freyr's death. I know it was my brother's fault."

She shakes her head. *It's this—all of this. The rape stone. My father's agenda—to subjugate all earth children. It's never going to end.*

I don't know what to say.

She turns toward me. *Unless* we *end it. Together.*

I blink.

I couldn't remove it.

"You said."

It's encased in gold—that's Jörð's domain. I think she placed it here, and that means it can only be removed by an earth child.

She could be manipulating me. Her father might have put her up to this. He might want the heartstone to be portable so he can take the fight to Ásgarðr. Things like this always have a cost—she's not asking for a small favor.

I think our only hope is to remove it together. Earth and sky. Will you help me?

I think about what she's said—if it's all true, she may be right. Among the vanir, there won't be likely to be many sky-earth pairings that aren't fueled by hatred. We may be the first. . .and we could easily be the last. I reach for the bond, and I close my eyes.

I've spent so much time shielding from it, so much time hiding, so much time being as separate as I can, that I'm not sure how to use it, not properly. But it feels. . .it feels solid. It feels. . .honest.

I think she's telling the truth.

"If your father finds us here, after the first time?"

He'll kill us both, she says. *If anyone saw us, if. . .*

She's risking as much as I am. That decides me. I reach for the stone, and then I hesitate. It's encased in earth. An earth child can remove it. . .but how? My hands won't do it. They're weak and soft. But the swords she had crafted for me—they're a joinder of two worlds, as we are. They're metal, smelted from the earth.

But they're also magic from the sky that allows sky to be harmed.

And I used them to protect her from the earth children who meant her harm. My own people. "You've betrayed your own people—and I've also betrayed mine."

But only to try and help both, she says. *We have done what I hope Veralden Radian and Jörð would have wanted.*

Before I start, I say a prayer. "Jörð, we don't know what you've endured, whether it was a theft or a loss. Either way, I'm sure it's painful, and I know there's great power, great magic, in this stone—the product of your loss or your wound. But no matter what happened, your children are struggling, and so are his. Freja and I are here to try and fix it. We want to change things between our people. We want to do it with your help and your blessing."

I wait, and I'm not sure why. What am I hoping for? It's not like the goddess of the earth is going to talk to me. Just as I'm thinking what an idiot I am, the heartstone begins to glow. The gold pillar around it lights up, too, turning almost red. I unsheathe my swords, and I plunge them into the gold on either side.

The sword blades melt in a hiss, the steam burning my face, and I jump back.

You are my child. You're a child of earth, but you saw the beauty in the sky.

So much for the vanir's claim that Jörð didn't love Veralden.

Because of your sacrifice, because of your open heart, I give you a gift of the sky.

Pain blooms across my shoulders, like someone's stabbing me, and then it spreads outward, radiating through my entire body until I'm bowed backward, almost insensate in my agony.

And to Freja, sky child who loves my own earth bird, what should I give?

For some reason, Freja looks at *me*.

I shrug, and I notice my shoulders are now—I have massive white-feathered wings on my back.

You have to answer her, Freja says. *Quickly.*

"I want her to gain an understanding," I say. "Just as, through her, I knew kindness from the children of the sky, I want her to know what it's like to be a child of the earth. Then she can know, as will I."

A wise gift requested by a wise child. My chosen child. Granted.

As my pain begins to ebb, I watch Freja's body stiffen, her head curling inward, her limbs contorting, and then there's a sound like the shattering of ice, and Freja becomes. . .like me. A child of earth. Her hair flows down past her back—white, silver, red, blue, golden, and brown. Iridescent like her scales, it ripples outward. She's clad in a gown of the iciest of blues, and when she opens her eyes, they're the exact same color.

You're my chosen now, so I shall name you. Gullveig, my golden bird. My sky child is the same but also new, so you shall be known instead as Freya. As your father made you, and as I shaped you. Both of you must serve as promised.

The heartstone falls loose.

I lunge forward to catch it, but Freya's faster. At the same moment that her hands, working for the first time, catch the heartstone, my swords also plunge downward. Miraculously, instead of being nothing but bare hilts, they each have blades, now burning crimson, like the sun.

New and different than before, just like Freya and me.

Earth-blessed.

Strangely, when I snatch them so the blades don't strike the ground, the hilts aren't even hot. The blades themselves cool quickly, fading from bright red to golden, to silver.

"We can't stay here." Freya sounds panicked, and I don't blame her. We just stole her father's treasure, and now, she's weak—weaker even than I am.

"Where will we go and how will we get there?"

"We certainly can't stay here," she says. "And you betrayed your people. Will they welcome us?"

I doubt it, but with the heartstone and no evil vanir with me, at least not as far as they can see. . . "It probably depends on what we take with us."

It's our best chance.

Her ability to talk to me the same way as before surprises me. When I feel for it. . .our bond is still there. I'm not sure what it means.

"We need to go," I say.

"The only way out is up," Freya says.

But when I look up. . .I have no idea how we could possibly get through there.

"She gave you wings," Freya says. "Use them."

I try. About four pumps later, I slam into the wall, knocking icicles to the ground. The shattering sounds echo loudly.

"We're going to die," Freya says.

I groan, but I pick myself up, and after a moment to recover, I try again. This time, I make it almost twenty paces before lurching sideways and crashing into the wall again. The room I found so uniquely beautiful has transformed into a total nightmare, full of erratic, low ceilings and sharp icicles.

"I hate this place," I say. "You'd think these wings might have come with a set of instructions!" I look around futilely. "You gave Freya clothes and the ability to speak. What do I get? Not even a padded jacket."

Blood's running down my arm from a gash where a sharp icicle sliced me open. There are two more lacerations on my legs and one on my back that hurts at least as much as my arm, maybe more.

"Gyda," Freya says. "If you can't fly us out of here

soon, we're going to die. My father left to deal with a group of humans they stole from the æsir, but that takes almost no time, and—"

But it's already too late.

Judging by the roar, Daddy's back, and he sounds really angry.

I t's happening every time I go to sleep now.

When I wake up, I'm not even a bit rested, and my heart's racing. "She's going to die. They're both going to die."

Are you alright?

Axel must be close—his voice isn't distant at all. "Did you wait all night?" I can't quite help my smile. "How pathetic."

I know. It really is, but at least I'm not the only one. Asteria's smiling like a complete imbecile at your sister right now because she thinks we're all busy with other things.

He and Gordon and Asteria all feel the same way, which is how I know none of the dragons' feelings—including Axel's—are the least bit romantic. I wish I could be happy that he likes me, at least, but it's almost worse.

He likes me, but not the right way at all.

Unrequited love is literally my least favorite trope in books and movies. That's probably why I'm living it. It's just how the world works.

Coral stretches and yawns. "Bad dream?"

I shrug. "My life. A nightmare. What's the difference?"

"Is it really so bad?" She frowns. "He still doesn't remember anything?"

I sigh. "I've been dreaming of either a past life or stuff I need to know in order to, I don't know, help stupid Freya play her mind games."

"What?" Coral's querulous expression makes me laugh.

"They're dreams that I'm living back in the times before the dragons left Earth. There were two main groups of them, and Axel's nanny says that much is true. They called themselves the æsir and the vanir. The æsir are basically the blessed, and the vanir are like the evil version of them."

"And?"

Yes, and?

I almost forgot that now we've bonded, he can hear most everything if he's close and wants to. "Last night, I dreamed about the heartstone—finally. It *is* a rock, and it was stuck in some gold pillar below Vanaheim. Freya's evil father Bjorn was using it to face off against the æsir and it's the reason he always won. Freja was my enemy, but then after my brother and hers both died, we teamed up to take it from Bjorn. Only, when we tried, Jörð gave me wings, which was cool, and she made my swords special. . .and then she turned Freja into a human, so that's kind of a bummer."

"Wait, Freja was a dragon, but Jörð, who is like, mother earth?"

I nod.

"She turned Freja into a person?"

"And she renamed me Gullveig—so Gyda and Gullveig are the same person, and renamed Freja so now it's Freya." I can't help my heavy sigh. "Which is bad, because now we have the heartstone, but we're trapped underground in a cave, and Freya's dad just showed up. I think we're both about to die."

"Freya can't die, not if she's the same one who's trapped under the volcano—Wait!" Coral stands up on the bed, flinging the covers on the floor. "You've met her. *Are* they the same?"

"Yes," I say. "They are. Which means somehow she escapes, but I'm not sure that I do."

"Is he about to burn you, then?" Coral asks.

I shake my head. "He's an ice dragon, so I don't think he can."

What? Axel's poked his head almost all the way through the doorway. He looks ridiculous. *An ice dragon? Those don't exist.*

"They were called the vanir," I say. "Remember? Euphrasia said they did."

"Then he can't be the one who kills you," Coral says. "The legends say Gullveig burns, don't they?"

"Not that I think I'm actually her," I say. "I'm probably just having freaky visions from Freya, trying to lure me back into the lava." Although, I did get wings in the dream, too. That's pretty. . .damning.

You're not going anywhere near that mountain, Axel says.

"He may not remember you," Coral whispers, "but he sounds *exactly* the same as before."

That makes me laugh.

Coral slugs me on the shoulder, hard.

"Hey, what's that for?"

"I heard you almost died again yesterday."

She did die, Axel says. *Asteria had to shock her back to life before I could bond her.*

"That's really not helping," I hiss.

We need to get ready. The ensnared are saying the executions are set for noon.

"Ixnay on the executions-eh," I say.

"Who's being executed?" Coral frowns. "Someone we know?"

I sigh. "When we're done with this, I am *so* teaching you Pig Latin."

"You already taught it to me," Coral says. "And besides. Executions starts with a vowel. Any idiot would understand executions if you just add 'eh' to the end of the word." She rolls her eyes.

But I've distracted her from the point.

"We'll be back later," I say. "I can shower then."

It's not like Axel's going to care how I smell—we're buddies, like drinking buddies. I could vomit on his shoes. No big deal. It's not like he *cares* how I look or smell or anything else, as long as I'm alive and kicking.

"I'm going to take up overeating when we get back from this," I mutter. "I'm going to get as big as a house. Chocolate. That's what I need."

"Are you alright?" Coral frowns. "You're acting really strange."

"I'm fine." I sigh. "But listen, no matter how you may feel, promise me you won't go bonding any dragons while I'm gone."

Her smile's sly. "Fine. I'll wait until you're back. How's that?"

I'm scowling as I fly out the door and toward the

hole in our building. Thankfully, Sammy and Jade are just wandering through the other direction.

"Hey," Coral says. "When you get back, can we go shopping?"

I freeze midair and turn. "What?"

"It's Christmas soon—we have lists."

For some reason that hits me like a slug to the gut. "Christmas?"

Sometimes, like when they're bonding dragons and taking care of each other, I forget how young they are. Christmas—in the middle of the end of the world? That makes me remember—Hyperion said they were talking about it.

"Sure," I say. "When I get back, let's make some Christmas plans, alright?"

"All I want for Christmas," Coral says, "is—"

"Don't even think about saying 'a flame blessed to bond,'" I snap.

She shrugs. "Alright, I won't say it, but you can't say I can't do it—you already bonded one." She huffs. "*Again.*"

How is it that the hardest child is the only one who listened to my rules? And how can I keep telling her no when her sister and brother already bonded dragons? Ugh, fill-in parenting is the worst. I don't even have the luxury of saying, "Because I'm your mom. That's why." Hopefully Mom will be back soon, and then she can take over.

As I wing my way over to the flat ridge overlooking Selfoss that has become our constant meeting area, I'm fuming. I still can't believe Jade and Sammy are bonded.

Axel's wisely flying quietly beside me.

"Hey, why are you golden today? I figured it would be a red day."

Because someone shot you yesterday?

"I mean. . ." I chuckle. "You do tend to go red when you're mad or worried." The wind gusts past me, buffeting me and sending a shiver through my entire body, wingtip to wingtip.

The air around us warms almost instantly.

"I've missed that," I say. "Definitely the best part of being bonded to a fire dragon in Iceland."

I warmed the air before we were bonded again.

"Not as often, and not as well," I mutter.

As we reach the plateau, the humans who have already gathered are freaking out. "What's going on?"

Norm's there, Phileas beside him. "Liz!" He waves, as if I didn't hear his shout.

"Hey." I land smoothly—much better at flying than I was at first. Worlds ahead of Gullveig. I will grant her that it was a little more difficult at first, and I did make my first flight after being launched out of lava like a pop rock out of a can of soda, but still.

"Did you hear?" Norm's eyes are bright, and he's exuding the same kind of shaky-energy that Fluff Dog gets when he hasn't seen me all day.

"Hear what? That my mom's being executed?" I can't imagine that would make him excited, but he's a little odd. Who knows?

Norm's face falls. "No—I'm so sorry about that, by the way."

"Oh." I glance around. "What then?"

Hyperion lands next to Axel. He's usually the first one here. I'm surprised he's just arriving. *The humans*

"An invitation?"

"Someone videotaped one of your presentations," Norm says. "One of the humans who wasn't bright." He bites his lip. "It went viral—popping up in new places before the government could shut it down. The people of Australia voted—they're all welcoming us to live there. No attacks, and no fighting, as long as we promise not to attack. They'll let the local humans who wish to bond one of us bond us. They'll also work with us to provide whatever sustainable food we need, and they said they have vast tracts of uninhabited land. Look."

He swivels the iPad around.

"How are you even getting a signal here?"

"Are you really worried about the logistics of that?" Norm shakes his head. "It's so nerdy that I don't even understand most of it, but you just brought one percent of the American nerd population to Selfoss. You didn't think they'd be able to get around a few military firewalls?"

I guess he's right. I snatch the iPad and start scrolling.

Article after article.

The funniest one was released by the Australian Prime Minister in response to the United States' outrage. One US general reportedly called Australia's offer, "the dumbest thing to come out of Australia since drop bears and Vegemite." He went on to say that, "Australia will regret inviting the dragon freaks to their barren little island—or they would if they survived it."

Australia's Prime Minister fired back in the best possible way. "Vegemite, drop bears, and photos of snakes and spiders were all designed to keep idiots exactly like General North away from our barren little island. And if the dragons are freaky, that's better for us. Have you ever heard of the platypus? What about wombats, kangaroos, or koalas? We've always been a haven for uniquely beautiful animals."

For some reason, I find myself crying.

It's been months since the world has shown me anything truly beautiful. It feels way overdue. I'm nodding as I bawl this time.

You're happy, Axel says. *I always thought the leaking was a symptom of a system malfunction when humans were overly upset.*

"Yes, it is that, usually," I say. "But sometimes we cry when we're happy, too."

"So will we all be moving to Australia?" Jean asks. "Because it's only been a few days, but so far, I *hate* Iceland."

"It's not so bad," Norm says, but he shivers as he says it.

"People told me it was gorgeous." Jean waves her arms around. "It looks like Sauron's playground. With snow."

I laugh. "Yes, I think we're going to Australia, which I think may be where they filmed *Lord of the Rings*. . ."

We may travel to Australia to bond humans, Hyperion says. *But we won't leave Eyjafjallajökull until we've recovered the heart.*

"I should probably tell you that I've been having some strange dreams," I say.

Axel straightens. *No.* His command is stiff and made on our private channel.

"It might be because of the strange Icelandic climate." I shrug. "Moving to Australia might be just the thing I need." Great. Now I sound like a total idiot. I turn to glare at Axel. *Why not?*

Tension pulses through the bond. I miss the colors I could feel when we were entwined, but even without them, I can tell he's serious. He must be worried Hyperion will chuck me right back in the volcano if he knows I saw the heart and it's a stone. "Alright everyone, let's talk more about Australia when we get back from saving Mom. It's—we have less than an hour."

"Talk about cutting it close," Jean says.

"Whoa." I look around. "Are you all here because—the rest of you aren't coming."

"We are," Norm says. "I've met your mom."

"This is extremely likely to be a trap," I say. "Think about it. They know you'll want to save the blessed they've been torturing, and they have to guess I'll come for my mom. They know now that Azar didn't die, and they saw us recruiting humans."

"Isn't that more reason you might want people you can trust to come along?" Norm asks.

"Don't deny us our first quest," Jean says. "Please."

I grit my teeth, but they're right. They aren't my siblings. Every dragon going is already risking their life —I can't expect all the humans to stay home, safe, while the dragons take every risk. "Fine."

As Hyperion's talking to them about the details of our plan, I pull Axel aside. *We didn't have much time to talk. My dreams—if they're real, and they feel real—the heartstone turned Freja the vanir into the same Freya that I met in that volcano—a human.*

And could she shift back again?

I'm not sure, I say. *I mean—I just don't know.*

Was she like the earth blessed, perhaps?

I shrug. *When I woke up from my dream, she was still stuck as a human. She didn't seem able to shift. In the volcano, I've never seen her shift either.*

My father would never have married a human, so it can't be my mother if she can't shift into a blessed form. He frowns. *For now, let's keep this between us.*

The private channel's so tiring. *Fine.*

But Liz, this is precisely the sort of thing you can't tell Hyperion. He's too hasty. We need more information before we do anything about it. He'd try to—

Throw me into the volcano again?

Axel's going to need dragon botox if he's not careful.

If Freya still has the heart and we recover it, we might be able to restore the earth dragons' ability to shift. Or maybe that's just my delusional hope.

I never really understood its benefit.

Of course he doesn't. *You liked it well enough before you forgot me.* I can't help my smile. *I imagine you'd appreciate it again.*

Why don't I remember? You know, don't you.

I could lie. I should lie. Hyperion's trying to get my attention. They're ready to go. My mom could die if I delay. But this *feels* just like that moment in every movie where they *don't* tell the big secret, and it always comes back to bite them.

I do know, I confess. *When you died, when Azar died,* I amend, *you could have released your bond to me—your memories, all of it—and you'd have survived. It was your refusal to give up on me, on us, that killed you. When I escaped from the humans and returned, only Axel was alive.*

He doesn't get it. He looks totally confused.

I was with the humans—Gideon killed me and brought me back to break our bond. When I escaped and returned, you bonded me again—just Axel. Azar was dead, and it was all my fault.

Emotions are flying across Axel's face so fast that I can't make them out, even with the bond helping.

Hyperion showed up the second I returned and insisted on dragging me back to the volcano. To try and keep me safe, you told Hyperion your secret, that you were Axel. You begged him not to throw me into the volcano, but he did it anyway. And while I was in there, you and Gordon and Rufus were being tortured—the vanir demons or whatever those creatures are—were feeding on you. Freya gave me the chance to set things right.

What does that mean? He's catching on. *Set things right* how?

She gave me the choice to restore your flame blessed form. . .and eliminate your memories of all our time together. Or you could stay as Axel and retain those memories.

You said I had already been given that choice. I chose to keep them.

It's so hard explaining what I did. *I—it was my fault Azar died. Memories of me are* why *you died, and memories of me are the reason you exposed your earth dragon secret. It was all my fault, all the damage you'd suffered, and suddenly I had a chance to make it all right. The only one who would suffer was me—you wouldn't even remember what you'd lost.*

He's straightening beside me, his eyes hardening. *You've been fighting with Hyperion all week because you*

*don't want anyone bonding a human without their consent.
You've been entirely insistent that it has to be their choice.*

I know. He's right. I can't even argue.

And you're telling me that you took my choice away.

That's what I'm saying, yes. My breath catches. *I'm sorry.*

You wouldn't do it again, if you had a chance to repeat that decision?

No. I shake my head. *I'd probably do it again.* I reach for him.

But he backs away, his eyes hurt, his nostrils flaring.

It was hard, but I did it for you.

I had chosen. He narrows his eyes. *You said I chose to live with the weakness. Did you restore me because you only liked me when I was flame blessed? As an earth blessed, I was too weak for you?* He looks like at least that, he would understand.

I shake my head. "No, that wasn't it."

Do not tell me it was for me again. It wasn't.

"It was," I insist.

I made my choice—you mattered more to me than my power. He leans closer, his eyes on mine. *In my entire life, I have never chosen anything but more power. It's all the blessed value. It's all that matters. If I chose to give up all my power for you—you should have known what that meant. If you knew me at all, you knew.*

"I couldn't be responsible for that loss," I say. "It's because I knew what it meant that I did what I did."

And you hoped to restore my memories if possible.

"Yes." I nod. "See? You get it."

He shakes his head. *No, you're the one who doesn't get it. You should have loved me, trusted me* enough *to let me lose what I valued less. Power. Position. We could have tried to regain my power, but you didn't honor my choice.*

He's right.

It was his pain, his vulnerability. His memories.

I was wrong.

Power to endure. I chose it the first time, but then I reversed my position later. *I'm sorry,* I say.

Axel shifts into Azar in that moment, glances at me sideways, and then makes a portal. *I'll be saving the blessed.* He tosses his head at me. *Hyperion will take Elizabeth Chadwick to save her mother. Thanks to our new bond, we can communicate across the seventy miles separating them. How convenient.*

Without another word, he flies into the hole and is gone.

Hyperion sets down next to me. *Something wrong?*

I'm leaking again. Stupid human tears. I swipe them away. "I think he finally gets what I did, trading Azar for his memories."

For what it's worth, I'm grateful to you. I think you made the right decision. Strength is always better than weakness.

Spoken like the strongest being on earth.

You're bonded again. It's been hard, but it was the right decision. He'll get over it eventually.

I'm not sure he will.

We're nothing like we were, but the one thing I have going for me is that Azar still doesn't remember what he lost. Hopefully that'll make it sting less.

All the information the nerds who joined us gathered on my mom was wrong.

Like, dead wrong.

The execution wasn't happening at noon, for one.

It wasn't in Iceland, either. When we portal into the camp where I was being held. . .it's empty.

"Uh." I land. "So."

Hyperion lands beside me. *I'm assuming this isn't what we expected.*

"I mean, we probably should have expected it." I sigh. "I kind of figured it would be a trap, but I should also have considered that they'd feed us false information."

So they can trap us?

I look around. If this is a trap, it's not a very quick-to-spring one. I take off flying around the very empty city of Reykjavik, wondering whether something might come to mind.

Blessed aren't being held in Borgarnes.

Looks like that was also a trick. *My mother's not in Reykjavik. No one is.*

"What now?" I land on the roof of the Harpa Concert Hall, according to the undamaged signage, and overlook the ocean. The waves are crashing loudly below, and I'm not sure I've ever felt more lost.

And cold.

Without Azar by my side, it's very, very cold.

At least, until Hyperion lands beside me, warming the air either intentionally or with his presence. *You can't wander off. Even if he's upset, if you're harmed, Azar will try to kill me.*

"Why haven't you bonded a human yet, Hyperion?"

He frowns.

"You better not be thinking of bonding Coral." I lean closer. "Didn't you hear that my swords pierce dragonhide?"

You threw one into *me. I remember.*

I cringe. "Forgot about that. Sorry."

You're not sorry.

"I'm not, no. You were about to chuck me into a volcano. You know, you really have no one to blame but yourself for the earth blessed glow-up and the needing-humans thing."

I don't blame you. He's staring off at the waves, at least as forlorn as me, and for the first time, I realize that he doesn't. He doesn't blame me at all.

"I've been having dreams." Axel and I aren't entwined, so he can't hear every little thing. He didn't want me to share this, but he got just a little ticked at me and left, so he gets what he gets. "I've been having dreams that I'm Gullveig. I think they're memories."

Hyperion doesn't even turn to face me.

"I think Freya has the heart—it's a beautiful stone—and I was with her, as Gullveig, when we pried it out of a cave underneath the earth."

He's still not registering any surprise—no emotion at all. I know the blessed aren't quite as emotive as we are, but this. . .

"Earth to Hyperion."

I'm pleased to hear you're gaining answers—answers we need.

I take a few steps until we're standing right next to each other, and I ball up my fist, and then I think again. Instead of hitting him with my bare hand, I kick him as hard as I can. And then I swear under my breath, jump from foot to foot, and cry. A lot. "Why are your scales so stupidly hard?"

You know how hard they are. Why would you harm your soft foot like that?

I roll my eyes. "Humans do stupid things all the time when we're angry or sad. I'm just not used to the blessed doing them." I arch one eyebrow. "So why are you, stupidly, waiting around until you die?"

I expect him to argue with me.

I expect him to make up all sorts of lies.

I expect him to beg me not to tell Axel, at least.

He doesn't.

From the time I hatched, I knew.

The doom of his people.

I can't even imagine living with that prophecy hanging over your head. "I'm sorry—for you and for Axel. It wasn't fair. Especially since. . .I think it was your mother who foretold that. I heard this alleged oracle was named Freya."

If my death can spare my people the doom that prophecy foretells, I'd be evil to go on living.

"What if your death sets this doom in motion?" I shake my head. "That's the problem with a prophecy like that. You can't live with it hanging over you, and it's pointlessly vague. Wondering before every action whether this will be the one that dooms everyone is just tragic. You have to let it go—make the best decisions you can at the time with the information you have."

You decided wrong, though. Axel's angry—he wanted you to let Azar die.

"And I told him I'd do it again," I say. "And I would."

Hyperion turns back toward the ocean. *There aren't any prophecies about you, so you have the luxury of doing whatever you want.*

"You're right," I say. "No prophecies about me at all. I mean, there's a little stone-carved insignia that shows how many lives I have left, or whatever, and I'm getting these weird dreams that indicate I'm some warmongering woman named Gullveig, and that I'm somehow connected to all the lava demons. But, you know, just a regular girl making regular decisions right here."

His lips curl upward. *I suppose you might understand better than most.*

"If you can tell me that you're glad I saved Azar, I can tell you that I'm glad you were there for him. Axel told me that out of all his brothers, you were the only one who didn't try to kill him."

He was an irritating hatchling.

I bet he was.

He was also brave. And kind. Kindness isn't appreciated among the blessed.

I can see that, too. "But you protected him. He told me you did."

Maybe more than he knows. Our older brothers—Odin had a wife before he married Freya. Her name was Frigg, and I'm not sure whether you know this, but—

"Freya's brother, Freyr, killed Frigg."

He freezes, turning slowly. *Did Azar tell you that? He hated talking about it.*

"I dreamed it," I say. "I was there when it happened."

As Gullveig? Hyperion sighs. *Perhaps your dreams are real. I hope they are. But for us, as hatchlings of Odin and Freya, it was hard.*

"Hard?"

To keep things simple, I'll just say that inasmuch as the flame blessed sons of Odin fought, we banded together for one thing—defending against Odin's children with Frigg. They hated us for our connection to their mother's murderer.

Wow. Azar never mentioned it. "You were in danger too, as the oldest?"

Only the oldest of Freya and Odin—the first hatched after our departure. And yes, we were all in danger. Always.

"Let's make a deal," I say. "You promise me to bond a human as soon as we get back—the second we reach Australia. And I'll promise that the moment I know enough, I'll go back into that volcano and face Freya. I think she has the heart, and I think we can get it back."

You're trying to motivate me to live by inspiring me that I might be part of the success, not the initiator of their doom.

"I'm not inspiring you, dummy. I'm promising you." I ball up my fist. "Don't make me punch y—"

Hurt your poor soft body again?

"Exactly," I say. "Because if you do, I'll tattle to Azar."

We found them, Azar says. *It's happening now, live. They're definitely hoping we'll come. Your mom's in Killeen, Texas, at a place called Fort Cavazos. Jean's on the phone with Norm.*

They'll have what Hyperion needs to portal.

"Alright," I say. "We have a new location. Round up the troops. We're headed for Texas again. At least it's warm." I pause by Hyperion. "They'll have ice spears."

He laughs. He actually laughs.

Where are you going? I ask Azar. *Where did they put the blessed?*

We're not sure, Azar says. *Possibly the same place. We're coming, too.*

You are? I can't disguise my happiness. I hate when he's somewhere I'm not. Maybe he's coming because he's not mad anymore.

Wanting you to be safe isn't the same as forgiving you.

I sigh and stand. Norm and Phileas are winging their way toward us, along with a dozen other dragons. "Where do you think all the humans who were living in Iceland went?"

Hyperion shrugs. *The difference between you and me, Liz, is that I don't care.*

"Baby steps, you big jerk." I slap his leg, but that hurts too.

You don't learn from your mistakes.

"Shut up."

As directed, we portal into the far east side of the base.

"Killeen's the largest military base the United States has, geographically," Norm says. He's disgustingly excited about this.

"You haven't forgotten that they're about to kill my mom?" I arch one eyebrow.

"I'm sorry." His shoulders droop. "I'm not trying to be a ghoul, but it's my very first real, live quest."

I wish it could be my last. I'm beyond tired of it all.

Liz?

I freeze in place, my wings only moving enough to keep me from falling. *Mom?*

You should leave. It's a trap. They're going to kill me the moment you reach my side.

I wish she was calling me to her side. Then I'd feel no qualms leaving. But if she's warning me off? If she's being a *mom* to me, which is exactly what she did when she helped me escape, then I feel compelled to find her.

Can you tell where she is? Hyperion asks.

Our plan, now that Azar can come as well, is basically a shell and pea game. Two red dragons. Lots of portals. Eventually we find my mom, and then we portal out.

Stick to the plan, I tell everyone.

I can sense Azar. He's flying-distance away now. *Mom, tell me where you are.*

They have the other dragons here too. They're going to kill them and *me to upset you. Just leave. Keep the kids safe.*

I can already imagine what she'll say when she

hears Sammy and Jade have bonded dragons. But if today goes well, she'll get to yell at me for years to come.

We're by the ropes course, I tell Azar. *Are you ready?*

Yes, start.

I hear it—his roar. He's calling the soldiers there and warning the people who are nearby to leave. Not sixty seconds later, he torches the ammunitions warehouse. I hope the people were all evacuated—please, please let them all have gotten out.

It's a military base, Hyperion says. *They chose this.*

I hear what he's saying. I do. It still hurts. *We're up.*

I swoop down first, careful to stay inside Hyperion's red bubble shield. It's not as big or as thick as Azar's, which is likely because he's exhausted. I'm totally going to tattle about his plan to Azar the second this is over.

Ropes course is clear, Hyperion says. *Advancing to location two.*

"At least call it the Air Cavalry Obstacle Course," Norm says. "Ropes course sounds. . .lame."

But then Hyperion's opening a portal, and we're flying through to the Warrior Way Gate.

At the Clear Creek Gate, Azar says. *No signs of your mother or any blessed.*

Liz?

Mom? Tell me where you are—what do you see?

I'm—I can't tell. They're trying to bring Azar here. I thought he'd died. If you come alone—they might not hurt you. They'll definitely try and attack him.

They might not hurt me? Does she think I'm delusional? They think I'm public enemy number one. I've seen the videos.

Two more hops, still no luck.

But in our fifth location, I'm waiting for them to clear the main buildings when I notice something strange. There's some kind of movement at the nearby dog park. We've been popping around for a while—more than enough time for everyone to hightail it with their canine friends. They must have seen us. . . So why are there still people out there? Or was it just a stray dog? I think about Fluff Dog and how scared he was when I found him.

I'm heading over to the dog park, I say, *because that's strange.*

Thanks to some kind of man they caught hiding with a handgun, Hyperion and the others are obsessed with thoroughly checking the commissary. No idea why—it's just a store. Hyperion glances that way, and seeing nothing, he shrugs.

As I draw closer, though, I feel it.

Mom's here.

I'm not sure how I can tell—I've never been able to feel her before, but now I can. Maybe I'm growing in skill, or maybe she was trying to let me know she's here. As I fly closer, I see her. There's an enormous orange, cartoon-cutout dog decoration made of molded plastic, and there's a green, plastic-coated wire picnic table next to it. She's zip-tied to the picnic table.

I can't help thinking of my mom before all this started. She was—well, she was the ideal mother. She never cared if I ate too much candy, not that we ever had a lot. She never cared whether I wore trashy outfits—she was more likely to borrow them. And she always patted my head and kissed my forehead. She and my dad fought a lot, but they also showed up for everything I did, my entire life.

She taught me to stand up for myself.

We made signs and protested the injustices of the world together.

In fact, she was probably the person I respected most in the world. She never compromised on what she thought, what she believed.

Which is why it hurt when she told me I was a monster.

When I realized my only real value was in protecting my siblings.

Watching her flinch every time I drew near. . . It didn't hurt as much as losing Azar, but it was close. I'll never forget the look on her face when she told me how I murdered that woman when I was kidnapped. It's seared into my soul.

But she's still my mom.

And she did help me escape. I just can't reconcile in my mind which one is her. The one who helped and raised and watched over me? The one who worked with Gideon to betray me? The one who helped me escape? Who is she, really? Which one?

Saving me landed her an execution. She may be a lure for me, but I don't doubt they mean to kill her. Gideon might want to spare her, but he doesn't have real power, not truly. The old, white-haired men running the US military aren't going to tolerate a young, up-and-coming MMA fighter among their ranks any longer than they're forced.

His knowledge of the dragons would only have gotten him so far.

If he's even in charge of his own post at this point, I'll be surprised. I wonder whether he regrets it. More even than my mother, losing him hurt. I know that sounds strange—my own *mother*—and Gideon's betrayal stung more.

But Mom was always all about causes.

I think I always sensed that I scared her on some level.

But not Gideon. He loved me. He helped me. He always would.

Until he didn't.

No one else is around as I fly toward her. When I come into her view, her eyes widen in alarm. "It's true." She swallows.

I land on the edge of the coffee table, and I'm grateful it's bolted down. My weight doesn't cause it to tilt at all. I look her over carefully. Other than having her wrists and ankles restrained, zip ties running under the holes in the table and back around, she looks completely fine.

"You're even wearing normal clothes." She always looked good in her blousy, embroidered shirts and yoga pants. "And they're feeding you, clearly."

"Liz, I told you not to come." She glances to the side, but no one's there. Just the big orange dog.

I unsheathe a sword and slice the zip ties on her ankles.

Between one second and the next, I freeze, waiting for something bad to happen.

Liz? It's Hyperion. *Where did you go? We were just clearing the commissary, and you disappeared. Azar's going to kill me.*

I found my mom. Dog park. Releasing her now.

"Checking in?"

"Could you hear me?" I step forward, leaning down to slice her wrist ties.

"I know the look," she says. "You rebonded him?"

"Actually," I say, "that wasn't Azar."

"Who was it?"

"Hyperion," I say.

Mom sits up, rubbing her wrists. "Did you bond *him* now? You just can't help yourself."

You're okay? Hyperion sounds a little panicked. *Phileas just found someone else—once we confirm he's the only one, I'm coming. Stay put.*

I'm fine. There's no one here. I drop down next to her, sitting on the edge of the picnic table. *Our distraction worked—no one's here.* "Mom, we need to get out of here."

She nods. "Give me one minute to catch my breath. Lying like that—I lost the circulation in my wrists."

"But you'll come with us, right?"

Mom eyes my wings. "You've changed even more than before."

"I have, yeah." I grit my teeth. "Do you really hate them? Because you helped me escape with them before."

Mom's frown is deep. Even her brow furrows. "I owe you an apology, Liz. You know, I buried my guilt deep."

"Your guilt?"

More soldiers here, Hyperion says. *A lot more.*

Here too, Azar says. *Ice spears, bullets, ballista.*

Hold tight, Liz. We'll tell you when we're clear. Hyperion doesn't sound upset. He sounds. . .excited.

I can hear it all behind us—the bullets, and the roar of Hyperion's fire.

"I—when I was pregnant with you, I went to the doctor." She starts breathing faster. "That's when I found out that you had died."

"Excuse me?" I lean closer. "I must've misheard you."

Mom touches the sword I'm holding in my hand, her fingertips tracing the lines of the hilt—almost pure gold. "You died. The ultrasound showed no heartbeat, but I couldn't take it. They wanted to do something called a D&C. Do you know what that is?"

I have no idea what to say. "Clearly I wasn't dead."

"They told me you were. They wanted to do a dilation and curettage, where they scrape the inside of my uterus until I've expelled the incompatible fetus." Her eyes are not focused. "That's what they called you, the incompatible fetus."

"Mom, I'm fine."

Her head snaps toward mine. "You weren't fine, but I had a friend." She narrows her eyes. "She said she had a way to fix it. She knew a woman—so I didn't tell your dad what the doctor said. I went to see this woman instead, and she promised she could fix it—she could restart your heart. You'd be fine."

"This sounds insane, Mom."

"She told me you'd be marked—bought and paid for, if I did this. I could have your childhood, but eventually, they'd come for you. One day, the woman who saved you would come to collect payment for what she'd done." Mom's crying now. "And she did." She chokes. "She—um, she had a fake leg."

I threw that woman into the same volcano Hyperion threw me into. Unlike me, she never flew back out.

"You were supposed to be a sacrifice. They came too early—far earlier than I was ready to accept—but even as a child, you didn't make it easy." She looks into my eyes. "It's my fault you are this way. You should never have been born."

Hyperion bursts through the building behind me, roaring. He's coming for us, so nothing she says can scare me. She may be insane, or maybe she did let someone perform some kind of dark magic ritual on me, but I'm still me. I'm not some kind of creature.

I'm not the monster she accused me of being.

I'm just Liz.

"You can't make me hate myself anymore," I say. "But you know what? I shouldn't have come." At least she answered my question—she's closer to the woman who called me a monster than the one who helped me escape.

She grabs the hilt of my sword. "Now," she hisses, pulling the sword free.

From behind the orange dog, Gideon steps out. She throws the sword at him, and he snaps the hilt from the air. "We're both trying to help you, Liz," he says as he slams the sword into some kind of prepared slot on. . .I can't quite tell what. "We're always trying to help you."

I jump toward him, but he presses a lever down, and the ice spear shoots. I recall what he said before I escaped, that they planned to use my swords against the blessed. The ice spears haven't ever worked—they're not strong enough to penetrate the flame blessed scales—but with the blade of my sword strapped to it, the spear slices right through the hide on Hyperion's chest and disappears.

"What did you do?" I ask.

"Actually, I should be thanking you," Gideon says. "Without your sword, this would never have worked." He's smiling. "I plan to tell them all that you voluntarily handed it over. That should get you the pardon you deserve, and if you die when the bond shatters this time, I'm ready to bring you back again."

"Gideon."

He reaches for my face, his hand soft. "You're a victim. I don't blame you Liz—I'd never blame the victim."

Hyperion's body slams into the ground beside us, writhing. In the center of his belly, there's a bright blue spear, pulsing with no way out.

He's shaking now, and I think that, although I missed it when Azar died, I'm about to see, front and center, what it looks like when a flame blessed explodes, opening up a massive chasm in the ground like the one I saw with the red scales wedged into it.

Liz! A portal opens on the ground next to Hyperion. *Get your mom! Let's go.* Azar's talons curl around Hyperion and he yanks, dragging his brother's massive, convulsing body through the portal. *Now!*

"I don't have a mother," I say. "As far as she's concerned, I died in the womb." I slam Gideon's hand away, and launch into the air. But just before I pass through the portal, I turn back. "You may not care about me, but you should care to hear that your son bonded Gordon Earth Blessed, and your daughter Jade bonded Asteria Strike Blessed. Your daughter Coral— she has even bigger plans. Looks like I'm not your only monster." I flap my wings intentionally hard, blowing wind in her face. "I guess we all take after our mother."

Then I pivot and fly down through the portal to Selfoss, watching with a smile while Azar closes the hole on Mom and Gideon's upset faces.

21

AXEL

From the moment I hatched, Hyperion was a legend. The prince who would doom us.

While I would save us.

You'd think it would be demoralizing.

Other than Euphrasia, I'm not sure anyone believed that prophecy. Dad might have, but even he didn't want it to be true. Mostly though, I was a reminder to everyone that the blessed needed to be saved.

Hyperion grew up in the midst of mocking and taunts about being our people's doom.

I grew up with the opposite.

Neither of us had it easy. The difference is that I had *him* to make it easier. When I drag his body through the portal. . . It hurts, watching him like this, limp, prone, and pulsing with unhealthy, ominous blue light.

Hyperion.

Liz wings her way through, and I close the portal. If I'd come sooner—checked on them instead of getting everyone else through, but I never thought Hyperion wouldn't be able to. . .

"It was Gideon," she says. "My mom and Gideon." She closes her eyes and shakes her head. "They used my sword. It's my fault."

It isn't, Hyperion says. *You wanted to save your mother—what they did was smart. It was one of the first smart things I've seen the humans do. That Gideon is almost a worthy opponent. He can't help being so small and weak.*

And now Hyperion's convulsing again.

"I don't know much about dragon anatomy," Liz says. "But this looks bad. Really bad."

We have to get that spear out, I say. *If we can't. . .*

"His body can't heal while it's in there."

Liz. Hyperion opens one great eye and stills. His legs are twitching a little, but he's clearly trying to stop. *We talked about this. It's time.*

Time for what? I ask.

Liz shakes her head. "No. We talked about this, and I said *no*. I told you that your plan's terrible—it makes no sense. Your death could be the very thing that dooms your people. Listen to me." She kicks him. Then she hits him.

That doesn't hurt me any more now than it did before. But Hyperion's smile is pained.

Liz spins on me, her eyes flashing. "He's giving up." She kicks him again. "No, you can't give up, you stupid brute. I forbid it."

He's lived his entire life with the weight of knowing that, if the prophecy is true, he'll destroy his people. But now, on Earth, he's done nothing to harm us. He hasn't betrayed the blessed. He's been brave, and strong, and good, and true.

Even so, I understand.

He wants to die, because he'll finally be free of the *weight* of it all.

Liz.

She ignores me.

She yanks the remaining blade out of the sheath on her back. "I'm cutting my sword out of your belly, you big jerk. Do you hear me? You can't keep it!" Before I can stop her, she scrambles up toward the top of his belly.

Liz, stop, I say. *I understand his desire. He's not insane. It's rational.*

"Just because you're stupid too doesn't mean it's right. We need him. The blessed need him. Don't let some idiotic thing—" Liz is crying, rivulets of tears running down her face. "My mom told me I was promised to the crazy people who came to kidnap me. She traded my life to those people who dragged me away from my home and tried to throw me in that volcano." She tightens both her hands on the hilt of her one remaining sword. "My mom made a deal, after I died in her stomach, that if they brought me back and I got a childhood, they could have me. She traded my life to them."

That's. . .insane. Hyperion coughs. I've never seen a dragon cough, unless they had a rock or a small animal caught in their throat. *She's insane.*

"You're just as bad as she is," Liz says. "Worse!" She looks down at the glowing blue spear inside Hyperion's belly. "I'm going to perform the first-ever dragon surgery, and I'm going to pull this stupid ice spear out of your dumb belly, and then you're going to bond a human and recover. Do you hear me?"

Before I can stop her again, Liz slices his belly open.

At least, she tries. Even badly injured, Hyperion's magic is strong, and his hide is even stronger. She's barely sliced through the scales when the blue line that's glowing inside his stomach *explodes,* tiny blue and red glowing specks swirling wildly.

What just happened? Liz is blasting her questions far and wide. *What was that? Is he—did that—*

Blessed are gathering now, flooding the flat top of the mountain north of Selfoss where we've been gathering. Gordon and Rufus. Asteria and a dozen of her strike blessed. They're coming from all over, and their ensnared have come with them, too. No one can look away from the blue and red lights chasing one another around in Hyperion's stomach.

I can't blame them. I'm staring, too.

His head has gone limp. His eyes are flat and dark.

He's dying.

You have to let him go, I say. *It's what he wants.*

"You have got to be kidding me. This is *so* messed up," Coral says, hopping off Asteria's back and jogging to Hyperion's side. Before any of us can stop her, before we can say a single word, she braces both her arms against the bright red scales of his right flank, and there's a sucking feeling, and then the room's flooded with a brilliant golden light.

The word Liz says is one I haven't heard very often, and she looks *very* displeased.

Coral straightens. "He's not dead yet, and now if he dies, I do too. So, tell me again what he wants, and how we need to let him go?"

Liz's face blanches. "We have to get him over to

that cursed volcano, *right now*. I think maybe only that heartstone can save him."

NO. I forbid it.

"It's Coral," Liz says. "She's bonded to him, so spare me the lecture, and fly your stupid brother to Eyjafjallajökull before I stab *you*!"

Ah, Coral. What a stupid human baby.

I have no idea what Liz thinks she's going to do at the volcano. Even if she leaps back inside, there's no way she's going to save him in time, but there's no reasoning with her. If I ignore her, she'll do something else just as drastic, and with her wings she could fly there herself.

So I open the portal.

And then I drag my poor, mostly-dead brother onto the warm, jagged ground in front of the mouth of the angry volcano. The second Liz flies through, the creatures milling around in the bubbling lava begin chanting. I may not be able to see them, but I hear them well enough.

Gullveig.

Hjartanu.

Gullveig! Hjartanu!

Gullveig! Bjargaðu okkur! Gullveig!

I hate them—more even than Liz's mother. I want to rend them into small pieces, or fly her away from here and never return. But it's not an option right now, because now that we're here, my stupid bonded human is literally sprinting toward the dumb lava.

I'm not going in again, Gordon says.

No one else will, I say. *That's an order.*

Before Liz leaps into the lava, she points at Coral, who has jogged through the portal after her almost-dead, bonded, flame blessed prince. "Do. Not. Die. Do you hear me? You take one hundred and ten percent of that stubborn, pain-in-the-ass nature that you have, and you cling to that for all you're worth until I'm back. Do you hear me?"

Coral nods, tears running down her face. "Please Liz—you made it out last time. Do it one more time."

Then Liz leaps from the edge of the rock into the lava. I'm only half a step behind her, but it's enough. I have to watch as her body hits the lava—which has a more substantial form than I thought it would. She hits it more like a wall than a pool. Her body blackens, and then she *screams*.

And then I hit too, and the world's nothing but fire and ash and *pain*.

22

LIZ

I could hear Azar behind me as I hit the lava—I know he was there, but here I am again, alone, in a sea of nothingness.

"This is the loneliest place I have ever been," I say. "I think it must have been terrible for you."

"Think of this like a foyer."

I spin around, and Freya's here.

"Hello, Freja," I say. "Nice to see you again."

Her smile's slow coming, but it's real when it arrives. "You're learning."

"Too slowly," I say. "Clearly. But I've remembered some things."

Freya tilts her head. "Sometimes I wonder which of us had it harder—remembering and reliving every last moment for all time, never-ending, never ceasing. Or what you had to endure—forgetting everything and being born anew." She shrugs.

"You're saying I'm like Azar," I say. "I've forgotten all that went before, and I'm acting like a complete idiot."

Freya tilts her head. "Not quite like Azar, no. His memories are there—if he will just do what it takes to reach them. Yours. . .you are Gullveig, and you're not. There was a softness to her that doesn't exist within you. It was burned away, perhaps."

"My mother tells me that I'm an abomination—a demon, maybe. She paid a witch to bring me back from the dead. Maybe that's where Gullveig went."

Freya laughs. "And you believed that nonsense? Her ridiculous midwife was wrong—you were never dead. The one thing a witch is good at is stealing things that aren't hers, and making unjust deals. Your mother went looking for demons, so she found them. It's that simple."

"I have so many questions, but I don't have time—"

"Because you're here to save your sister."

"And your son."

It's small—almost imperceptible—but I know Freya better now. She flinches.

"He's dying, an ice-spear in his belly, and I don't know what to do."

"It's not precisely ice as you understand it. It's liquid hydrogen. One of your soldiers is doing their homework, because it's absolutely cold, and also highly combustible. Thrusting it into napalm, basically, was ingenious."

"Can you save him?" I ask.

"You've heard my prophecy, I assume?"

"It was yours?" I shake my head. "Your stupid prophecy wrecked both your sons, you know. They had to drag that weight around, and that's why Hyperion's here. He was willing to die—because he didn't want to cause his people's doom."

"And ironically, he's here, doing just that."

"What does that mean?"

"You already know." Freya begins to circle me slowly. "It's why you brought that with you." She eyes my sword, still clasped tightly in my hand. "I had no idea when I commissioned those, that you'd use them to. . ."

"To what?"

"Liz." Freya smiles. "Do me the credit of admitting what you already know."

"You have the heartstone," I say. "And I need it, to save Hyperion." I shake my head. "But why can't you use it to save him? You have it, I know you do."

"I don't *have* the heartstone. You can do better than that." She lifts her chin, her eyes on me.

"You *are* the heartstone?"

She smiles. "You're closer."

"You can't use it—because it's already being used."

Now she's nodding. "The heartstone fused with me when—you'll have to remember that for yourself. I could never explain it properly, not here, not like this. Suffice it to say that I can't *use* it in the way you would like. I'm stuck here as surely as the cursed are stuck. They all should have died as part of my spell, but Odin didn't do his part." She fumes. "So here we all are, alive and miserable, forever."

I ponder that for a moment before remembering that Coral's life and Hyperion's life, they're both hanging in the balance now too. "I don't have time to reminisce," I say. "No matter how much I might want to. What do I have to do to save them?"

"Looking for a baby to skin?" Freya sighs. "Sorry, warrior Liz. No babies here, only me."

"Where's Azar? He followed me through."

"Azar, Axel, why the two names?" She lifts her eyebrows. "When you sacrificed for me, a sky child, you were reborn as Gullveig. I don't hear you switching back to Gyda."

"I'm Elizabeth Chadwick," I say. "But you people persist in calling me Gullveig. It's not that hard to explain, honestly. Apparently I'm not the only one with dumb questions."

"But my son's not two people—he hasn't lived two lives. He's one person with two masks."

"Two masks?" That's a strange way to put it. "What do you mean—"

"No time for stupid questions," Freya says. "Remember?"

"They aren't stupid." I swing my sword at her. "I can't remember anything important, *remember?*"

She dodges and smiles. "Now we're getting somewhere."

"What does that mean?"

"You have a big choice to make today, Liz. You can let Hyperion, and by extension, your sister, die. Or you can take the heartstone for yourself and heal him."

"By killing you."

She lifts one hand, turns it over, palm up, with a flourish, and inclines her head. "Even so."

"You're not even armed."

"Don't be deceived. This entire place, the whole construct, is what I want it to be. Why do you think I've been so polite?"

"You think I can't do it," I say.

"No, I *know* you can't, because thousands of years ago, the first time you tried, I killed you." Freya's eyes are sad. "If I hadn't, you'd be the one stuck here, not me. Not my finest call, was it?"

"Then why don't you let me kill you?"

"More ignorant, thoughtless questions," Freya says. "Those make me maddest of all." In the blink of an eye, I'm not looking at Freya. I'm staring at the ice dragon from my nightmare, and when she roars, the floor that isn't a floor shakes.

I really, really wish I had both my swords, and not just so that the second one wouldn't be stuck inside Hyperion.

A snippet of a dream. That's how much time I spent 'training' with Freja before. That's what I remember. But Gullveig, the Gullveig who needed that training, wasn't a warrior.

And I'm not Gullveig.

I'm Elizabeth Chadwick, and the one thing in my life I've been prepared for is this. My whole life has been a sequence of attacks.

What's one more, even if I'm outmatched.

I'm *always* outmatched.

It's never stopped me before.

Freya opens her mouth and blasts me with shimmering ice, and I raise my hand without much idea what to do. . .and the red magic from Azar simply flows through. Even without being entwined, I'm able to pull from him, and it's enough.

Freya blasts me for what feels like an hour, but finally, she gives up.

"Are you just trying to kill time until he dies?" I shout and lunge at her. "You can't win. Not this time."

My sword hits nothing but air.

She's already disappeared.

Vapor—that's what she is every single time I strike, over and over.

But I'm learning the rules of engagement. When she materializes a few swings later, I'm ready. I *almost* hit her before she disappears. I'm not sure how long we go round and round. She blasts me, and I block. I strike, and she disappears. She almost catches my leg with her snapping teeth once, and I slice her hindquarter another time, but neither wound is significant.

I can't help trying to track time—is Coral already dead? It makes me desperate, but then I start to think.

What does Freya want?

Why hasn't she simply killed me?

She could burn me into ash by releasing me back into the lava. She could call her fearsome beasts over to eat me. She could materialize with her jaws already around my torso and snap me in two.

Why, then, are we fighting?

She doesn't want me dead, but she can't let me win.

Why not? What other option is there? What am I missing?

The next time she appears, I drop my sword. It clatters on the nonexistent ground, and her eyes widen. She shifts back to her human form with the same ice-shattering noise I heard that first time. "What are you doing?"

"You don't want me dead."

"No." Her nostrils flare. "I don't."

"But you don't want to die."

She sighs. "I have to die."

"Yet you won't let me kill you." I shake my head. "You're very frustrating. Why can't you just tell me the third option?"

"It must be freely given," she says.

"You want me to take your place," I say. "Not take the heart to save my sister and Hyperion—you want me to accept this place from you. They're chanting for me. . .because I can become their new master."

Freya sighs with total exhaustion. "Thousands of years, Gullveig. *Thousands of years.*" A single tear forms in her right eye and rolls down her perfect, inhuman cheek. "Please, please take it."

"Or, I could kill you and take it."

Her grin this time isn't compassionate. It's not understanding. She's enraged. "That's the wrong answer."

"You want me to take it, because the vanir wanted to enslave the humans. They were bad, bad creatures."

"You know that much already," she says. "But if you knew how bad they've become in all this time, trapped here and suffering for thousands of years? You'd never even consider an alternative that would release them."

"You're right," I say. "If I knew the truth, if I knew how things were, I'd do exactly as I was told, right?"

She nods. "Exactly."

"What would I have to do, exactly, to take over for you?"

Freya's shoulders soften. Her mouth parts, and she exhales. "Bless you, Gullveig. You never were selfish." She steps closer. "First, you take my right arm with your left." She holds her hand out. "Then we clasp one another's wrists, and you rest your head on my shoulder."

I do as she asks, stepping toward her slowly.

She feels like a bright, fresh spring meadow.

She smells like fields of lavender just unfurled into brilliant blooms.

She sounds like sunshine and ocean waves and laughing children.

She's devoted her entire life to ending the suffering that she and Gullveig swore to stop. She and Gullveig made that vow to Jörð, to honor the love she had for Veralden Radian. They both wanted to set the world's wrongs right, and she's suffered terribly for it.

"Now," Freya says. "Repeat after me."

"Okay," I say.

But instead of repeating the words she begins to chant, I clasp her hand as tightly as I can, and I channel Azar's energy into a shield to hold her in place, and I kick the hilt of my sword upward with my toe.

I grab it with my right hand, and I plunge it into her heart.

And I never once let go. I never waver.

Her voice is pained. "Gullveig."

Even here, in this strange place, standing on a floor that's not a floor, holding a blade that she gave me, blood bubbles up out of her mouth and splatters *everywhere.*

Apparently dying sucks everywhere, and it's always messy.

"I'm sorry," I say. "But I'm not Gullveig, and I never made a vow, not to Jörð, not to you, and certainly not to Veralden Radien. In fact, he can burn, for all I care."

I pull the blade out, and as it's almost loose, it grinds on something.

I smile as I reach my hand inside and yank the heartstone from her chest. "I bet this freaking hurt for the last few thousand years. You must have been choking on it all the time." I shake my head. "And I know I should feel really terrible right now, but here's the thing."

I back away from her, the heartstone pulsing in my hands. "In the world out there? No one's perfect. So I know there are devils in here, but there are devils everywhere. Keeping them penned up? It didn't fix anything."

Freya collapses to her knees. "You've just brought my prophecy to fruition." She coughs again, covering my one decent tunic with even more red splatter. "You'll save Hyperion, but the blessed will be doomed in return."

"Good thing I'm bonded to their savior, then," I say. "And if you'd be a doll, could you give your son his memories back before you die?" I toss my head. "Because it has really *sucked* for him not to know who I am."

"Only he can retrieve those," Freya whispers. "But, old friend, I have one last thing to share." She grabs my wrist and pulls me closer. "The one thing you truly desire, it's always been in your grasp." Her smile—I can't tell whether it's kind or smug. Before I can ask her what the heck she means, her eyes close and she gasps.

"You couldn't have told me how to use this to heal Hyperion first? Really?" I stand.

I should probably be sad, but I barely know Freya,

and let's be real. She lived a long freaking time. It's tragic she had to die, but she had it coming.

Before I've even figured out where the door is, the white-but-not-substantial walls around me start to literally crumble. *Azar!* I push the call as hard as I can. *Where are you? We need to get out of here,* now!

❦ 23 ❦

AXEL

The last time I entered the lava, it wasn't by choice.

I think that makes a difference here.

My last experience, I forgot as soon as I left. It was part of Liz's deal with Freya, and while I hate that she did it, I understand why. Here, with my memories intact, I understand entirely. Liz has been the one suffering, really, not me. I'm sure it's been harder on her than I can even imagine, especially knowing how angry I was with her when she was trying to do the right thing.

More than any being I've ever met, Liz always wants to do the right thing. She's as opposite the monster she fears as anyone I've ever met. And all she does for her bravery, for her self-sacrifice, is suffer more. I'm standing in my human form for the first time since, well, since right before I was hurled into the lava by the very brother we're here trying to save.

Hyperion always meant well.

He *means* well, I repeat, because I'm still holding

out hope that Liz might somehow save him. She'll do anything to save him now, because Coral's life's hanging in the balance. Losing that little spitfire would *wreck* my warrior queen.

I wish I knew where Liz was.

Instead of writhing in lava while creatures come at me, I'm floating in a room that isn't a room. It's somehow an overlook—like I'm standing on a balcony overlooking a courtyard, only the courtyard's lava, and the overlook doesn't actually exist. When I focus on my feet, it's especially strange, because while it *feels* solid, there's nothing underneath them.

I hope Liz found Freya, because I've got nothing.

The creatures who look distorted in the lava are sharp and clear here. They are humanoid, sort of, but they have horns, and massive underbites with protruding, bestial teeth. Some have small horns and some large. Some have teeth the size of my thumb, but much taller, sharper, and they're stained dark yellow and orange. Others barely have incisors at all. They're sitting, standing, milling around, arguing, snapping, and snarling.

Not a one of them looks happy.

But they aren't burning, either. Most of them are walking around in what appears to be relative comfort, wearing only bizarrely shredded loincloths, metal-studded leather strips, and various rags. But when I look out a little farther, the lava looks hotter, brighter, and *meaner* in a way I can't quite explain. The creatures out there are watching something.

I have to assume that's the entrance of the volcano.

The closer they are to the outside world, the

hotter and more miserable it becomes? It's an ingenious kind of trap—stay away from the exit, or you suffer even more. If this Freya is my mother, she's at least clever. I can't tell quite what I'm doing here, though. As I watch more closely, I realize that some of the creatures are male, and some are vaguely female. They're all so unattractive and deformed in appearance that it's hard to differentiate at first.

I lean over the nonexistent ledge and call out. "Hey, beasties. Can you see me?"

Their heads snap sideways and they rush toward me, climbing on top of one another, clawing their way toward me.

Whoops.

"Food," one of them snarls—in our language, not the English I've almost grown accustomed to using in this form.

As if the others just needed a little encouragement, more come from seemingly nowhere. At this rate, they'll reach me in the next two to three minutes by flinging themselves on top of one another and rising to my level from sheer mass. They seem to be limitless in number, coming from I can't tell where, and I'm regretting drawing attention to myself.

I cast around for any sort of weapon. In this weak, useless form, I can't use my claws, my teeth, or my tail —honestly, it's a miracle the earth children have survived like this at all. They do use their brains well, sometimes. Every interaction I have with that cursed Gideon makes me wish I'd eaten him the first day we met.

I'm not sure Liz would ever have forgiven me, but otherwise we'd all be way happier. . .

The pile of snarling and snapping creatures are less than twenty paces away now, still mounding up like rats in a pit. Only, these rats have massive, sharp teeth, long, curved, wicked black claws, and bulk that even I can't match. At least, not all tiny and powerless in my humanoid form.

I pull on my magic to try and shift, but it comes up blank.

I try a few of the human swear words I've learned from Liz, which helps me feel better, but offers no real benefit. "Come on, Axel. You have to think. You called them over here—now figure out how to get away."

That's when it hits me. I'm standing on. . .nothing at all.

Why can't I simply shift up higher?

It works. The second I imagine myself in a higher position, I am.

The creatures bellow and roar below, clearly irate that I've figured out how to prolong their torture. They don't *look* emaciated and starving, so something's clearly keeping them alive, but that doesn't mean they aren't suffering from terrible hunger pangs.

I can understand that whole concept.

The blessed don't require as much in terms of physical consumption as earth children, because we bring in energy from other locations. We might not even die without eating for an extended period, if we weren't expending a lot of energy, but we'd suffer.

These guys look like the poster children of suffering.

I've just shifted upward a second time when the walls that aren't walls begin to shake. It's not constant, more like trembling from the impact of. . .something. I'm not sure what, but it's not reassuring.

Liz?

Or what if, here, like me, she has all her memories, even the lost ones? Who would she identify as? What name would she answer to?

Gullveig? I call out. *Gullveig? Elizabeth Chadwick? Are you there?*

No reply from Liz, but the creatures double down, upon hearing that name. It's clearly one they know.

Gullveig! They all start shrieking in a demented sort of rasping unison. And then, without warning, they begin to shift.

The great, hulking beasts with monstrous fangs, frightfully corded muscles, and curved, blackened claws take on much larger forms, surging upward rapidly, expanding in size as they turn into their blessed—or cursed, as Liz called it—forms. They're black, dingy grey, and the purple of a vibrant human bruise.

And they seem to be even angrier.

Rabid, even, snapping, snarling, and agitated. They almost reach me before I practically fly upward. A simple glance shows no ceiling, thankfully. "Why do you all want Gullveig? Do you hate her? Do you want to kill her? Or do you want to serve her?"

Salvatoris! they shriek. *Dimittis!*

Some of them think she'll save them, and others count on her for their release. I'm not sure they should, since I doubt Liz will differ in her opinion from me. *Liz,* I call again. *There's a horde of demons here, and they all want you. They think you're going to free them, but I vote against it.*

I shift upward more often now, ever more upward. The creatures seem to measure into the thousands or more, never ending. Churning, snapping, snarling, and hissing.

I hope Liz is alright, and I hope she can save Hyperion, and I hope when I go back to Earth, I'll remember her.

And I'd really like to touch her—in my human form.

It's a lot to ask for, I know. It's greedy.

Saving Hyperion would be enough.

But now that I'm here, even fleeing increasingly higher from nasty critters in my human form, I can't help yearning for her. Even without memories, even not being able to touch her, I did finally figure out she was special.

And I never forgot she was *mine*. It was like that truth was embedded in my soul. But there's something about the earth children's tactile comfort, something about their quiet moments and reassurances that just isn't the same when I have scales.

Just the thought of her—and now with her wings, scowling or laughing—she's glorious. I *ache* for her. In this form, in this place, knowing what I know, remembering her fierce bravery, her tenacious insistence on doing the right thing—I love her. I miss her. I yearn to get that back.

Liz! I shout. *Please, please get back safely. Please.*

Distracted by my internal stress, I don't shift upward fast enough, and one of the beasts catches my leg, biting down hard. The pain radiates upward, and I cry out.

In that same moment, the walls-that-aren't-walls

shudder and cracks run up the sides of the entire construct. Chunks begin to fall, one of them smashing the cursed-blessed that's currently clamped onto my leg in his ugly face. He releases me, thankfully, and I spring backward, barely avoiding being struck by a similar chunk of. . .nothingness. And that's when I hear her.

Azar! Where are you? We need to get out of here, now!

I'm here! I scramble backward, avoiding another large chunk of debris. *What do I do? Where do I go?*

Azar!!

The entire world around me *shifts* in a very uncomfortable, very unsettling way, and then I'm beside her. "Liz!" I reach for her, and she collapses in my arms, sobbing. Her clothing—the only clothing she has to fit her new wings—is spattered in red. "What happened?"

She's sobbing against my chest, a hard, bright, strange object clutched against her belly. "I—Azar." She looks up into my eyes. "Axel! It's you!" She freezes, her eyes widening. "Do you—" She swallows. "Do you *remember* me?" The hope in her face—it's heartbreaking.

I kiss her then, pressing my mouth against hers too hard—too insistently. But she doesn't shy away. If anything, she presses harder, her fingers digging into my arms, pulling me closer. Our mouths move against one another's frantically for a moment before she pulls away.

"Hyperion," she breathes. "Time isn't the same here, but we have to get out now, or I won't be able to." She shakes her head. "And Axel, Azar, whatever, I don't know—you clearly remember me now. Right?" Her eyes are so terribly hopeful.

It hurts me, and I nod, desperate to kiss her again while I can.

"I'm not sure if you'll remember me when we get out, and I'm not sure if you'll be able to shift either."

"I know," I say. "I know. I'm sorry for being angry. I didn't understand."

"You do now?" Her mouth is soft, her eyes frantic. "Do you really?"

I pull her tightly against me, so *healed* by feeling her body against mine. But the large, hard thing's digging sharply into my side until I release her. "I do—I know why you did it—I might have done the same if I'd been forced. But what *is* that?"

She glances down, trembling slightly. "It's the heart." She offers it to me.

I back up a step, blinking and shaking my head. "It's—that's it?" It's the reason we came here in the first place. Now that we've found it, we'll have no reason to stay. I almost. . .I almost want to chuck it into the nothingness that's falling apart all around and leave it here in the rubble.

If I have the heart, what will I do with Liz? What excuse can I use to stay, especially if I don't remember how much I love her once we leave this place?

"You should know." She chokes up, tears welling in her eyes. "I had to kill your mother to get it."

My eyes snap up to meet hers. "You had to—"

"I'm so sorry." Tears roll down her face. "There was no other way. It's—Freya—she *is* your mother. I'm not sure what went down between her and your dad, but I don't think it was good, and now she's. . ." She glances backward, and I see it—the bloody, broken body of a human woman with a massive, gaping chest wound.

That's the red on her body. My mother's blood.

Liz is sinking to the ground, the stone clutched to her chest. "I'm so, *so* sorry. If there was any other way, but Coral." Her voice catches. "And Hyperion."

My eyes widen. "Yes, right. We need to get out there and save them." But I'm still staring at the dead woman. I feel like I should recognize her somehow, if she is my mother, and like I should *care* more than I do. "Let's go." I force my eyes up. "Do you know how to do that?"

"Do you—do you want to. . ." Liz shakes her head. "I don't even know what I'm asking. What could you possibly do? She's dead. I'm just so very sorry. I wish—I tried to pull you to me then, before, but I didn't have the stone. I think I could only do it once I took it, and it was *inside of her.* I really liked her, Azar. We were friends, back when I was Gullveig, and I wouldn't have killed her if I could have. . ." She cuts off again, clenching her free hand at her side. "I'm sorry."

I step toward her, dragging her against my body again, tightening one arm around her, and pressing our bodies together from her shoulder to my hip. "I know you had no choice. I'm sorry you had to do this." I press a kiss to her forehead. "Thank you."

"I don't know how to get out of here," she says. "But the last time. . ." She closes her eyes and inhales, and then. . .

"Wait." I press my free hand to her cheek. "Liz." I drag one finger down the side of her face. "When we get out—"

"I released them all," she says. "I killed your mother, and that freed all the beasts she'd trapped. They're escaping even now, as this place crumbles, and. . ." She exhales. "I got the heart your people need, but I'm afraid I've destroyed the earth in the process."

Sky or earth.

She had to choose, and she chose me.

My heart swells even more than before. "I love you, Elizabeth Chadwick. I love you wildly, as much as a selfish dragon prince ever can. I hope you know that. I will help you keep your earth safe from the creatures. And I hope you can remember how much I care for you when I turn back into a beast."

"Maybe you won't change back this time," she says.

"Maybe not." I feel something odd happening to me. Something I've never experienced before. My eyes. . .are leaking. "But I fear I will forget you, and I fear I'll forget *us*." I shake my head, "But I still love you, even then. I just don't understand yet. Believe that."

She kisses me again, and then she nods slowly. "Thank you."

The walls around us disappear.

And so do I.

This time, when I'm expelled from Eyjafjallajökull, I have no trouble course correcting and flying, which is good, because Hyperion looks *bad*. Azar hurtles through just behind me, and that's also good, because we aren't the only ones shooting out—demon-encrusted vanir are shooting out like t-shirts from a cannon at a corny football game.

Only, these prizes won't just give you a black eye or break your nail.

They're literally ravening, and also, their charred, ragged bodies are smoking. They all look like they're three-quarters baked. . .by a blow torch.

"Shield," I say. "Azar! I need a shield!? Please?" I'm clutching my sword in one hand and the heartstone in the other, so when the closest vanir-beast stumbles toward me, his massive mouth open, drool hissing as it slides down his oversized chin, I slash at him, opening up a massive gash on his beefy arm.

Azar looks a little dazed at first, and then he

frowns. A second later, he pops a giant red shield around Hyperion, Coral, and me. *Thank you.*

But there's no one protecting Azar—at least, not until I see a lightning bolt strike the demon vanir that are closing in on him. All three of them go down like bowling pins to a strike.

Asteria's in the corner, Jade unfortunately on her back, but she's an absolute goddess, her eyes sparking, and lightning bolts arcing outward from her claws, from her head, and from her chest, striking vanir right and left. She's not the only one fighting them, either. The blessed have come out in impressive numbers to help us, and I've never been more grateful in my life.

Grateful or not, Coral looks even worse than Hyperion.

Her skin's a terrible shade of pale grey.

My hands are trembling as I drop the heartstone beside her and reach for her neck. *Please, please, please let me find a pulse,* I beg. *Please let her be alive. Let this not all be useless.*

There's nothing.

I'm too late.

Her skin's clammy, even in this hot, miserable place, with demon creatures rocketing past us, slamming into the red barrier, and fighting all the dragons on the other side of this shield.

I killed Freya, my friend, Azar's mother, and I'm too late.

She's already dead.

Tears roll freely down my cheeks, and I fall back on my knees, sobbing. "No," I cry, my voice utterly broken. "No! No!!" I grab the stone, and I shove it up next to her tiny body. "Coral Whitney Chadwick, you cannot be *dead*!"

Her eyes flutter open.

I nearly drop the stone. "Coral!"

"I'm not dead," she wheezes. "You just *suck* at taking someone's pulse."

And now I'm crying harder, but there's no time for that. "Okay, right, okay. Then I need to heal—well, not you. You're not hurt. I need to heal Hyperion so he doesn't drag you down with him. Right." I spin around, regaining my grip on the stupid heartstone, and then I stumble toward Hyperion, dragging my sword along. With that awful liquid whatever inside, not to mention my other sword, he's not going to get better until we eliminate it.

It takes me far too long to crawl up on top of his massive form.

"Oh Hyperion, why do you have to be so ghastly huge?" I'm puffing when I reach the top of his belly, and I realize that thanks to my wings, I may have let my other training slide just a hair. "Coral, plug your ears. If he's awake, this is going to hurt, and he's going to be a big old baby about it."

I wrap the dumb stone up in my shirt and knot it closed—it sort of exposes my bra, but it's not like anyone on this miserable rock cares. Then I heft my blade with both hands, and I throw all my force into it, praying to Jörð for her help, as if she even likes me, and I plunge the sword as far into Hyperion's meaty belly as I can.

It sinks a few inches.

"Eh, hopefully that's enough." I flip around and shift my hands, and then I haul on it as hard as I can.

It reminds me of trying to saw through an overcooked turkey with a butter knife, but I am making some progress, however small.

Bright, flashing sparks start billowing out of him, along with a lot of nasty, reddish brown goo. The blue sparks explode as soon as they hit the air around us. The first one scalds my arm, and I yelp and jump back.

Which is good.

Otherwise, the second and third would have taken my head off.

I slink back, but this time, I pull on poor Azar's magic a little more, creating a small shield around myself as I gut Hyperion, one painful, agonizing inch at a time.

I keep glancing back at Coral—still alive, I think— and Azar, fighting hordes of awful, blackened vanir who are swarming, but he's also alive.

And I keep sawing away. It takes what feels like ten minutes, but might have been more, before I finally see it. Down, down, down, a good two feet into Hyperion's belly, in between gushes of exploding blue blobsparks, I find my sword.

My hand trembles as I brace myself with the other, leaning over the chasm I carved in his belly, and I lean down, down, reaching. Sparks explode around my hand as I reach, and then just before I touch the sword, I grit my teeth and release the shield so I can grip it.

When I grasp the handle, a spark beside me explodes.

The pain—oh, the pain! My hand burns like lava has eaten it down to the bone, but I don't let go. I pull with every part of my body, shaking and miserable, and then I keep pulling, and slowly, the stupid sword Gideon hurled as a killing blow gives way, sliding upward.

Another spark explodes, and another, but finally, I pull it free.

My arm and hand are blackened, like I'm part vanir.

"I should've used my left hand," I mutter, and then I drop the disgusting, dragon-blood coated sword to clatter on the ground beside Hyperion. Sparks explode all the way down as they shift and come in contact with the air, but none of them hit me. I stare a little numb at my hand, which is still working, miraculously, but looks like grilled chicken left on the smoker for far too long.

A groan beneath me reminds me of what I came to do.

He'll die like this, splayed open like a grotesque science experiment, unless this dumb heartstone can finally do something good. I fumble, my right hand not working anymore, pain shooting up my arm and radiating through my chest, but I finally manage to pull the heartstone out. Both my swords are gone, the first discarded when I went for the other, but that's good. I can only hold one thing at a time, and even that's hard with a blackened stump and one non-dominant hand.

I'm not sure what to do with this dumb thing. Maybe if I'd had more dreams about it, or maybe if I had more time to fiddle around, but I don't. I can feel the blood—or whatever it is—oozing and exploding out of Hyperion, and I can tell we're at the end of his energy.

So how do I fix him?

I can barely hold the stone up, but I take all the parts inside of me that I usually use to channel Azar's magic, and I press against the stone, and I'm flooded suddenly with a brilliant light.

It's not golden.

It's not blue.

It's not any color I can identify, and it's all the colors—like Freya. That feels right, since it was inside of her. I gather up all the new light that I've gotten, and as I shove it at Hyperion, I realize that it's like the sun and the moon and the stars, all rolled together. The night sky and the midday sun, and the strangely combined strength of both.

I try to braid the energy somehow, giving it the form I wish Hyperion's body would follow, knitting his bloody and broken body back together, but it's not quite right.

Because there's still a lot of bad inside him.

First, I gather it up, like chasing dirt with a hose, until it's all down at the bottom, huddled, and I flush it up and out, and it explodes all around me.

I haven't put up a shield, but the energy inside of me surges outward to keep me safe. It's handy stuff—I could get used to this. But then Coral gasps, and I refocus, pushing all the light that's left inside of Hyperion, and instead of trying to knit him back together, I shove it at his heart—his center.

DO something with this, you great moron. I—I have no idea what to do to fix you.

Hyperion's body ripples, and I'm flung off and away. I'm grateful once again for my wings, or I'd have broken something for sure, but now Hyperion's belly wound's closing up, lit up all along the jagged, unsteady length, and he begins to scream, like a newborn baby, if they weighed nineteen billion pounds and had lungs the size of a dumptruck.

What in Eyjafjallajökull are you doing to me, human?

I can't help my smile. If he's yelling, he can't be dead.

She's trying to save your very unworthy hide, Azar snaps. *Just like the rest of us. You did just what they said—it's your fault all these awful little buggers are being released into the world. Demented, fricasseed blessed, all of them trying to eat whatever they can find, including us.*

They were calling for Gullveig, Hyperion says, groaning. *Not me.*

But he's getting to his feet again, and Coral's not quite as grey.

Liz only went in there to save you. You should be thanking her. Azar sounds ticked.

You need lessons in slicing, Hyperion says. *That was the slowest, most agonizing way I have ever seen anyone cut anything.*

"You felt that?" I shudder. "It was pretty bad. I'm sorry."

Coral's sitting up, thankfully, and she rubs her eyes and looks around. "Liz!" she shouts. "Your arm."

It's still blackened, which isn't ideal. It does—mostly—work, so that's promising. "It's not my best look."

I'm sorry about that.

Azar's roasting a whole flock of flying vanir, but they're starting to reroute. When they spring from the lava, they fly up and out, circumventing Azar and Asteria and the whole lot of them.

"They're fleeing," I say.

It's a good thing, Azar says. *I'm not sure why, but I'm terribly tired.*

"The volcano does that to you." I feel a little weak-kneed right now, too.

"How many are there?" Coral's watching, wide-eyed, as they stream past in an almost never-ending line.

"Thousands," I say. "Hundreds of thousands? I can't tell."

"We need to get out of here," Coral says. "But we can barely move."

"Australia," I say, turning. "Hyperion, can you get there? Could you portal?"

He blinks, turning a little more and getting his feet underneath him.

There isn't really room for him to stand, not under the shield Azar's holding over us. I hate to remove it, but we're going to have to, soon. I'm not sure how much longer Azar can hold it, for one, but for another, Hyperion definitely can't portal through from inside this tiny area.

I think so, he says. *But if their offer was a lie. . .if it's a trap. . .*

As weak as he is? They'd kill him for sure. It's a gamble, but staying here feels like a war of attrition that we'll lose. "What do you think?" I glance at Azar, still fighting all the straggling vanir who become distracted and break away.

I think it's a rational risk. I'll follow as soon as I can break away.

"I'm not leaving you," I say. "No way."

Azar looks at my arm and flinches. *You're injured. You'll go now.*

"I'll stay by your side, with my shining rock, and my two earth-blessed swords, and you'll stop arguing with me."

He rolls his eyes, but he listens. Mostly.

Asteria, Jade, and a dozen other blessed go through with Hyperion as an honor guard of sorts, and it takes a solid half hour for Azar and me to break away from the fleeing vanir—and even then at least two hundred of them follow us back to Selfoss. Luckily, there are lots of angry blessed there willing to help us dispatch them.

It's too bad we're so tired.

It would be a great time to try and deal with all the vanir. After spending millennia trapped in a volcano, they're at their weakest point, presumably. A few hundred earth dragons pursue the fleeing column, attacking, ripping, and rending the vanir as they flee, but there are too many of them.

The line of creatures must continue for almost an hour as we gather the blessed to leave.

By my best estimates, there are almost a hundred thousand of them, to barely more than ten thousand of us. It's not an inspiring comparison. But our two best fighters, Hyperion and Azar, are not in fine form right now. I won't risk the dragon I value most, and if Hyperion goes, so does Coral.

After I've frantically gathered the few things I have, and Sammy and Jade have done the same, we open a portal to the same place Hyperion did, a town called Darwin in the Northern Territory of Australia. I tried not to show my anxiety, but I've been low-key terrified since Hyperion portaled out.

What if Australia's offer was a trap?

I wouldn't put it past Gideon to lure us somewhere new, only to attack us upon arrival, and sending a weakened flame blessed with a tiny human who's also not doing great would be like sending a fruit basket for the US Government.

Only, it wasn't a trap.

The hot and humid air of Darwin, Australia hits me like a warm, gloved hand when I fly through the portal, much like the unwelcome embrace of Houston's summer air. I drag in a heavy breath and scan the area around the Charles Darwin Lookout, where the reports all invited us to come.

Then, like a sunrise over the mountains, I see them. On the edge of the lookout, there's a platform. It's been piled high with fruits, vegetables, grains, and other things, like piles of what look like candy? On the open, grassy areas between the lookout and the parking lot, there are blessed standing around in small groups.

It's easy to find Hyperion, thanks to his color, and when I do, I finally relax. He's sitting on the ground, beside Coral, eating what looks like gobbets of some kind of freshly butchered meat—disgusting—out of a large metal tub. Across from him, the Australian Prime Minister's smiling and dabbing at his face with a napkin, sitting at a long table. If he's nervous, he's good at covering it up.

It's like a scene out of a movie or something—utterly unbelievable.

"Oh." Coral stands and waves. "The others are

coming." She points at the portal Azar opened and waves us over. "My sister's the one with wings, there."

The Prime Minister stands, smiling broadly. "We are just so happy that you decided to join us here in the Northern Territory." I land close to the table, but Azar opts to land quite a bit farther away, possibly out of caution, or perhaps in an attempt to be polite.

"It's impressive you're here, welcoming us yourself," I say. "We certainly didn't expect that."

"You know, we didn't rush into this," the Prime Minister says. "Well, we did, rather, but we've been dragon-friendly since you first landed."

"Dragon-friendly?" I can't help lifting my eyebrows.

"Watching the United States, it just didn't seem like they were handling things with prudence." His smile is mild. "I know you're an American, and we generally like them, but you never seemed bent to destruction or domination. You could have done far more damage if you had been."

"That's true." Though I do recall hating the dragons myself for quite some time. "But are you sure your people won't change their minds? A government's composed of a lot of groups, and the troops don't always agree with everyone else."

"Indeed," the Prime Minister says. "But in this case, the reason we offered you the Northern Territory is that their very small population of right around two hundred thousand, in a very large area, voted almost unanimously to invite you."

"Oh?"

"Yes, the country came in right around seventy percent in support of inviting you here, but this particular area. . .” He chuckles. “Even more than the rest of Australia, the people who live here have always dealt with and appreciated. . .unique fauna and flora.”

“There’s a plant here that, if you touch it, will burn for *days*,” Coral says. “Like, it’ll hurt so bad you can’t even sleep.” She looks far too delighted by that.

“Tell me you didn’t already discover that yourself,” I say.

She rolls her eyes. “Come on.”

“The poor child would be curled up, screaming, if she had,” the Prime Minister says. “We’ll be sure to give you each a briefing, inasmuch as you want one, but the government has agreed to offer you all the government-owned land in exchange for a few reasonable requests.”

I’ll just bet.

“I’m sure we can come to terms on all that,” I say.

“Oh, no.” The familiar voice is one that has me jogging behind me, where I heard it.

“Sammy?” I look around, and I don’t see him, but then I see Gordon. “Where’s Sammy?”

He’s—Gordon’s frowning. *Rufus isn’t doing well.*

Behind Gordon, he’s right. Rufus is lying on his side, his large body barely rising and falling.

“Don’t be mad, Liz,” Sammy says. “Okay? Promise?” I see him, then. He’s standing near Rufus, his arms around his neck.

“Don’t be mad about what?”

But before I can even try to stop him, Sammy’s entire face squints up tightly, and all the blessed around me gasp.

Rufus shudders once, and then twice, and then he

shakes himself off and stands. When he turns toward me, he's smiling.

"What just happened?" I ask. "What's going on?"

Your little brother has bonded a second *blessed.* Azar looks perversely pleased.

"But he can't. . ." I shake my head. "That can't be done. Right?"

"Why not?" Sammy shrugs. "Rufus needed me, too."

The Prime Minister's watching us carefully, which means this isn't the best time for me to freak out.

"We're still learning how to navigate some parts of the human-dragon bond," I say. "Clearly."

"It's an exciting thing to be a part of," he says. "I look forward to many discussions with you about it."

"What exactly do you want from us?" I arch one eyebrow.

"We didn't leave ourselves a lot of negotiating room, for sure," the Prime Minister says. "But I think you'll find we're not really asking for much. We can get into all that later. For now, we have plans set in motion to see that you have what you need while you're getting established." He leans toward me a bit and drops to a whisper. "What exactly do all the dragons eat?"

"Actually, about that," I say. "Many of the dragons won't be able to eat at all, not until they bond a human."

He blinks. "So that's what that one needed?" He swallows. "He needed to be bonded to a human?"

I nod slowly.

"And how do humans know whether they're. . ." He clears his throat. "Eligible for a bond like that?"

I smile. "I'm guessing you'd like to give it a go?"

He blushes a bit. "I really, really like the flame blessed." He glances at Hyperion. "But this little girl, your sister, if I understand it, says she's just bonded the only other one on Earth."

I chuckle. "That's true. As you know, I've bonded Azar."

"The electro dragons—the strike blessed, that's what they call themselves, isn't it?" He glances back at Asteria. "They're also very stunning."

Can you hear me? Azar asks.

His eyes widen, and he adjusts his glasses before nodding slightly. "That was quite strange."

"You're a very lucky man, Mr. Albanese," I say. "I think we may be able to work something out that benefits all of us."

"I do think very few countries will be keen on fighting with us in the future." His smile widens, and he glances back at the strike blessed like Christmas has come early.

Since it's December fourteenth, or maybe the fifteenth?

I think he may be right.

25

LIZ

Even with Azar's magic to pull on, and the heartstone, it takes several *days* for my disgusting arm and hand to heal. Every time I moved and saw the gleaming white bones from my arm poking through the charred tissue, I almost threw up.

But it *does* heal, eventually, thank heavens.

And I have plenty to distract me from the pain. It's a chaotic few days, finding enough brights and semi-brights for each dragon. But these brights come with the added advantage of already having places to live, at least most of them.

As an added bonus, they don't have to leave their homes behind.

For the first time, in Australia, we're not conquering.

We're integrating.

It's a land that's rich in metals like gold and silver, which the earth dragons love. They make visors for all the new recruits—including me—and it's almost disturbing to see my siblings walking around wearing them.

There are also an abundance of precious gems hiding in the ground in the Northern Territory, and discovering the dragons could easily uncover them, well, that created challenges of its own. Integration is better, but also harder in many ways.

Finding places for the blessed to live has been a bit of a struggle, but with the powered-up earth dragons, even that works out simpler than I expected. Axel—using his earth powers—has already made us an amazing home overlooking the tempestuous Timor Sea. The very first day in our new home, I saw a huge *crocodile* swimming in the saltwater. It made me happy to know Azar's always nearby and that Sammy's closely watched as well.

Most of the main structure's made of rock, reshaped and formed from the bedrock up, to exactly the size and form I wanted. There's a good mix of massive rooms to accommodate several dragon forms, with soaring ceilings and massive doorways through which dragons can fly, slide, or climb, and smaller chambers where I don't feel like I'm speaking into an airplane hangar.

The front of the house opens over the ocean, but the internal rooms, blocked by fixed red shields that allow me, Sammy, Coral, and Jade to pass, are smaller and more intimate. There are four main rooms in the center, each of them large enough for one dragon, and one human. Coral, Sammy, Jade, and I all live here, with our dragons. That's not something I ever thought I'd say.

My mother would have a heart attack.

Once my arm's healed, I spend *days* acting as the intermediary between the blessed and the Australian government, hashing and rehashing the rights we're allowed and the concessions we'll offer. Now that they know how adept the earth dragons are at locating and refining precious metals and stones, they have a new set of demands. And of course, they're keen to employ the water dragons to police the nearby Indian and Timor Seas. It's a little tiresome, but mostly we're happy to help after their generosity.

I'm not sure why we even want to stay, Hyperion says when I come back with the latest round of requests. *We have the heartstone. We can go home.*

"Are you sure?" I ask. "We can't go home until we confirm that recovering the stone was enough to restore your ability to procreate." I lift my eyebrows. "Have we had any confirmation of new eggs being laid?"

It takes time, Azar says. *From mating, it can be as little as five or six days or as many as a dozen before a female lays an egg.*

I think I have quite a lot to learn about dragon biology. "Well, once we've confirmed it's working, we can talk about a timeline for you to leave."

For us *to leave?* Azar frowns. *Our bonded will come with us, surely.*

"What about you staying here?" I ask. "Why can't we talk about that?"

We're working things out with Australia under the belief there are ten thousand of us, Hyperion says. *I wonder how they'd feel about eighty thousand more showing up?*

Oh, and don't forget that we'll actively be making eggs for baby dragons, Azar says.

Are you really saying dragons? Hyperion rolls his eyes. *It's degrading.*

"It's not," I say. "It's just our word for your kind."

We should probably encourage our people to mate, Azar says. *You could set the example for them.* He raises his eyebrows.

Hyperion turns his head slowly, his lip curled. *Excuse me?*

You were happy enough to shove me into mating with Asteria before.

I'm a delight, Asteria says. *You'd have been lucky to mate with me.*

I can't help smiling a little, now that Azar seems uninterested in that possibility. He may not remember anything before his factory reset, and he may be stuck in dragon forms still, but I'm making progress.

What are you smiling at? Hyperion snaps. *Why would you even want us to stay?*

He's right that I haven't exactly experienced the warmest welcome from my own family for my new. . .calling? Is that the right word for being Azar's bonded, winged human?

"But we have the Prime Minister on our side now," I say. "He can't leave Australia, not while he's still in office."

Again, once we confirm the heartstone's working, we can talk about a departure plan, Azar says. *As things stand, we don't even have much to report to Father. What if this is merely a beautiful rock, and nothing has changed?*

"The heartstone?" I don't mention that I carved it from his mother's chest. I'm kind of relieved he doesn't remember any of that. "Pretty big coincidence, if the heartstone that released all those vanir and healed your dying brother wasn't the very thing you needed."

Even so, Azar says.

"I think the biggest reason you can't leave yet is that you promised to defend Earth against the vanir," I say.

I remember no such promise, Azar says.

"Well, that's convenient," I say. "But you made it twice—before you lost your memories, and again in the lava. I'm beginning to think your brain's a bit like a sieve."

A what? Hyperion asks.

"Forget it," I say. "But do you really think it's fine to just pull up stakes and fly away, when saving your brother and stealing your heart released a horde of demons on the humans?"

The humans who were more than prepared to attack us, Hyperion says.

"They've successfully killed only a handful of you. Think about the vanir—they really *do* want to dominate and conquer."

Still not our problem. Hyperion frowns.

"Precisely your problem," I say again. "You released them."

No, Hyperion says. *You released them.*

I gnash my teeth. "Only to save your ungrateful, unworthy—"

"We'll stay here until we can figure out what to do," Coral says, like that decides it.

Hyperion's face softens.

I want to laugh. I mean, how ridiculous is that? "Just because—"

"I think rushing off would be a mistake, too," Jade says.

As do I. Asteria's agreement surprises me the most.

She has softened since bonding Jade, but she's not usually much of a fighter, as far as I can tell. "Really?"

There are many things in life we don't want to do, but if they're the right thing, we must do them. I've seen you make many decisions like that, Elizabeth Chadwick. Whether the princes want to take responsibility or not, our return prompted the release of the blessed-cursed ones, and the humans are not equipped to deal with them.

Fine, Hyperion says. *We slay the creatures, and* then *we leave.*

I can't help thinking about the battle between the æsir and the vanir—how it went on and on. I haven't remembered quite what Gullveig and Freya did or why, but this feels like it'll become a harder task than Hyperion's making it out to be.

Still, at least they're not packing up right this minute.

"How exactly do dragons mate?" Jade asks. "All I heard is that they *fly*, if they can, and the water blessed can't do that."

"You know, in my dreams of the past, they could fly," I say. "All the dragons could."

"Even earth dragons?" Coral asks.

I shrugged. "There weren't earth dragons, at least, none that I saw, and I saw all the other blessed, and a few weird kinds of vanir."

"There weren't earth dragons?" Coral blinks.

"Water dragons could fly?" Jade asks.

They would love that, Azar says. *They're complaining even more now than before.*

You would be too, Asteria says, *if the one thing you desired was given to another group instead of to you.*

They've been so obnoxious since the earth blessed got wings, Hyperion says. *Far whinier than the earth blessed ever were.*

But I'm not listening to Hyperion. Asteria's words are still echoing in my brain. It feels like I've heard them before, and then it clicks. That's very nearly what Freya said to me, when she knew she was dying. Her last words were, "The one thing you truly desire, it's always been in your grasp."

Are you alright? The others are still chattering away, but Azar's looking at me with concern.

We've come such a long way from when he was expelled from the volcano with no memory—nothing but contempt for the human whom he'd previously bonded. We're in a much better place than we were, but she's right.

I do long for something—two things, really.

I want Azar's memories returned, but she said only he can do that.

And I want him to be able to take a human form. It's selfish—it benefits no one but me, but I yearn for it all the same. Except, then I recall what I said to Jörð when I was Gullveig, what I asked her to do for Freya.

. .

I asked her to know.

It is selfish that I want Axel to take a human form again, yes. But it's also a gift that the goddess of earth gave herself, to help Freja understand us. I'm not sure where the earth dragons came from, or why they're so different, or even why there weren't any back in my memories.

But becoming human, it's not *just* for me. It helped the dragons too.

It helped them understand us—it helped the children of the sky live in harmony with the children of earth. It helped bridge the wide and difficult divide between our people. So while they're all talking, I creep back into the back room of our new home, to *my* room.

And I pull the heart out from the carefully carved box where we keep it. It's pulsing, even now. It's stunning, and it feels almost alive, like a real heart. I stroke it carefully, and then I bow my head over it, and I reach for the light and energy that always surges inside it.

Once I'm full of it, the bright light, I pause. "Please, Jörð, please grant me this wish. Let me help Azar to know—help Axel to understand. Let him take a human form again."

And then I wait.

All the light churns and surges with nowhere to go.

After a few moments, I release it back into the stupid rock, disheartened. Azar's standing in the doorway, his head tilted. *Are you alright?*

I sigh. "I'm just being greedy, I guess."

How so?

I flop back on my tiny bed, shoved into the corner of the still cavernous room. "You used to be able to turn into a human."

Useless ability.

"I know you think that," I say, my voice small. "But I miss it."

He walks carefully toward me and lies down beside my bed, his enormous scarlet head resting on his front legs. *I am sorry my lack of humanoid shape upsets you. I don't like when you're upset.*

"I know." I shake my head. "And it's fine. Things are—well, they're better than I could have hoped, especially with the release of all those vanir, and you know, everything else." I close my eyes.

But you wanted to try and restore my ability to shift?

I don't want him to feel like he's not good enough. "It's not that I don't like you as you are," I say. "It's just that—Freya said this weird thing. She said that I always had the ability to have the thing I most desired, and other than your memories coming back, that's what I want most."

Maybe I should take a nap. I'm clearly cranky.

"I just wish—I've wished for a very long time that Jörð would allow you to take a human form again, like me."

Why?

I drop my voice to a whisper. "I miss it." My heart contracts. "I miss having you beside me. I miss your fingers brushing against mine. I miss you asking me questions about kissing. I miss knowing you in that form. I miss connecting with you—I miss the Axel I had started to love."

There's a strange sound then, like the roaring of a sports car engine, and I slowly open my eyes.

And then I sit up.

Because Axel—the Axel I've longed to see—black hair shaggy and full around his face, is standing in front of me. He's wearing the weirdest clothing, though. I can't help laughing. "What on earth are you wearing?"

He looks down at his clothing. "It's the same thing Norm was wearing when we first met."

It's a red, stylized medieval jacquard coat with gold buttons. It looks utterly ridiculous.

And entirely delicious.

I stretch up to my knees, and I hold out one finger, curling it back toward me. "Come here. Now." And then, I purr.

26

AXEL

I'm small.

I'm so very, very small.

This body is strange. Everything *feels* different. Everything *looks* different.

Including Liz.

Instead of being tiny, so tiny that I have to be careful not to crush her, she's almost the same size as me.

When she stands up, her wings flaring behind her slightly, and she beckons me with a finger, "Come here. Now," something inside of my strange body *shivers*. My heart beats faster, and I experience a bizarre desire and also an unfamiliar fear of listening to her. We're bonded, and I know she would never hurt me, but she sounded almost predatory when she made the trilling sound after ordering me.

I liked it.

I liked it a lot.

I haven't lamented the supposed loss of being able to shift into this human form, and when she's spoken of it infrequently, I mostly discounted her words, but now I'm starting to understand how this shape might help our bond deepen.

"You want me to come onto the bed?" My spoken voice is strange—deeper and rougher than Liz's.

Her eyes widen, and she blinks. "Oh." She shakes her head. "I'm—you don't even remember—it's just." Her entire face turns a bright red. "Never mind." She plops back on the bed, her legs crossed, and her wings tucking up behind her.

"Are you alright?" I can't help peering at her, from her level this time.

It's nice.

"I'm fine," she snaps, clearly irritable for no reason I can fathom.

"I'm in the form you wished for, am I not? Or do I look different than I did before?"

Again, her face flushes. "No, I mean, yes, you look exactly the same." But she's staring at her hands, and then she clenches her fists. "She told me you *couldn't* shift anymore after I chose to make the earth blessed stronger." When she looks up this time, her eyes are flashing. "Your mother—she's just the *worst.*"

"I've never met her," I say. "I'm. . .sorry?"

She stands up again, flouncing across the length of the bed, her wings fluffing out and then tucking again as she moves, balancing her easily. She's gotten much better at using them. "Of course you're not sorry. It's between me and Freya."

"I am—I'm confused," I say.

She hops down so that she's standing right in front of me. "Your mother—it's like she hit the pause button on us, but we didn't have to pause. I think she did it just to *mess* with me. She should've told me flat out, but she let me flounder around." She shakes her head. "That was just. . .it was mean." She jabs me in the chest, but she leaves her finger there, pressing against me. Her eyes widen, her nostrils flare, and she inhales sharply. "I forgot how beautiful your chest was." She drags her finger down a little, still staring at it.

Beautiful. . .my what? I look down to where her finger's *still* pressed against my front. "It's beautiful?"

Again, with the reddening skin.

"I think your thermal regulation is off," I say. "It is a warm day, so I'm not sure how much I can help, but—"

She whips her hand back, palm flat out, fingers splayed. Her eyes dart from the spot she was just jabbing back up to my face. "I'm sorry. It's really strange, when you've been longing for something for a very long time, to suddenly have it, but also *not* to have it."

"Longing?" I arch one eyebrow. "Define longing." I'm smiling, now. I may not have any idea what she's doing, but I find that I like all of it. "This situation's unique, but I find it entirely pleasurable."

Liz's mouth dangles open.

I reach up with one small, human finger, and press underneath her chin until her mouth closes. The feel of her chin, her human skin, under my finger—it's nice. I like it, too. "This is all very. . .interesting. I intend to spend a lot of time in this tiny shape, whenever no villains are threatening, of course."

"No freaking way." Coral's standing in the open doorway, her eyes wider than Liz's were. "No fair!" Her eyebrows shoot up her face, and she turns, pointing. "I want you to fix Hyperion."

"He's not an earth dragon, dummy." Now Jade's beside her. "But Gordon is, and Rufus too. Can you fix them for Sammy? He's making me crazy, asking to play Candy Land and cards."

Liz looks a little sick, like she wishes no one else knew. "I—" She shakes her head. "I'm not sure. It just happened." She glares at the door, like she's wishing it would spontaneously close on its own.

Usually she's very pleased to see her sisters. I'm not sure why she's upset. I expected them to all celebrate together, or with me, perhaps, now that I'm size-appropriate for the leaping around and cheering. I decide to show her that I've been paying attention to their human customs for excitement. I leap up and down, wiggling my arms and then I yell. "It's great news, though, right?"

Liz's eyes widen further than I've ever seen and she takes two fumbling steps backward, stepping on the edge of her wing and falling. I reach and grab her hand, yanking her back upright, but I overestimate and pull a little too hard.

She tumbles forward, her hands both flattening against my chest.

My *beautiful* chest.

I can't help smiling at her. "Was that authentic human excitement?"

"This is the funniest thing I've ever seen," Jade whispers from the doorway. "We should have been recording it."

"No kidding," Coral says. "She'd do *anything* we asked just to keep anyone from ever seeing her like this. She's like Bambi, in that scene when he can barely walk on the ice."

They're both laughing, clearly delighted, but Liz straightens, her eyes flashing. Faster than I could have imagined in this defective form, Liz dives for the bed, lunges for a pillow, and whips it at the door.

The girls disappear behind a barrage of fluffy pillows aimed at their heads.

"I think they're gone," I say.

"You wish." She shakes her head and straightens. "Vultures. They're like tiny, doe-eyed vultures."

"I think they're just happy," I say. "As am I."

She laughs then. "What on earth was that jumping in the air thing?" Her laughter's beautiful. I may not understand why she thinks my perfectly flat, normal humanoid male chest is beautiful, but any fool could see that her face, suffused with joy as it is, is a thing of unparalleled loveliness.

I could stare at it all day.

"What?" She finally stops laughing and straightens. "What are you looking at?"

"You," I say. "You look. . .different to me when I'm like this." I look down at my hands and move them at the same time, wiggling them. "I—I understand more about why you lamented the loss of this shape."

She stands up, stepping toward me. "Because when you're like this, when you're like *me*, we can connect in a way we can't when you're scaly." She traces a finger down the side of my face and shakes her head. "You're so heartbreakingly beautiful." She's leaking again.

"I hope this is one of the happy-crying times," I say.

She nods. "It is." Her finger reaches my chin, and then she takes her finger away.

I hate it, so I inhale, leaning forward a bit.

She presses her finger against my mouth, staring at my lips.

My heart speeds up again.

She steps closer, her mouth near mine. "What do you remember about this?" Her eyes dart up to mine. "Anything?"

I shake my head, but my hands move toward her, my fingers spreading out as they *feel* her body, tightening on her hips. "Nothing."

"Would you be opposed to trying something that *I* really like doing with you?" She looks almost nervous when she looks up at me this time, her eyes. . .vulnerable. Like she's exposing her throat.

It's a heady feeling. "No. I'd like it."

"This," she whispers, her breath washing over my face, "is called a kiss." Then she presses her mouth against mine.

My heart had already accelerated, but now it's beating so fast I can almost hear it behind my ears. Probably another human design flaw, but I find that I like it, too. My hands tighten more on her body, and she makes a sound, a whimpering noise.

I pull back. "Did I hurt you? With these puny hands?"

She's laughing now, but her face is still close enough that I can *feel* her laugh against me, her breath soft and warm. "Not at all, unless you call pulling away *hurting* me, and I think it almost qualifies."

When I look down at her, my eyes drop lower to

her mouth, and she breathes faster again, like a small creature, scared and ready to dart away, and I like it.

I *like* it, like it.

A lot.

I lower my head to hers again, but this time, I press my mouth against her cheek. Then her jaw. Then the space between her lip and her nose, and then I finally press my mouth where I wanted to press it all along—against her lips. The sensation of her mouth against mine is unique, and it's different, and I fall into it, forgetting almost everything else as I taste her.

Mine.

The claim pulses through me, strengthening and deepening, and I almost pulse with a desire for *more*. I'm not sure *what* more I want, but I think Liz will know. I pull her closer, and I kiss her again, her tongue darting *inside* my mouth, and I groan.

When I do, her arms slide around my waist, her fingers splayed, and they pull me even closer, until our soft, human bodies are touching almost from my chest to her knees. I tighten my hold on her hip, and she makes the same little sound, and now that I know it's not from discomfort, it makes me even more excited.

Excited.

That's the best word yet for how I feel.

Mine—she's mine, and she's beside me, and she likes it, too, this connection. Being with Liz, touching her like this, I finally understand longing. I hate having to do it, but I need to confirm something. I pull back just enough to ask, "Not having this." My voice sounds strange. Deeper. Rougher. I clear my throat. "Not having your hands on me, your mouth against mine,

that's what you mean when you used the word *longing*."
I inhale. "Yes?"

Her eyes look a little glazed at first, but then she
nods. "Yes." She smiles. "Yes, Axel, that's longing."
And then she leaps on me, her legs wrapping around
my waist. "And I've been *longing* for you to figure that
out for a very *long*, very painful time."

Well, I switch to this method of communication,
because I don't have to pull away from her again. *You
won't have to* long *for me again any time soon. I don't plan to
move away.*

Except, in that moment, when Liz looks ready to
eat my face, something happens. Something horrible.

Portals make a very distinct sound.

Most blessed probably think they sound the same
—mine, Hyperion's, and my father's. They probably
can't tell a difference, but I can. In fact, of the
hundred or so creatures like me who are capable of
making a portal, I can differentiate each one if I'm
really paying attention.

But when I'm distracted?

There are maybe only three portalling sounds I'll
always recognize.

My father's, which sounds like the screaming of a
thousand dying blessed. My sister, Gersemi, because
hers sounds like the ringing of bells.

And my brother, Thunar, because for most of my
childhood, the sound of grinding and crashing at the
same moment meant one thing: my life was in terrible
danger.

Hyperion couldn't help me, either, because Thunar
could kill us both.

There isn't another single blessed I would less like to see, and my father would have known that. His sending Thunar is a clear message: deliver results, or get dead.

Liz and I are out of time.

****** I hope you enjoyed Embroiled. If you have time to leave me a review wherever you like to read, that would be AMAZING. Reviews help readers to know the book is great. The fourth book, Embattled, will be out summer 2025. You can preorder it now—preordering helps authors out so much!

If you want to make sure you get updates and information on my next release and on other series, you can sign up for my newsletter on my website at www.BridgetEBakerWrites.com. I'll send you a free book when you sign up. <3

AND if you want something else fun to read while you wait, you might like my HORSE shifter series, starting with My Queendom for a Horse (Yes, you read that right! It's a HORSE shifter series! I had a lot of people tell me that no one wanted that, but you know what? I've never worried too much about what people want...)

· · ·

O R I have a humorous fantasy series that's also a lot of fun, and it starts with My Pigeon Familiar. If you like the jokes and twists and turns in the Dragon Captured series, I think you'll love that one as well.

ACKNOWLEDGMENTS

I have five kids, eight horses, four dogs, two cats, and thirty chickens that my HOA does NOT know about... I have one husband, and I'm guessing you can already tell that he's a saint. I tried to find a publisher for years for my books, but after being told over and over that they weren't something anyone wanted to read, I decided to test that myself. I've been indie since 2018, and I've never looked back. I kickbox almost every day (to address my excess cookie-making), so if you don't like my kids, my cookies, or my books, maybe don't tell me in person.

The Birthright Series Collection, Books 1-3

The Anchored Series:

Anchored (1)

Adrift (2)

Awoken (3)

Capsized (4)

The Sins of Our Ancestors Series:

Marked (1)

Suppressed (2)

Redeemed (3)

Renounced (4)

Reclaimed (5) a novella!

A stand alone YA romantic suspense:

Already Gone

I also write women's fiction/romance books under B. E. Baker.

The Scarsdale Fosters Series:

Seed Money (1)

Nouveau Riche (2)

Minted (3)

Loaded (4)

Filthy Rich (5)

The Finding Home Series:

Finding Grace (1)

Finding Faith (2)

Finding Cupid (3)

Finding Spring (4)

Finding Liberty (5)

Finding Holly (6)

Finding Home (7)

Finding Balance (8)

Finding Peace (9)

The Finding Home Series Boxset Books 1-3

The Finding Home Series Boxset Books 4-6

The Finding Home Series Boxset Books 7-9

The Birch Creek Ranch Series:

The Bequest

The Vow

The Ranch

The Retreat

The Reboot

The Surprise

The Setback

The Lookback

Children's Picture Book

Yuck! What's for Dinner?

www.ingramcontent.com/pod-product-compliance
Lightning Source LLC
Chambersburg PA
CBHW060855210726
48293CB00006B/1805